SHE WORE ONLY WHITE

SHE WORE ONLY WHITE

Dörthe Binkert

Translated by Lesley Schuldt

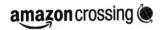

Text copyright © 2008 by Deutscher Taschenbuch Verlag GmbH & Co., KG
English translation copyright © 2012 by Lesley Schuldt

She Wore Only White was first published in 2008 by Deutscher Taschenbuch Verlag GmbH & Co. KG as Weit übers Meer (Far Across the Sea). Translated from German by Lesley Schuldt. First published in English by AmazonCrossing in 2012.

Published by AmazonCrossing
P.O. Box 400818
Las Vegas, NV 89140

ISBN-13: 9781612182919
ISBN-10: 1612182917
Library of Congress Control Number: 2011960936

For Peter

Freedom is the sure possession of those alone
who have the courage to defend it.

—Pericles

Prologue

She stood, tall and thin, in the lilac light of dusk. It was as though the world stopped spinning for a split second. At least that's how I remember it. I saw only her, a solitary figure in the middle of a crowd.

The sounds all around me fell away.

On my skin, I felt a breath of wind, as though the hot summer day had fanned itself.

Then the chorus of voices and harbor sounds returned, and the air was filled once again with shouting, laughing, barking dogs, and the echo of wheels and horses' hoofs on the cobblestones.

Like so many others, I had been at the harbor for hours to see the *Kroonland* cast off at midday, which was when it was supposed to start its passage from Antwerp to New York. But there had supposedly been a technical problem and the ship was still tethered to the dock at the Rhine quay.

The passengers, the majority of them emigrants, were crowded on the decks. They hadn't been allowed to leave the ship once they had gotten their berth assignments. I was there to see a friend off, but he had disappeared onto one of the lower decks, and I had lost sight of him.

The quay was in a state of chaos. Many of the first- and second-class passengers had disembarked once it had become known that the ship's departure would be delayed for several hours. The Red Star Line employees were having trouble keeping track of who had already gotten their accommodation assignments and who hadn't. All the while, they were attempting to assuage nervous passengers expressing concern about the reason for the delay.

The day had turned muggy. The perspiration of countless sweating bodies mixed with the salty odors of the harbor. A faint trace of decay wafted through the air.

It was July 23, 1904.

As I looked out toward the ship, still trying futilely to find my friend, a carriage stopped a few steps from where I stood. The driver jumped from the seat, opened the door of the coach, and sullenly offered a hand to help his passenger down the steps.

Initially I watched the scene without much interest. Then I saw a white silk shoe emerge from the carriage onto the cobblestones. It was followed by a hem of openwork lace, and then the other foot. A woman climbed out of the carriage, then turned back toward it, as though she wanted to bid farewell to someone inside. She grasped the train of her evening gown with her ungloved right hand, turned around, and stood directly in front of me.

Like everyone around me, I took a step back.

Her dress was white, though in the waning light, it had the wintery glimmer of blue pearls. Her splendid shoulders were bare down to her cleavage. The back of her dress fell in a long train, which streamed from a fold beneath the laced-up bodice and spilled out like a waterfall onto the litter-covered cobblestones.

The crowd inspected her with blatant curiosity; the women craned their necks, whispering to one another in astonishment. Through it all, the lady in the white dress just stood there. Eventually, she fished some change from her evening purse and pressed it into the driver's hand. He scanned the coins with a practiced glance, nodded his head, took off his hat, and climbed back onto his seat. He gave the two bays a light lash of his whip to get them moving again. The bystanders fell back and gave them room to leave.

The woman looked around. The ship was straight ahead, its gleaming black side rising out of the river like a massive, impregnable wall.

The passengers' luggage—heavy trunks with metal fittings, knurled baskets tied up with ropes, all manner of odd-shaped boxes and bundles—had been carried aboard several hours before. Several tons of coal had been unloaded from trains into the ship's hold. Thanks to two new propellers, the boilers were now working properly, and the *Kroonland* was finally ready for launch. There was a sudden frenzy to board.

I realized that the woman before me was looking for the gangway and that she planned to leave everything behind. I was overcome with an inexplicable feeling of exhilaration, which was interrupted by an equally inexplicable current of sorrow.

"Madame, wait!" I called, composing myself. "Let me take you to the ship!"

It was only then that she noticed me. I wasn't much to look at. Just eighteen, I was thin and lanky, a fresh-faced lad with little more than peach fuzz on my rosy cheeks. I was ashamed of my outdated suit, which I had inherited from my older brother, and had never been more conscious of the fact that I didn't even begin to fill the shoulders of the jacket.

She looked at me and smiled. The blood rushed to my cheeks. To hide my embarrassment, I turned away from her abruptly and began to pave the way for her to the ship. I broke through the gaping crowd, pushing the stubborn bodies to the side so that she could pass through unmolested. I glanced back twice to see if she was following me. She was. But with every step forward, I realized that she was one stride closer to disappearing from my life. She had entered it like a shooting star flashing across the night sky—and she'd evaporate just as quickly. As I walked her toward the ship, I wondered, why was I making her departure so easy?

We arrived at the gangway. I reluctantly stepped aside to clear the way for her. She put a foot on the gangplank, paused, and looked straight at me.

Seagulls flew up and screeched, spinning and diving around the ship, letting themselves be carried away by the evening breeze, and then swooping down again.

The woman stood still for a moment, as though she wanted to give me the opportunity to memorize her figure. Her gaze was almost tender, but that was certainly a delusion on my part. Again the seagulls flew up. And again I was distracted by the dry sound of their feathers beating the air and their harsh, pervasive cries. Then the stranger suddenly pulled her wedding ring from her finger, grasped my hand, placed the ring in it, and closed my fingers around it.

"Thank you," she said in a voice that I still remember today, more than thirty years later, and would recognize anywhere.

I looked at her incredulously, but she had already turned to the ship's officer who was standing on the landing.

"Would you take me on board?" I heard her say, firmly but pleasantly. The officer tipped his cap and politely offered her his arm. She took it and stepped onto the ship. She did not look back.

I closed my eyes. Just as when the bright circle of the sun is delineated sharply and clearly on the inner eye when we close our lids, her face was etched in my mind's eye. She was a few years older than I. Her eyes were wiser than mine; her lips were full, but not sweet. A tiny cut split her upper lip, and I knew that I would spend the rest of my life asking myself how she had injured it and what could possibly heal her.

A Night on Deck

Henri Sauvignac had moved into his stateroom on the *Kroon-land* several hours earlier. Now he leaned against the upper railing and watched the goings-on from a new perspective. He liked the metallic smell of the machine oil; the bitter taste of the coal, whose particles filtered down through his nose onto his tongue; the creak of the loading cranes bumping over the tracks; the sight of the horses pulling heavily laden carts; and the crowds milling around on the dock.

Ever since he was a child, Henri had loved the harbor. It was the heart of Antwerp, served and driven by the river, the Scheldt, which carried a seemingly endless stream of people and goods to and from distant countries. Though the river had once been filled with sailing ships, steamships had taken over in recent years. As a young man, he had often gone to visit the river at night, loitering around the Het Steen fortress and the Jordaens and Rhine quays. At night, the dockworkers ignited kerosene fires in barrels. Their glow illuminated the quay with a flickering light that threw shadows over the workers and didn't go out until dawn, when the night shift ended. In the morning, the sailors, having just emerged from the nearby brothels, sat in the quayside bars alongside those workers who could afford a coffee, beer, or schnapps at the end of their shift.

The ocean liners of the Red Star Line arrived on Mondays and put out to sea again on Saturdays, as punctual as the trains. People worked around the clock to discharge each shipment, transfer the coal into the ship's hold, haul new cargo on board, and to restock the ship with all of the provisions needed to sustain the crew for the nine-day crossing from Antwerp to New York or Philadelphia.

In the early morning, the cries of the fishwives resounded in the market and the widow Georg served the better-off travelers breakfast at the middle-class inn Zum Schweizerhof at 22 Zand Street. Henri had occasionally stopped by for a bite. Most of the emigrants, certainly those traveling by rail and those who had started in Russia or Poland, didn't stay here or at Francis de Meyer's Boarding House or even at the hotel Skandinavia, but rather at a dreary boarding house that didn't advertise the quality of its rooms and board so much as the possession of disinfection equipment.

The stream of emigrants, the state-of-the-art Belgian train, and the twenty-seven shipping companies in Antwerp enriched the city that Henri so often watched come to life in the early morning hours.

A hackney cab stopping on the quay near the *Kroonland* tore Henri from his thoughts. To his astonishment, a woman in a white evening gown alighted from the coach. She was not wearing normal traveling clothes, and she was quite alone, not—as he would have expected—accompanied by a man. Mesmerized, he stared at the peculiar figure—a strange, white spot in the crowd.

Henri suddenly had an image of death, death in the form of a bride. He was horrified by the thought, and yet an aura of poise and calm emanated from her. That is, until a young man, almost still a boy, broke away from the crowd and blazed a trail to the ship for the woman. Before she stepped onto the gangway, she turned back to the youth. Henri didn't recognize either of them, but he noticed that she slipped a ring from her hand and gave it to the boy. There was something somnambulistic about the scene, and Henri touched his forehead as if he had seen a Fata Morgana mirage. Then the woman disappeared inside the hull on the arm of a ship's officer. The boy was lost in the crowd.

Henri guessed that the woman was in her mid-twenties. She was slender and strikingly tall. Though he hadn't spoken a word to her, the stranger touched him in some way. He didn't consider words to be all that important anyway. He was a sculptor and relied on his eyes and his hands—and on an intuitive understanding of body language. In this case, the woman's body appeared to be asleep. She wore a tight corset, which made her waist look fragile, almost childlike. But he could tell that her body wasn't fragile; it was only numb. Locked up.

Henri chided himself. *My God, stop speculating! She will be on the ship with you for nine days…*

Their paths would cross. Inevitably. And Henri Sauvignac was a patient person. Anyone who worked with stone knew that it was a mistake to rush.

Most of the passengers stayed patiently on the deck, waiting until the gangway was pulled in, the chains and cables released slithering and rattling from the bitt.

Not far from Henri sat a young girl in a wheelchair that had been pushed right up to the ship's rail. The girl could scarcely see over the railing, despite trying to sit up straight to see over it. She had long dark brown hair, tied up with a wide green velvet bow. Her hands lay virtuously in her lap, but you could see that she would have loved to bend over the railing of the towering ship and see whether she would get vertigo. Impatiently she tugged at her bangs. A man in a dinner jacket bent over her and Henri heard him say:

"Lily! Mama doesn't want to wait any longer for you. And she would like you to get dressed for dinner."

"Oh, Papa! Look, they're pulling the gangway in, can you hear the machine? We're putting out to sea right now…"

Indeed, at that very moment, the ship's horn sounded, a melancholy bellowing sound that carried across the breeze, pulling the soul along like a siren's song.

"Now we're going, do you see? We're going!" called the girl, jerking back and forth in her wheelchair. "I have to wave. I'm going to America!"

Henri liked the little girl. She had probably had polio; her long green and blue diamond-patterned skirt covered her legs, but he could see that they looked as thin as sticks.

The ship forged ahead into the current and rapidly gained speed. The people who had remained on the quay turned into a patchwork of dark and light spots, like in the pictures of the modern impressionistic painters, and soon became indistinct in the evening light. The undulations of the waving hands faded away.

The girl noticed that Henri was observing her. She looked unsettled, even a little angry that she was being stared at, and blushed. Henri could see that she was obviously no longer a child.

Henri smiled at her. She didn't react, but instead turned to her father and said, "OK, Papa. Take me to the stateroom. The ship's chambermaid can help me change." Her father undid the brakes on the wheelchair and pushed her away. Two ship boys hurried by to help her down the stairs.

Lily looked challengingly at the smiling stranger as she was rolled away. Henri decided he liked Lily. He really liked her.

New York would just be a way station for Henri Sauvignac; he planned to go on to the world's fair in St. Louis, where some of his sculptures were going to be displayed in the Belgian pavilion. The Belgian government had paid for a first-class passage for him. Although Henri wasn't entirely comfortable mingling with the upper classes, the government expected him to act as a Belgian ambassador of the arts on this trip. He had even had to borrow the appropriate wardrobe because he didn't own enough suits, especially not of the type that he would need to fit in in first class.

"I guess it's time to change for dinner," he said to himself, sighing, and turned to go.

The lady in the white evening gown must have been standing behind him for a while. But Henri wasn't sure whether she noticed him when he turned to face her now. Her expression was vacant, as though she were looking straight through him. But she didn't turn away either. Amber, he thought; her eyes are the color of amber.

The first-class staterooms were spread out over multiple stories in the center of the ship because the rolling motion of the ship was less noticeable there. Henri had brought only a trunk and an overnight bag, which he had already unpacked. His stateroom was comfortably furnished with a washbasin and electrical lighting, but Henri was used to moving about in a large, airy studio. He felt cramped in this tiny berth, which seemed like a dollhouse for little girls, and he kept banging his elbows every time he turned around. Nevertheless, he managed to shave and change. When he put on the black patent-leather dress shoes he had borrowed, he thought that they looked ridiculous on him.

The passengers gathered from different parts of the ship in the spacious wood-paneled vestibules, which led to stairs that descended in a theatrical sweep to the dining room. For a week, for better or worse, this community of strangers would share its fate, in death and life, trusting in modern technology's ability to defy the elements as it traversed the open sea.

Although the thick red-patterned carpeting on the first-class stairway absorbed some of the noise, scraps of conversations could easily be overheard. Henri wasn't in any hurry to enter the dining room, so he settled onto a plush sofa in the hall and watched the guests parade past him.

The delayed departure had obviously been cause for some confusion regarding dress etiquette. Some of the passengers were in evening gowns, while others still wore their traveling clothes.

"Look, Philippe, I told you others would change," complained someone near Henri. "You didn't want to believe me because you didn't feel like changing into something else. How embarrassing...," said a woman in traveling clothes.

"It doesn't matter what you are wearing, *ma chère* Clothilde..."

"What are you trying to say? You can be so insulting!"

The pudgy, red-cheeked man took his wife placatingly by the arm, but she shook off his hand with a short practiced movement. Henri thought he recognized the woman's shrill voice. Weren't they the neighbors to the left of his stateroom? Clothilde's voice grated in a way that you didn't quickly forget.

Ah, and there was Lily, suitably dressed in a dark blue skirt and white blouse, with her mother, who wore an elegant, dusty pink buttoned dress with a voluminous dusty pink hat. Lily's father smiled at his wife and Henri overheard him say, "I hope the two of you will enjoy the crossing and that you won't argue…"

"That's completely up to Lily…," retorted his young wife coolly.

Henri would have given anything to see Lily's face, but at that moment, he was distracted by a strikingly odd-looking couple. Tall and thin, the man was about thirty years old, and he was so handsome that everyone—not only women—couldn't help but stare. Henri instinctively sucked in his stomach when he caught sight of him, but no snide comments came to mind that could have soothed his ego. He had the charisma of a person who has been so often assured of his charm and good looks that he has finally begun to believe it himself, even if a bit reluctantly. Although the woman at his side was dressed meticulously and had an alert look about her, she seemed almost pitiably nondescript by comparison. She was substantially smaller than her companion. Diminutive though she was, she had grasped his arm and linked hers through it. It appeared that she could lead him better this way. Henri followed the couple with his eyes. Did she not have confidence in herself? Or did she lack faith in the man at her side, even though he appeared to be walking meekly beside her?

Henri thought for a moment about how this connection might have come about.

Just then, he was distracted again, this time by a gentleman who walked past him with his companion and almost stepped on his foot. Henri recognized him, albeit only from the newspaper, where he had seen this face a few times. He tried to remember the man's name, but he'd had a terrible memory for names since his mid-thirties. It seemed that names were simply not as interesting to him as bodies.

Although the name eluded him, he knew the man was an industrialist of some kind, involved in railroads, steel, or something like that. He knew the man had substantial wealth at his disposal and didn't have to be good-looking to have a beautiful woman in tow. Henri didn't find her particularly attractive, but he could tell she was the type that was considered beautiful. She wore a brilliant red evening gown, and Henri didn't like red dresses on blonde women. He grimaced. Why was he even wasting time thinking about her? Perhaps because there was something tantalizingly empty about her, which he tried to fill with his own imagination…

A middle-aged woman herded her three children ahead of her: two boys and a small girl, about nine, six, and four years old, all in navy outfits with white sailor collars. The oldest boy led the way, while the middle kept tripping up the line because he stopped to look at the pattern in the carpet or to feel the banister railing with his curious fingers. The littlest one, with a large white bow in her hair, grabbed for her mother's hand. The father retained a certain irritating distance from his family so that it wasn't clear whether he belonged to them or not. Clearly annoyed, the woman said something to him, but he carried on as though he hadn't heard anything. At this treatment, his wife blushed angrily and hollered to the middle boy to settle down. The woman gripped the little girl's hand tighter.

Henri looked around. But he didn't see the woman in the white evening gown.

Henri finally entered the dining room, which was filled with long, white-cloth-covered tables, each set for twenty to thirty guests.

The steward put Henri between two married couples who had not attracted his attention previously. He didn't have any interest even now in speaking with them. A refined but nondescript man in his forties sat across from him with his young companion, whom Henri assumed wasn't his wife since the man was rather overly solicitous of her. She was pretty and smiled spontaneously at Henri when he sat down.

Henri felt uneasy. The red velvet swivel armchairs were fastened to the floor, so that the dining guests sat neatly in perfect rows, which made him feel distinctly uncomfortable. Henri decided to leave the table as soon as possible, and excuse himself to the smoking lounge or to the deck.

He simply wasn't accustomed to polite chitchat; he was bored by it and would rather listen than talk himself. He found that spirited conversations were rare, and that he couldn't start them himself. His thoughts often digressed when he was with others. He thought of his work, of drafts to be made, of material that he needed to order. But before he got the chance to disappear into his own thoughts, Madame Borg, seated beside him, started peppering him with questions. They exchanged the usual empty pleasantries, while Henri tried to concentrate on the menu.

"Monsieur Sauvignac, permit me to ask a question. Half of the ship is speaking of it: did you see the lady who boarded the ship in an evening gown shortly before we set sail?"

"Why, Madame," replied Henri politely, "what did you see?"

"Well, actually, my husband saw her. I had called the ship's chambermaid and was in my stateroom. She was supposed to..."

Henri didn't want to know what the ship's chambermaid was supposed to do and turned toward her husband. "Then you saw her, Monsieur Borg?"

"Yes," he replied.

"And?" asked Henri. "How was she?"

Monsieur Borg bent slightly across the table in order to be able to look around his wife at his neighbor.

"She…" he fell silent again.

"Just tell us what she was like," pressed Madame Borg, sweeping an impatient look around the room. "She isn't here. Was it an angel who appeared before you? Just tell us what you saw."

Monsieur Borg leaned back in his chair and threw Henri a beseeching look behind his wife's back. Then he said, "You know I didn't witness all that much. She turned into the corridor that I had just come down. She came toward me; I made room to let her pass. That's it."

Madame Borg was not satisfied with her spouse's response. "In doing so, you must have gotten the chance to inspect her. Since you made room for her, you must be able to describe what she looks like!" She hit the edge of the table with her cloth napkin as though she wanted the table to take the place of her husband's legs.

Monsieur Borg replied reluctantly, "What are you imagining? It wasn't all that bright in the corridor. I stepped to the side; she nodded gratefully and continued on her way."

Now his wife turned to Henri, gave a withering smile, and said, imitating her husband, "She nodded and continued on her way."

"She wore a white evening gown," Monsieur Borg added wearily and turned his attention to dessert.

The sculptor leaned toward Madame Borg, took a sip of red wine, looked her straight in the eyes, and said, "I saw her briefly on deck. She was only a few feet away from me. It's not just that she wore a white evening gown. She is also gorgeous."

Madame Borg said nothing for a moment and cleaned one or two breadcrumbs from the tablecloth. Then she said, to no one in particular, "I wonder how the weather will be for the crossing? It was so muggy the last couple of days in Antwerp. I don't like thunderstorms."

She laid her hand on her spouse's. "Wilhelm knows that." She laughed nervously. Monsieur Borg didn't respond.

Henri was eager to leave the table, but, as though fastened to the chair, he couldn't bring himself to leave. He asked himself how he was supposed to keep this up for an entire week.

The nondescript man who sat across from Henri had noticed that the conversation at the table was threatening to peter out.

"Mister...Monsieur Sauvignac?" he intruded. "Did I understand your name correctly...? May I ask to where you are traveling? Are you going to stay in New York or do you have to continue on?"

"I don't know yet," Henri answered without enthusiasm, unwilling to embark on yet another new conversation. "And you, Mister...?" He had already forgotten the name of his colleague, even though it hadn't been more than an hour since they had been introduced. He took a breath, "Excuse me, could you tell me your name again...?"

The man laughed indulgently and said, stroking his sparse, curly blond hair: "William Brown. A common name that is easily forgotten. We—" he motioned to the lady at his side, who obviously couldn't or wasn't allowed to speak for herself and whom, Henri noticed, William Brown hadn't introduced as his wife— "are on the return trip. Mrs. Henderson and I know each other from Philadelphia and we met on a street in Antwerp—there are such coincidences!—only to discover that we were returning on the same ship at the same time." He smiled and looked at Mrs. Henderson, as though surprised to discover her beside him. "A very agreeable surprise!" he added charmingly.

"I can believe that," Henri answered, who didn't care one way or the other. Mrs. Henderson remained quiet. She reminded Henri of a young woman who had sat for him as a model in Paris, except that Mrs. Henderson's hair was more tightly curled than Lisette's had been. Yes, that had been the name of the girl in Paris.

Henri liked brunettes, and Mrs. Henderson was a brunette. She had wide, prominent cheekbones and a pointed chin. Her cheeks were pink, though Henri couldn't tell whether they were rouged or flushed from the wine she had drunk at dinner. She looked at Henri briefly, a frank glance from blue-green eyes. Henri noticed that her nose bent very slightly to one side of her face, and he suddenly pictured her standing in front of a mirror trying in vain to straighten it. However, Henri liked the small abnormality in her pretty face. It made it more interesting.

"Did you enjoy your time in Europe?" he asked Mrs. Henderson. She nodded earnestly.

"Oh yes. Very much!" She looked at her companion, as though expecting confirmation from him then stopped to think for a moment. Then she said, turning toward Henri again, "Have you ever been to Rome? I was in Rome for the first time in my life. I'm telling you, I could rave about it all day long. I could never have imagined that there was anything so beautiful." She paused again, putting her right index finger to her nose. "In Rome I understood for the first time what beauty is." She looked over at Mr. Brown, who looked uneasy. Then she continued, unperturbed. "I never thought about what beauty was before. That is," she sighed softly, "it hadn't been a theme in my life until now, anyhow. But now, I've given it some thought. Beauty is that which can't be expressed. We say something is perfect when we think it is beautiful. But that isn't it. It is something different. Beauty is something vulnerable that we would like to save from ruin. Yes. Beauty is beautiful because it is so vulnerable…"

Mrs. Henderson had spoken with such enthusiasm that the pink in her cheeks had become more vibrant. Mr. Brown interrupted her by briefly touching her arm, as though he wanted to ask Henri and the entire table for forgiveness for Mrs. Henderson's exuberance.

"May I top off your water glass, Billie? You too, Mr. Sauvignac?" said Mr. Brown.

Mrs. Henderson looked rattled, and then said in a firm voice, "Thank you, William. I know that I talk too much. But I'd like another glass of wine, if you would be so kind. The waiter didn't notice that my glass is empty."

Mr. Brown stroked his hair, which he did quite often, as though he wanted to be sure that it was still there, checked that his black bow tie was still straight, and hurried to refill Mrs. Henderson's wineglass.

"I find what you say interesting," Henri said to Mrs. Henderson. He had forgotten the bolted-down chair for a moment.

"Thank you," she said.

"You're welcome. My pleasure," said Mr. Brown.

Mrs. Henderson took a sip of her wine.

"Do you know," she continued, gazing intently into Henri's eyes, "I saw many ruins in Rome. And I loved them. They were beautiful, even though they were incomplete. Or perhaps because they were incomplete." She paused and looked penetratingly at Henri.

"And that kept me busy." With this afterthought, Mrs. Henderson stopped talking.

Ienri didn't respond. He thought about whether Mrs. Henderson had made the discovery about life and the fragility of human dreams in Rome or just now.

Mr. Brown was quiet too, thankful that Mrs. Henderson had finished her monologue.

With a graceful movement, Mrs. Henderson put her napkin next to her glass and said, "It's late."

And Mr. Brown said, "That's true. It was a long day. You must certainly be very tired."

"Oh no," she responded with a disarming smile. "But I would be grateful if you would bring me to my stateroom. I am afraid that otherwise I will get lost. Tomorrow I will certainly be able to find my way better."

At that, they rose from the table, and Mr. Brown offered Mrs. Henderson his arm.

Valentina wrapped herself tightly in the blanket that the ship's deckhand had brought her. The night was Valentina's ally. The night turned her into a shapeless shadow; under the cloak of darkness, she could disappear, just like little Charles had disappeared from her life two years ago today, on July 23, 1902.

A half-moon low on the horizon cast a reddish glow on her dress. "My queen," Viktor had called her the first time he had seen her in it, "my queen of the night," and he had led her off to dance. Viktor, who danced so well. She hadn't danced anymore after that, and Viktor had chosen other queens and ladies-in-waiting.

Now, after all that she'd endured, it seemed that fate would have her in this dress, a prisoner of the ocean and of this ship, when she would rather have been plunged to the bottom of the sea.

She had waited a long time before leaving the stateroom. She had only slipped out once nothing could be heard other than the quiet thumping of the ship's engines. She had cautiously left the door ajar and hadn't met anyone on her way up to the deck. After all the commotion caused by the delayed departure, the passengers had disappeared into their staterooms shortly after dinner. Only a few voices from steerage below penetrated the darkness; anyone who felt like it could sleep out in the open.

Valentina hadn't expected that a deckhand would be making his rounds on the deck at this hour and was dismayed when the youth suddenly stopped in front of her. But she quickly regained her composure and asked him to bring her a blanket.

What had she done? It was rash, horrible, and stupid, and—worst of all—irreparable. Had she lost her mind? If so, then why did she feel so calm—which was in itself disconcerting?

When she had stepped onto the ship on the arm of the ship's officer, oh yes, then she had been afraid. Afraid of being caught, of being found, of being dragged back into her old world, which was only separated from a new life by a gangplank. Most of all, she had been afraid that her heart, which had almost burst out of her chest from nerves, would betray her.

But she wasn't afraid anymore.

She had left everything behind. Everything that she knew, loved, and hated. Even her fear.

Tomorrow morning she would look for the captain early.

And she had to speak with Jan, without fail. Jan.

When the deckhand made his final rounds for the night, he discovered Valentina asleep on a deck chair. He whispered softly, asking whether she might like to be taken to her stateroom? But she didn't stir, so the deckhand let her sleep.

When Henri got back to his stateroom, it seemed even more claustrophobic than it had been during the day. He knew he wouldn't be able to sleep, so he slipped into his comfortable daytime shoes with a sigh and headed off once again for the promenade deck. The filthy trail of smoke that rose out of the smokestack mingled with the dark sky; the smell of burnt coal hung in the air.

Soon the ship would reach Dover and pick up the remaining passengers, but after that they would only see water for days.

Henri ran his hand over the ship's railing. The wood and metal were damp from the fine mist that rose from the water. A few deck chairs still sat out forlornly, the moon bathing the wooden planks of the deck in a soft light. Even though the sky was vast and black and infinite, Henri felt trapped outside, too.

Why was he stuck in his friend Jean's borrowed tails on a ship bound for America? What did he want in America anyway? His statues had already been shipped; workmen at their destination could put them in place without his help.

Water wasn't his element. Everything was suddenly formless, fluctuating, blurred; he couldn't see the dark shoreline, even though he knew it couldn't be very far away. Henri didn't have the slightest desire to see the world's fair, and he didn't want to go to the New World. He also hadn't, like so many of his fellow human beings, discovered the joy of traveling. And writing postcards, the ridiculous greetings from Athens, Rome, and Florence, grated on his nerves. "Send me a postcard from New York and from St. Louis," his mother had requested, as though they'd be proof of something. Henri wanted to be home in his studio, pulling on his work coat, wrapping a clay model with damp cloths—it had been difficult to find someone who would keep the clay damp during his absence—and labor quietly on his work.

Henri Sauvignac didn't wish for anything other than his studio. It was there that he found his freedom, his place, his life.

A deckhand went past and greeted him. Henri returned the greeting, stood up, and left the deck.

Henri didn't know that what he felt was loneliness. He hadn't noticed that the lady in the white evening gown sat on the other side of the deck, only a few yards away. Only the black-coated smokestack separated them from each other.

"It was already late in the evening. I made my requisite rounds to see if there were any passengers still on deck. As long as someone's still there, we have to stay on duty. It was a beautiful, warm evening, but there were hardly any guests outside. The first night, passengers are always busy in their staterooms. They really like to settle in, even though it's only a nine-day journey to New York. Really just a stone's throw. The trip used to take two weeks.

"The lady that you asked about sat in a deck chair. I'd made a couple of trips across the pond at that point, but I'd never seen anything like this; I mean, such a beautiful dress. Completely white, covered with lace, and with a long train. The moon was red that night and the moonlight shone on her. She was alone, without an escort, which I found a little odd—that such a beautiful woman sat there all alone. She asked me politely if I could bring her a blanket because she wanted to stay outside, the sky was so beautiful at night. I asked her if she needed anything else.

She thought about it briefly and then said, 'No, thank you.' Then she said, would I perhaps be able to bring her a glass of water. 'Of course, Madame,' I answered. I remember thinking: Maybe she is a princess who wants to have some peace and quiet, who wants to be left completely alone because she normally has an entourage around her. Why she only wanted to drink water, I didn't understand. I would have ordered champagne.

"OK fine, I brought her the blanket and the water. Usually I got a tip, but she didn't give me one, she just thanked me. I found that strange, that she was so friendly, but didn't give me a tip. But then, I thought, princesses don't carry money. They never have to pay for anything. They probably can't even imagine that other people need money to live. Our bosses always say that we shouldn't think at all: 'Just serve and don't think and keep your mouths shut.'"

Ton Wilton, deckhand on the Kroonland
at an interrogation after the arrival of the ship in New York

Henri tossed and turned fitfully in his sleep. He dreamed that Mrs. Henderson, the lady from Philadelphia, stood in his stateroom telling him about the Roman ruins. He didn't interrupt her, just touched her face very lightly with the tips of his fingers, kissed her cheeks, her neck, her collarbone, the left, the right, and her cleavage. She laughed softly, looking for more words to prove to Henri that he couldn't distract her. In the dream, Henri began to undress Mrs. Henderson as she told him a story about the Baths of Caracalla and the floor heating in the ancient world. Henri said that if he were a photographer, he would like to photograph her. She twisted her mouth, pressed her right index finger to her nose, and said, "No, not that. What are you imagining!" Her features then became fuzzy, and Henri was no longer certain whether it was Mrs. Henderson or Lisette standing in front of him.

He awoke. Lisette had enjoyed the idea of being photographed; that he knew. She had run to the photographers whenever she could. She was fascinated by every technical innovation, and the notion that a bath in mercury vapor could conjure up her likeness on a small piece of celluloid delighted her. Henri rolled over in his bed.

The ship berthed in Dover. The noise woke everyone, but it was late, and none of the passengers with staterooms had any desire to get dressed again to go on deck and watch the new passengers come on board. Many people who couldn't sleep in the stifling accommodations in steerage had made their way to the decks, where they lay on the bare floor or leaned against walls and luggage.

Henri could hear snippets of English as the new arrivals settled into staterooms down the hall. These were punctuated by deep men's voices speaking what sounded like Russian. The sounds were loud, almost ominous, as they echoed in the darkness.

Henri lay awake. He thought of the mysterious lady in the white dress and of Mrs. Henderson, who—presumably—had spent the night with Mr. Brown.

And again Lisette pierced his thoughts. She stood in his Parisian studio and was about to leave. She wrapped herself in an old brown comforter. "I'm cold," she said and looked out through the dirty window at the unkempt garden. "It's always cold in your studio. And even if your arms are warm, your heart is unreachable, like the dark side of the moon."

❧

"Do you want to know what I think? It is simply a scandal. At first I only wondered how it was possible for a woman to come on board a ship without a male escort—and on top of that in evening attire. On board an ocean liner traveling to New York! Yes, a new century has begun, but have you ever heard of such a thing? A society lady without an escort of any kind, without a husband, without a female companion, without servants. At first no one knew whether her family was already on board. From the start, I thought that seemed extremely unlikely.

"You should have seen my husband. He met her in the corridor before we went in to dinner. He was bewitched after this meeting. Jinxed, I tell you. Acted absentminded, was completely distracted.

" 'What is it, Willem?' I asked him. His name is Willem.

" 'Nothing,' he said. 'Nothing.'

" 'What nothing?' I asked. Normally he gives me an answer if I ask him something, a completely normal answer.

" 'Just nothing. What do you mean? I took a stroll over to the navigating bridge and now I'm back. You'll want to freshen up.'

" 'But there must be something! You look as if you've just seen Christ appear. I can tell. You're acting strange.' But he didn't want to say anything more. The only thing he told me was, 'I met a woman in the corridor. She was very unusual in appearance. She was wearing a very elegant evening gown. You'll certainly see her at dinner in the dining room.'

" 'And?'

" 'What and?'

" 'And? Was she alone? Or with someone?'

" 'Yes. No. She was alone.'

"My husband and I have been married for over twenty years, you know, and he has never kept a secret from me. He isn't like other men who only see their wife at meals and if they have certain needs, if you understand what I mean. But at this moment, I just knew that there was something he wasn't telling me. Such scandalous women are poison for men. Men are easily seduced, but you have to keep them reasonable. It's a lifelong endeavor, I assure you. Such women undo in the blink of an eye everything that a wife has painstakingly done to keep her husband behaving rationally. Heaven knows what thoughts she unleashed in him!

"I couldn't have any children and that is a strain on any marriage. My husband is a successful contractor, but he doesn't have any heirs, any successors. After it was obvious that we wouldn't have any children, he didn't bother me anymore, if you understand what I mean. He never reproached me. He has always behaved impeccably. But nevertheless: Maybe some part of him is unsatisfied. Even if he always says, 'Everything is as it should be. Nothing is missing. You know that.'

"In any event, women like that, who behave so brashly and indecently, trigger unrest in men. And that isn't proper. If you had any idea what a woman has to put up with in a marriage. And then someone like this comes along and turns men's heads."

Henriette Borg, passenger on the Kroonland

"I am the last person who would know anything about this woman. Why are you even asking me? I met her in the corridor when she came aboard. I thought she was going to her stateroom. What else was I supposed to think? But I'll admit she was on my mind. I'm not young anymore, almost in my mid-fifties. Things are as they are; I can't change much about it anymore. I probably wouldn't want to either. I have a construction business that yields a passable profit; I'm married—unfortunately without children. My wife and I are, as much as can be expected at our age, healthy. I've done better than my parents. What more could I want?

"But when I saw her—she nodded politely to me when I made room for her so that we could pass one another in the corridor—I suddenly thought: Yes, so it is. When this unknown, gorgeous, unexpected being approached me, I stepped aside and couldn't help but stare. As she passed me in her expensive dress, with her tall, slim figure—like a vision—I couldn't help but feel that I had simply passed on life. That I don't really live anymore, perhaps never have lived, that I am simply managing my life until it is over. It was like a sudden cold breeze. I'm horrified by these thoughts.

"Naturally I wouldn't say anything of it to my wife. But that's how it was."

Willem Borg, passenger on the Kroonland

Sunday, July 24

"We passed Dover. No other stops until New York. The open sea lay before us. It was Sunday morning, a beautiful warm summer morning. Bright blue sky, the seas blue and quiet as well. The barometer indicated that fickle weather lay ahead, so we were expecting some treacherous conditions in the coming days, but for now, everything was still quiet on board.

"In the early morning, the ship belonged to the crew, and that's when I love my job most. It was about eight thirty when one of the stewards from first class came to me, a pretty boy, blond, tall, with a charming laugh. I always pulled his leg because the ladies devoured him with their eyes—many of the men, too, I might add. He had broad shoulders, narrow hips, a dimple on his chin. Everything that women like and that most men don't have. At least, not after a few years of marriage. I would love to see his tips, though I might be tempted to jump to conclusions, if you know what I mean.

"He clicked his heels at me and put his hand on his cap.

" 'Yes, what is it, Longden?' I asked. 'Will it be a successful crossing for you? When you were serving at dinner last night, did you already make a preliminary selection of the most beautiful ladies?'

"But Longden didn't respond to my banter. He seemed to have a problem.

" 'Sir,' he said, 'I found a lady on deck. She had asked a deck-hand to bring her coffee and an officer. But he came to me first. When I found her, the lady was standing at the railing, not in traveling clothes, but in a low-cut evening gown with a long train. At first I didn't believe my own eyes. The woman looked as though she came from the highest social circles. When she saw me, she said to the deckhand, 'I wanted to speak with an officer, not with a steward.' But she didn't appear angry. I explained, 'Excuse me, Madame, I will get the first officer immediately. But the deckhand has to follow the regulations and notify me first.'

" 'That's fine,' she said and smiled.

"Longden deliberated. 'You're right, sir,' he said then, 'I saw many beautiful ladies last night at dinner, but none like this one...'

"I interrupted him. 'Before you lose control, Longden, I want to see for myself. Take me to her,' I said. Then we went below together to make our way to the promenade deck.

"The woman was looking out at the water, with her back to me. A couple of trailing seagulls circled above us.

"Her hair was marvelous, very thick, and dark blond. A few strands had unraveled from her loose bun, and these coiled around her neck. I stared at her neck, the slightly tilted throat, her statuesque figure. I saw her face only in half profile, but that was enough. I had to agree with Longden. I took off my cap, straight-ened my uniform jacket, and cleared my throat.

"She turned around. Her eyes were stunning, I have to say.

" 'Good morning, Madame. You asked for an officer. My name is Anton van Broek; I am the first officer. What can I do for you?' Longden and the deckhand stood rooted to the deck.

" 'Good morning,' she answered. She barely smiled, but she didn't seem unfriendly, just preoccupied. She kept one hand on the wooden railing of the landing, grasped the train of her dress with the other, then turned completely toward me and said, 'I would like to speak with the captain. Would you be so kind as to bring me to the captain, Monsieur van Broek?' Her demeanor left no doubt that she wouldn't be giving any further explanation. She hadn't even told me her name at that point. I sent Longden and the deckhand back to work and pointed in the direction of the captain's quarters.

"I didn't have any idea what she wanted with the captain. She wasn't properly dressed for the daytime, and someone would certainly point that out to her. But otherwise she behaved like a perfect lady, so I withheld all of my questions. Discretion is a matter of honor."

Anton van Broek, first officer on the Kroonland

"In third class there's a stowaway every so often. Someone who mixes in with the emigrants.

"Most of the thousand or more passengers on each crossing, seven hundred to eight hundred of them, are emigrants. There is always a tremendous crowd when people board. Even though the stewards do everything they can to bring the travelers to their staterooms and their sleeping quarters in an orderly manner, a certain amount of confusion cannot be avoided. People don't get their bearings right away on a ship; the corridors are narrow, the staterooms are too; and everyone is getting accustomed to the various decks.

"The ship is like a large, swimming city. With each crossing, it must be reinhabited anew, with everyone figuring out their places and what role they'll play. That takes a while. And you'll find everything on board that you have on land: every layer of society, misery and glamour, friendship and envy, strife, greed, deception. Hatred and love.

"That said, I have never had a situation like this one in all the years I've been at sea.

"My first officer, Anton van Broek, knocked on my door, opened it, saluted, and said only, 'Sir, a lady would like to speak with you. It is urgent. Therefore she has asked to be brought to you. May I bring her in?'

"I wasn't thrilled with the idea of spending a Sunday morning solving the urgent problem of an unknown lady. So I just nodded, without asking whether van Broek knew what it was about. He probably wouldn't have been able to tell me much anyway. It's not his style to get to the bottom of things. He's a very discreet man.

"A lady, he said. I imagined it was probably a typical first-class problem. About a dog, one of these lap dogs, perhaps. It's all the rage now to take these little dears along on a cruise. And then Schnucki doesn't like it on board, the deckhands don't walk him like he's used to, and the food doesn't meet the standards of Chèri, and, even more importantly, those of Madame.

I was still thinking of Madame Binoche's yappy Pomeranian, an obnoxious animal that had snapped at the stewards' and deckhands' calves the entire journey from New York to Antwerp, when I turned toward the door and realized that van Broek had already brought the lady in and was waiting for permission to leave. The captain's cabin is covered with thick carpet and I hadn't heard their steps as they entered. I was surprised to see that the lady was not the least bit like the small, corpulent Madame Binoche with the triple chin. But I digress.

"The woman who stood before me looked as though she had come straight from the sea. She was a siren, a mermaid incarnate.

"I still hadn't personally welcomed all of the first-class passengers, but I had seen most of them in passing at that point—but not her. It was as though she had emerged from another world.

"I welcomed her and asked her to sit down.

"She sat very straight in the chair without leaning back and glanced back to make sure that van Broek really was gone. She wore long white dress gloves that reached above her elbows. Her hands lay in her lap, clutching an evening bag embroidered with pearls. It was an extraordinary picture at nine in the morning.

"When I sat down, she finally said, 'First of all, you would naturally like to know with whom you are dealing.' She looked like she was concentrating intensely. 'My name is Meyer, Valentina Meyer. I got on board in Antwerp without a ticket.'

"She paused for a moment, as though she wanted to give me the opportunity to familiarize myself with this unusual state of affairs. She was a stowaway, the most beautiful one I had ever seen. She looked down, as if she now had to pluck up a certain amount of courage, and continued, 'And I don't have any money.' She fell silent and waited to see what I would say. But I didn't say anything. The whole situation had taken me by surprise, and I literally couldn't think what to say. She leaned toward me, keeping her back straight, and laid one hand on the top of the table as if she wanted to make me an offer. With her other hand, she gripped the back of the chair.

" 'I am not destitute. I will pay for the trip when we arrive in New York. I know I am causing you trouble; I am a stowaway.

That alone means a lot of inconveniences for you. For me as well. But I could,' she gripped her ear involuntarily, 'I could give you my diamond earrings as a guarantee that I will cover all of my expenses.'

"I had listened very carefully, but I still didn't say a word. She could see that I was thinking, that I was going through the relevant regulations in my mind. The problem was just so different from the lap dog problem that I had expected.

"She knew that I had to report the incident and that there would be trouble when she got to New York. She smiled fetchingly at me and slid her hand across the table closer to me, almost as if she wanted to take my hand. Before I had the opportunity to say anything, she said, 'I am certain that you won't press me.' Her voice, which had until now been so calm and composed, suddenly took on an almost pleading tone. She continued, 'And that the personal life of a lady will be respected. If you desire it, I am a prisoner on your ship and I assume that you will treat me like a gentleman.'

"That was a very smart move.

"She stroked her brow lightly with her right hand and then placed both her hands back on her evening bag. Then she leaned back and rocked slightly back and forth. It looked as though she wanted to set her swivel chair in motion and simply fly away or return to the sea as a mermaid with a twist of the chair and an incantation.

"I needed some time. There were certain things that I had to arrange to meet with regulations, but there was some leeway in what the next few days could look like for her.

"I'm afraid I can't depict this first meeting any more accurately than that."

Richard Palmer, captain of the Kroonland

The confrontation with Jan Bartels lasted only a few minutes and yielded exactly the result she expected.

"Do you recognize this lady, Bartels?" the captain asked.

The ship's officer looked briefly at Valentina and answered, "Yes, sir!"

"Could you tell me when and where you have seen her?"

"Yes, sir." The officer stood very straight and looked past Valentina and the captain. Then he glanced back at the captain and continued, "The lady boarded the ship yesterday evening shortly before departure."

"And how is it, Bartels, that the lady was simply allowed to pass through even though you were on duty on the gangway?"

"I thought the lady had already moved into her stateroom and had disembarked like many of the other first- and second-class passengers, sir."

The captain's voice was menacingly calm.

"In full evening attire and without an escort?" he questioned.

"Well, yes," answered the officer. "I didn't think of that, sir."

"You meant to say, 'I shirked my duty,' if I understand you correctly?"

Palmer's face had turned crimson.

"Yes, sir."

"Dismissed. I will inform you of the consequences."

The officer saluted and left the room.

An unfamiliar face was bent over Valentina when she opened her eyes. The face smiled. "You fainted," said the man with the trimmed white beard who stood before her and helped her sit up. She found herself on an examining table in what was obviously a doctor's office.

"I am Dr. Kirschbaum, the ship's doctor. I was supposed to examine you on orders of the captain, but before I could even introduce myself, you were gone." He smiled again, which was somewhat unsettling.

"Nothing bad, don't worry. I believe you are just hungry and thirsty and are wearing a very tightly laced corset. I have asked that tea and toast be brought."

When a tray arrived moments later, Dr. Kirschbaum handed her a cup. Valentina had to smile.

"Thank you. I am Valentina Meyer. Nice to meet you. Thank you for the tea. It's true, I haven't had any breakfast yet. And hardly any dinner. It hasn't exactly been a normal Sunday morning for me."

"So I've been told," responded the doctor. His white hair stuck out like a tidy wreath on his face. "That's why I have to examine you. Stowaways have to be examined right away after they are discovered."

"I wasn't discovered," answered Valentina. "I went to the captain myself."

"I'm just explaining why you are sitting here. I wasn't expressing an opinion about your character. And it isn't a bad thing that we are drinking tea together. You should eat some toast before you say anything else."

Dr. Kirschbaum poured himself a cup of tea, too, and continued, "By the way, I need to listen to your lungs and examine your eyes later."

He didn't want to say anything else. He turned toward his desk and leafed through a few notes. Valentina took a bite of toast, though she was embarrassed to eat in the presence of the doctor. But he didn't even look at her.

"You are very kind," Valentina said finally.

"Good, then I would like to examine you quickly. It won't take long."

Dr. Kirschbaum couldn't discern any obvious illnesses. Her lungs functioned normally, her eyes were clear. Anyone suffering from lung or infectious diseases wasn't allowed entry into the United States, but it didn't look like that would be an issue in this case.

"I am charged with bringing you to a stateroom after the examination. Luckily we aren't full in first class. You must have made a good impression on the captain if he is housing you there. You won't be allowed to leave your stateroom during the day since the dress code does not permit anyone to move about on board in formal clothing during the day. But I will see what I can do. Maybe I can find you a dress that is suitable for daytime..."

He hesitated a moment, then said, "Permit me one more question. You don't have to answer, but is there anyone in America who can pick you up in New York and vouch for you to the immigration authorities? We have to report you, and your case will be investigated on arrival."

Yes, of course. Even in America, freedom isn't simply handed out to anyone without question. Valentina shook her head. "I don't even know if I want to stay in America. I didn't even board the *Kroonland* to travel to New York. I am here because this ship happened to be in the harbor in Antwerp and..." she broke off. Her sigh sounded very genuine. "I wanted to get away from my life."

She sat back down on the couch. The space had suddenly begun to swim before her eyes again. Dr. Kirschbaum pulled up his swivel stool, sat down, and was quiet.

"You have to be able to imagine a future if you emigrate," she said. When he said nothing, she continued, "When the children die before the parents, there isn't a future anymore."

She had just answered one of the questions the doctor hadn't yet asked: why, in God's name, wasn't she just a regular passenger on this ship? Now he had a tiny clue.

"I am already old," he said cautiously, "and I have two grown children who will hopefully outlive me. You are young and have, if I understand correctly, already lost a child. It would be presumptuous to say that I understand your feelings. I don't know any more than you do whether there can be a future for you." He looked at her calmly. "Whether or not you want one someday. Or whether there is suddenly a future there for you because you have stopped struggling against it."

He saw that she relaxed a bit. She started to breathe easier, and some of the rosiness returned to her cheeks.

"I don't know much about life. The longer I am a doctor and the older I get, the less I understand. But I know that some events border on the miraculous. If I were a believer, I would speak about miracles."

He cleared his throat, suggesting perhaps that he was uncomfortable talking about miracles and beliefs. "Who can hope for these 'miracles' other than a doctor such as myself who is always working at the very fringes of life itself? Or I could give up and abandon the world."

Dr. Kirschbaum stood up. "Anyway, as you see, I am still a doctor."

He went to the door. "I'll get a chambermaid. I will instruct the girl to bring you some toiletry items and linens. The stewards will take care of your meals."

Valentina nodded. Dr. Kirschbaum squeezed her hand.

"Feel free to call me whenever you want to, not just when you have medical problems. You may find you'd like to exchange a few words with someone every now and then."

He opened his stateroom door.

"Oh, excuse me," Valentina called after him as though she had suddenly remembered something important. "Would it be possible for me to speak with the officer who was on duty on the gangway? His name was Bartels, if I understood correctly. I want to apologize. I have inconvenienced him…"

"I'll try to send him to you shortly. And in case you would like to notify anyone in New York or the States, we have new technology on board that makes it possible. It's a miracle, too. We can actually transmit messages to the mainland with the help of the Marconi transmitting station. If the station is working, that is."

Jan still couldn't comprehend it. His Valentina was on his ship. He had to pinch himself on the arm to be sure that he wasn't dreaming. They would slap him with a disciplinary punishment, that was clear; but what did that matter when she was right here on board with him!

The day before, Jan had entered the kitchen at Boulevard Number 19, where his mother worked, to find her gutting some fish under running water that she had bought at the market that morning. Griet, his mother, had shaken her head disapprovingly, not because of his arrival, but because the insides of one of the fish had an unusual appearance that filled his mother with a sense of foreboding. She wiped her hands, red and swollen from the cold water, on her apron and retied the bow in the back before embracing her son. Apart from her cold hands, she was already uncomfortably hot in her long black skirt and black stockings. She hated these muggy days. With both hands, she pressed Jan onto a chair and looked at him—he recognized the look well enough—with skepticism and concern.

"It's great to see you, my boy. You've been gone for months. But I don't know, Jan. That doesn't exactly make a mother happy. You're always at sea, and your father was a seaman, too, God rest his soul—if he should be dead. I know it's in your blood and I can't stop you. I didn't raise you, and my mother didn't drive out this nonsense." She began to chop parsley on a wooden board. "She always let you do what you wanted. But can't you at least work on a regular sailing ship for my sake?"

She paused and drew in a breath, sighing as she began to peel onions. Her eyes became moist as the onions released their pungent fumes. "Do you have to go off on this newfangled steamership? Look at the harbor. Aren't there enough beautiful sailing ships? Do you want me tossing and turning night after night as I imagine you crossing the sea on this monstrosity with the gigantic chimneys and that hell-fire burning below in the ship's hold?"

Jan laughed. He would have liked to kiss his mother, but that would have seemed odd to her. Valentina had always been her favorite; his mother had always rocked her in the kitchen in her strong arms and pressed her to her expansive bosom.

"But the new steamships are much safer than the sailing ships, Mother! They are safer and faster. I'll be home sooner if I travel on the *Kroonland* to New York and back than if I cross the sea in a sailing ship. And imagine how much more elegant and comfortable it is to travel on a passenger liner. There is a first and second class and multicourse meals like at the best restaurants in Antwerp. With wine, coffee, and chocolates. It's another world on these modern steamships. You have no idea."

Jan paused and bit his lip. "In a nutshell, you'll get used to it. Soon all ships will be using steam, you'll see. There is even a radio station on the ship that can transmit messages to the shore. Do you know what that means? Your Jan won't disappear to sea anymore without someone knowing what is going on with the ship. If a ship is in distress, it will be able to get to another shore. The ship can always stay in contact with the mainland."

Griet looked at him uncertainly. "I've heard of that," she said. "Frans, the carriage driver, told me about it. Spirits whisper in the air and now someone can pick up their voices out of the air with an apparatus." She sounded disapproving.

"Nonsense!" replied Jan. "Someone picks up signals that have been sent from a radio station. Through the air. But they're not the voices of the dead!"

Now Griet contradicted him firmly. "If someone can pick up these other signals, why can't they also pick up messages from the dead?"

Jan scratched his head. "Nonsense," he repeated. He tried again. "You're happy to have a kitchen with running water and a bathroom with a toilet that flushes. And it's the same with me. I would rather work on the *Kroonland* than on an old schooner."

Jan sighed, realizing that no matter what he said, his mother would never agree with him. As they were talking, she had salted the stomach of the fish, filled it with tomatoes and parsley, and squeezed lemon over the whole thing. "I don't have a lot of time at the moment," she said. "Babette and Frans are coming by to eat before they have to serve their master and mistress their noon meal. In any case," she added emphatically after a short pause, determined to have the last word, "I have a bad feeling about that steamship of yours."

Jan knew how superstitious Griet was and decided to let the matter drop. Since his mother had brought up the master and mistress, he finally found the right opening.

"How is Valentina?" he asked. "Is she home? Do you think I can see her?" Jan, tall and thin, looked as helpless as a child as he asked.

Griet shook her head.

"No, my boy. Get that out of your head. The chambermaid announced first thing this morning that Madame isn't receiving anyone. I asked whether she'd like something for lunch, but she doesn't. Monsieur will dine alone. And he hates that."

Griet had sat down and looked her son in the face. "Nothing has changed since the last time you were here. It's been like this forever. My poor little Valentina. She doesn't want to see anyone. She doesn't go out, she doesn't sing, she doesn't play the piano, she doesn't eat properly. She doesn't receive any invitations anymore. The trouble that I go to just to get her to eat! She won't let Monsieur near her and that makes him crazy. Sometimes when he's been drinking, he forces open her room. It frightens me that one of these days he might lay a hand on her. He has Frans, the driver, keep an eye on her and has asked him to report her every move—what she says, what she does, who she sees."

She shook her head again.

"He is obsessed with the idea that she betrayed him. He thinks that's why she steers clear of him. He is so jealous, Jan, you can't even imagine. And God knows," she sighed, "all men are jealous."

Jan didn't answer. His Valentina. His strong, stubborn Valentina, with whom he used to climb trees and run secretly to the harbor to look at the ships. How they had loved those ships that traveled down the river to the sea and out to the world. His Valentina with the amber eyes had always enchanted him, and even back then, when his mother still cooked for Valentina's grand-mother, he'd have done anything she asked. Shortly after he was born, his mother had sent him to her parents in the country because she couldn't be a cook in the mistress's household and look after him at the same time. She had visited him whenever she could—but that hadn't been often.

Whenever he had come to visit his mother in Antwerp, he had been allowed to play with Valentina. That is, until she got older. Then she wasn't a playmate anymore, but rather a young woman from a good home who wasn't allowed to have any contact with a servant's son. Jan had gone off to work at sea, but he had always continued to think of her as his Valentina.

"So I can't see her," he said and stood up abruptly. "Then tell her hello for me."

There was no other reason to stay.

"Take care, Mother. Until next time." He gave Griet an awk-ward hug. "The ship is supposed to set sail this afternoon. But we probably won't leave before ten because of a technical problem. We have to wait for the next tide."

Griet only nodded. Jan came and went; that's how it had always been. He was her child, but he had never fully belonged to her.

Back on the ship, Jan was thinking about his mother and how someday, when he had saved enough money, he would like to take a trip with her. If only he could persuade her to...

The ship doctor's voice jolted him out of his thoughts.

"Bartels, the gorgeous lady in the white evening gown would like to apologize for the inconvenience she has caused you. First class, stateroom 10."

Henri Sauvignac woke up late. He didn't have a full-blown head-ache, but he felt a certain pressure in his temple and had a furry taste in his mouth. Toward morning—after the disruptively noisy stop in Dover—he had fallen asleep again. Judging from the bright sunlight shining in through the round stateroom window, he guessed he'd been asleep for quite a while. From his bed, he reached for his pocket watch, which lay on his clothes. Its silver cover was delicately engraved and bore the initials of his father. It was an heirloom that Henri cherished. Every day, he buttoned the fob to his vest and slid the watch into his pocket.

It was nine o'clock. Normally Henri got up early. He loved the morning more than any other time of the day. He liked to compare the early morning to a woman who hasn't yet put on her makeup; a woman who has shared the night with him and squinted at the dawn light entering the room.

And again Lisette came to mind.

"You monster," she said. "Again? I'm still sleeping." She stretched as he caressed her, eventually sliding his fingers into her. As she began to turn her head back and forth, back and forth, Henri watched the pattern made by her brown hair as it coiled and fell in new shapes on the pillow. He grabbed her hair with one hand, held down her head, kissed her on the mouth, and in this manner they welcomed the day, together. Lying hot and limp, yet awake, body to body. With his hand still between her thighs, Lisette's thoughts drifted to strong black coffee with two lumps of sugar and Henri thought about the newspaper. She slapped his fingers lightly with the palm of her hand and said, "Come on, get up and make me some coffee. And open the window. Open it wide so that the morning air can come in…" Then she began to sing: *The wind should caress my stomach...* A fictitious, wistful melody.

Lisette is like the morning.

No.

He loved the morning because the morning is like Lisette when she wakes up.

But Lisette, where is Lisette?

Far away.

Henri lay on the narrow stateroom bed, where there was no lover, only wallpaper, in a floral pattern of green, brown, pink, beige. Carnations and dog roses, carnations and dog roses, leafy branches, and more carnations and dog roses.

Red- and green-patterned garlands were intertwined on the carpeting. A wild affair. The ceiling in the stateroom was white lacquered wood. Henri missed the smell of fresh earth in the morning, even if it was only the somewhat moldy scent wafting from the garden behind the house. He missed the smells of city life and the sounds of voices coming from his neighbor's open windows.

Most of all, he missed the smell and the voice of Lisette.

He knew he'd better get up. He washed at the basin, spraying water all over the garland-patterned carpeting. Henri snorted and looked in the mirror that hung above the vanity. He decided he needed to visit the ship's barber as soon as possible; his hair looked like an overgrown black jungle. At the barber, he would get his hair cut, get a shave, and have his walrus moustache trimmed. Henri ran his wet fingers through his hair and smoothed it down on his head as best he could. His dark five o'clock stubble already had the look of a three-day-old beard. He was tired of the beard and the constant shaving. At one such moment of weariness, Lisette had looked at him and said, "Men would really like to be women. That's why they treat them poorly." Then she'd nipped him on the cheek, a quick, painful little bite, and said, "And women sometimes would like to be men. Even often."

Then she had laughed and was gone. She was studying painting at the Académie Julien and spent a good deal of time there. Sometimes, when she came to sit as a model for Henri, she corrected his sketches. He was surprised that he let her correct his work, but he had to admit that she sketched brilliantly.

He put on a light linen suit, dark brown vest, and a white shirt with a comfortable sailor collar, and took a look at himself in the mirror. Yes, he looked good. Shortly the barber would make a somewhat civilized person out of him.

Henri was just closing the door to his stateroom when a chambermaid headed toward him. She was still just a child, a blue-eyed little girl. The girl wore a ruffled white apron over her blue- and white-striped dress and a bonnet on top of her braided white-blond hair.

"Excuse me, Monsieur, if I am disturbing you. But we must use the room next to you…" She smiled apologetically, unlocked the stateroom door with a heavy set of keys and held the door open. The new guest…

…was the lady in the white dress.

"My name is Lotte and I have just assumed the position of ship's chambermaid on the *Kroonland*. This was my first trip. And straight away something exciting happened. Not everyone is lucky enough to experience something like this. My mother will never believe me when I tell her. She would rather that I worked for a mistress in Antwerp or in Brussels, but I thought it would be more exciting to be on an ocean liner. Then you can see the whole world.

"We have to get up at night if someone rings for a chambermaid. But you don't get free time anywhere—except for going to church. I wouldn't be able to visit my mother in Antwerp any more often than I do now.

"Since all of the older chambermaids were busy, I was allowed to bring Madame to her stateroom. It was odd that she hadn't moved into a stateroom yet, since we were already at sea. It also struck me as strange that the deckhands and stewards didn't bring in any luggage. I heard later that she had simply gotten on board without a ticket or luggage. I would never dare to do something like that. I can't believe that she had the courage to do that at her age!

"Madame was very elegant, even if she was older. I am fifteen and she was easily twice as old as me. I think she must have just had enough of everything. I can't imagine how anyone could have had enough of everything if they have a house, a husband, money, and servants. Actually, I'm just assuming that she had a house and a husband. I don't really know.

"I can't marry, especially if I were to accept a position in the country. I would have to live with my mistress and be available whenever she needed me. If I got married, it would have to be to a man who earned enough that I could give up my position. But how I am to find such a person? Maybe I could work at the post office or the telegraph office. But most of the women there don't have husbands either, according to my sister. She should know because she works there."

Lotte Breughel, chambermaid on the Kroonland

The chambermaid had said she would bring her a few small necessities right away. The girl was named Lotte, a friendly child.

How Valentina yearned to strip off her evening gown, freshen up, brush her hair, and simply lie down, but first she had to speak with Jan and consider what to do next.

For two years, she had refused to think about what the next day would bring. Now she had maneuvered herself into a situation that forced her hand. She had no choice but to take her fate into her own hands. Viktor, with his mistrust and his jealous ways, was no longer steering her. Nor was little Charles, whose death had plunged her into such a miserable state—a no man's land between life and death—where there was no tenderness, no blue sky, no laughing, and no music.

The doctor was right. She had to make a decision. The ship would dock in New York in a few days. Then what? What would she say to the immigration authorities, to the police?

She imagined what it would sound like to tell them the truth: "I ran away. I ran away from my life. I couldn't stand my husband anymore. My house. My city. The view. Myself. Above all, myself. I didn't want to come to America. I wanted to go overboard on the first night, to merge with the blackness of the sea and the sky and never be found. But I didn't do it. I should have done it on the first night. I can't say why, but I didn't do it."

No one would believe her.

What had stopped her? The feeling that she couldn't do that to Jan? No one other than Jan would have known. But he would have had to live with the guilt of helping her do something for which he would never forgive himself.

If she was honest with herself, Valentina wasn't sure that Jan was the real reason. Perhaps she had simply been afraid of the black sea.

Or was it the simple fact that she had made a decision and taken action that saved her?

She had to think, think, think. When her mind was filled with doubt, she couldn't really think. Her thoughts just swirled in an endless circle and never came to any conclusions.

What had Dr. Kirschbaum said? Did she know anyone in America who could vouch for her?

Valentina rubbed her hands over her eyes. Why hadn't she thought of that? It was so obvious! There was someone in New York that she could turn to. Someone who was maybe even still waiting for her…

When Griet had told Valentina that Jan had been there and had asked about her, she had been angry that Griet hadn't brought him to her. Of course she would have wanted to see him; he was like a brother to her and had been her confidant since childhood. Griet was dense on this point: she had insisted on treating Valentina like a "mistress" ever since she had grown up. When Griet had told her that Jan was traveling on the *Kroonland* and would set sail later that day for New York, she had suddenly felt electrified. She couldn't banish the crazy idea that came to her. Now. Now or never. On the ship. Away from here. Jan would help her…

All she had to do was send a letter off with Babette, the maid, to the ship. No one would know a thing.

There was a knock on the stateroom door and Lotte entered with linens, soap, towels, and even eau de cologne.

"We found a dress," she said, "I'll bring it right away."

"Oh, Lotte…! Your name is Lotte?" Valentina called after the girl. "Could you also bring me paper, quill, and ink please?"

In the barber's mirror, Henri's father stared back at him, just as he remembered him from childhood: the broad Slavic nose; the dark, twinkling, slightly almond-shaped eyes; an unruly walrus moustache; thick black hair; and a complexion that reminded him of young olives. Henri looked more like his father every year. The barber had folded a white towel into his collar and set out his paraphernalia as meticulously as if he were a surgeon. He smelled of pomade and a cloyingly sweet toilet water. A fan on the ceiling spun over the barber's chair, its blades whirring softly. Henri studied the barber, trying to decide whether the barber dyed his eyebrows and his carefully twirled moustache; perhaps he only had that impression because the brows were so carefully plucked and the moustache shaped so precisely. His hair gleamed with pomade.

I couldn't achieve that effect with an entire pound of pomade, Henri thought. The stone dust had made his hair dull and brittle over the years. Wistfully he remembered how Lisette would take hold of it as though it were a horse's mane when they were making love. No matter how violently he shook his head, he couldn't shake off her strong little hands when she held tight and wouldn't let go.

Henri decided to have his hair trimmed, but no more than that, in memory of Lisette, who liked longer hair on him. After several unsuccessful attempts at dragging Henri into conversation, the barber went about his work in a quiet and professional manner.

Going to the barber with his father was among Henri's earliest memories. He recalled sitting on a greasy leather chair designated for those who were waiting. Knee socks covered his perpetually scraped-up legs, which dangled above the floor. Henri remembered how his father, with his strong, authoritative voice, frightening manner, and a dangerous gleam in his eye always turned meek under the barber's hands. He always remained very still and spoke animatedly as the barber wielded his sharp scissors and straight razors. His instruments obviously put him in a position of power.

His father's mother, Henri's grandmother, was from Armenia, and everything that Henri's mother didn't understand in the behavior of her husband, she attributed to his foreign ancestry: his violent outbursts, but also his way of expressing his feelings without shame, even though he was a man.

Henri's father owned a hauling company, which young Henri had liked since he loved the stocky draft horses, with their soft, dark nostrils. He fondly recalled their warm coats that twitched and darkened with sweat. When the horses were unharnessed after work, the drivers threw blankets over them—prickly, rough blankets that smelled of animals. He loved it when the horses snorted, shook their manes, and drank water; when they curled their lips and took a carrot from his hand in their yellow teeth, making crunching sounds as they chewed. Henri loved the smell of the stalls and the straw—even the round horse droppings. He used to watch intently as the carts were loaded with oak barrels, gunnysacks, rough-hewn wooden crates, and heavily laden wooden baskets.

As a child, he wanted to touch everything: skin, hide, fabric, grass, stone, wood, iron, glass, clay, plaster, earth, flower petals, tree bark, earwax, mortar, the slimy surface of trout, sand, leather, and wool. He learned the difference between organic and inorganic textures. His fingertips were endlessly curious, and he learned to close his eyes and not interrupt his fingertips as they studied some new surface, entering it into memory through the pores of his skin. He also explored through taste and smell, learning how water, blood, and wine tasted, and compared them to salt and sugar, lemon and vinegar, closing his eyes to focus his senses. He tried to train his ear as well, but the variety of sounds was too overwhelming. He came to trust only that which he could touch. And he learned one final thing: bodies don't lie.

He wasn't a good student; he couldn't add particularly well, and he was often distracted in his lessons. He ended up listening to the noises in the street instead of his teacher and the laborious efforts of his fellow students.

He should have taken over his father's hauling company. Henri's father had a terrible temper and was apt to throw tantrums at the smallest thing—if the cook hadn't prepared a dish to his taste or if Henri wasn't sitting properly at the table—so Henri was surprised when he agreed to let Henri, at age fourteen, start apprenticing with a stonemason.

Henri remembered the day he asked for permission. After asking the question, he had stared anxiously at the black tuft of hair that grew out of his father's ear, then fixed his gaze on his father's stiff, high collar, and then on the fabric-covered buttons on his vest, all to avoid looking his father in the eye as he scrutinized him. Then, when Henri fell silent and didn't offer any further explanation, his father had cleared his throat cautiously and said, "Do it, Henri, my son."

Henri had never questioned why his father had allowed him to pursue this calling. His mother was unhappy that Henri wouldn't be taking after his father, who was a good businessman and had built a successful company, but simply attributed his inexplicable decision to the Armenian ancestry of her spouse.

The hairdresser had done his job well. Henri was thankful to see that he looked much as he did before, only groomed. He nodded when the barber asked whether he would be allowed to trim back his walrus moustache.

Afterward, the barber dusted some powder over Henri's smoothly shaved cheeks and dismissed his customer without a finishing splash of eau de cologne, which Henri had declined.

A satisfied Henri pressed a tip into the barber's soft hand and was sorry that his father, who had died more than a year ago, could no longer make his cherished daily visit to the barber.

It was as though Dr. Kirschbaum had turned on a light in her memory and dredged up something that Valentina had buried long ago.

Yes, there was someone she knew in America; she even had his address memorized: R. Livingston, Madison Square/Corner Madison Avenue, New York.

Valentina lowered her head and undid her bun. She unraveled the thick braids with small, practiced moves, enjoying the lovely release as her hair tumbled down over her shoulders. Then she unbuttoned the hated white dress, so confining that it made it difficult to breathe, loosened the dreaded corset, and lay on the bed, which smelled of fresh soap. As soon as her head hit the pillow, she released a long sigh of relief.

I'll only rest for a moment, she thought. Just a short moment.

When he had listened to her lungs, Dr. Kirschbaum had asked if she had been sick recently.

"No," she had answered, "not really sick. But there was a period when I wasn't well."

She had considered whether she could trust the doctor and then added, "I didn't have any appetite. Dr. Koch, a close family friend, sent me to do a health cure in the mountains in the fall of 1902." She recalled how she hadn't been hungry for anything—for food, for music, for light, for touch, even for air.

After her son's funeral, she had given up everything that was part of a normal life. In addition to losing her appetite, she didn't leave the house, she didn't sleep at night, and she stopped speaking. Mathilde, her grandmother, had wanted her to visit her in the house where she had grown up, thinking that would help Valentina recover. However, Viktor and Griet had protested.

"A wife belongs with her husband," said Viktor. "Valentina's home is with me."

In the beginning, he was patient with her. "How are you today, my little dove?" he asked every day. She never answered, and the more he asked, the more tight-lipped she became.

"Surely, you'll be fine soon," he said helplessly. Over time, an angry and impatient tone crept into his voice. She pushed his hand away when he touched her, turned her face away when he wanted to kiss her, sat across from him in the dining room without touching her plate, or laid down her fork after slowly, and with infinite difficulty, taking a couple of dainty bites. Although he was ashamed of it, Viktor felt a rage growing in him. In contrast to Valentina, he wanted to continue living. Despite himself, his anger grew as the beautiful creature he had married faded away before his eyes like a flower.

Griet, too, was hurt that Valentina, whom she loved and had nurtured since infancy, rejected the foods that she had thoughtfully prepared and that she turned away from the comfort of her strong arms.

Mathilde and Dr. Koch tried to convince Valentina and Viktor that she needed a change of scenery. Dr. Koch wanted to send her to do a health cure, preferably in the mountains, before the early winter began up there.

He hoped that the fresh mountain air would awaken Valentina's appetite and that walks and spa treatments would strengthen her nerves. "It is a tedious trip," he said, "but a few weeks in such different surroundings will distract you and do you good. If you are in agreement, I will telegraph them right away to find a hotel for you."

To Viktor, who felt uneasy about having his wife out of his sight and traveling alone, Dr. Koch said sternly, "Monsieur Gruschkin, your wife's nerves have been attacked. You must take a step back from the events. If you want to help your marriage, let her go, and let her go alone. Everything that reminds her of the death of her child—and by that, I mean you, too—has to stay behind. When she returns, she may be more receptive to the idea of having more children—an idea she wouldn't even consider now."

However, it wasn't just Viktor who fought against Dr. Koch's suggestion. Valentina didn't seem to want to go either.

"I don't need a health cure," she said softly but with unmistakable defiance. "I am not sick. I just want to be left in peace. We all know that *Maman* needs spas. I, however, do not."

Maman was virtually nonexistent in Valentina's life. Or rather, Maman had reacted unhappily to the fact that she had a daughter. She spent her life traveling to different therapeutic baths in Europe to cure her various gynecological disorders. And Valentina didn't want to be anything like her mother, Henriette.

Dr. Koch's suggestion that Valentina should undergo a cure was not only devastating, but also humiliating in Valentina's eyes. Was she already following in Henriette's footsteps? Maman was hysterical, demanding, discontent, restless, and selfish. Was Valentina destined to become the same? Even her grandmother was no help.

"Grandmaman," she said pleadingly, "I can't believe that you agree with Dr. Koch, that you too think I should be sent to a cure. Do you really think that is the answer? To have me follow in Maman's footsteps? You said yourself that she is incapable of returning to real life!"

Valentina looked reproachfully at her grandmother, who had appeared together with Dr. Koch at the Gruschkins' home to appeal to Viktor and Valentina's consciences.

Mathilde took Valentina's hand in both of her hands and rubbed them to warm them up.

"Valja, don't get upset," she said. "Your mother is your mother. The spa cures can't do anything for her, that's just how she is. Even the best doctors and the best spas can't help someone who doesn't want to be healthy. That's true, my dear," Mathilde looked Valentina straight in the eyes, "The same is true for you."

Valentina looked at the floor and didn't respond. What did they all want? Her child was dead; how was she supposed to behave otherwise? She stuck out her chin stubbornly, as she had done when she was a child.

"Valja," Mathilde knew the gesture all too well, "don't be petulant. You know very well that I don't mean that you shouldn't grieve. But you need support, help, so that you won't be so unhappy, as your mother is."

Valentina continued to look at the floor. Dr. Koch went into the other room to speak with Viktor and left Mathilde sitting alone with Valentina in her boudoir. She clasped her granddaughter to her. The faint scent of her grandmother's perfume suddenly transported Valentina to her grandmother's garden. She had been perhaps seven, a little girl with honey-blond curls. She pictured herself crouching on the warm ground, mapping out a square with a stick in the loose earth where she wanted to lay out her own garden. It was a sunny spring afternoon. Suddenly a shadow fell across the grass, right over her future garden. Valentina grabbed her straw hat and looked up to see who had come up behind her.

"Maman," she called, surprised. "Maman!" With a small cry, she jumped to her feet. She wanted to throw her arms around her mother, but hesitated, realizing she had dirty hands. She noticed that her mother hadn't thrown open her arms like Griet and Grandmaman did or even bent down to her. Valentina wiped her hands nervously on the blue gardening apron Griet had tied around her. A small perpendicular wrinkle of disapproval appeared between her mother's eyebrows. "Valentina! Just look at you! But come here and say hello!"

Valentina looked up at her mother shyly but with adoration. She wore a pearl-gray silk dress with pink passementerie and a pink hat. In her left hand, she held a small pink and white striped parasol. Her unbelievably small waist was accentuated by her bustle. Valentina, whose grandmother always dressed simply and had impressed her dislike of ribbons and rosettes on her granddaughter, questioned whether her mother could even sit down.

She dutifully presented herself to her mother, who finally bent down and kissed her on the forehead. A whiff of her expensive-smelling perfume wafted past Valentina's nose. Even today,

Valentina remembered the exotic scent, one of her few memories of her mother. She learned later that the mysterious scent was a *chypre* perfume, a blend of aromatic wood notes from the Mediterranean Sea. As she inhaled the scent, she thought, yes, that was her mother, a mysterious, elegant, inaccessible woman smelling of a foreign world.

"You've grown," said Henriette. "You have my hair." She grabbed a curl that had spilled out from under Valentina's straw hat and let it slide through her thin fingers, fingers that had certainly never laid out a garden bed. Her mother didn't say anything about Valentina's eyes. Valentina looked up at her mother's, which were an intense blue. She thought that her papa had surely fallen for her because of those blue eyes.

"Come inside," her mother said. "There's tea." She held out her hand and Valentina grabbed it quickly, as though she knew the opportunity might disappear. The warmth of her mother's hand penetrated through the fine material of her glove, and Valentina felt secure.

As they entered the house, hand in hand, Valentina plucked up her courage and asked, "Are you going to stay with us now, Maman?" Her heart beat so intensely as she uttered the question that the words came out breathlessly.

Henriette stopped, let go of her daughter's hand, looked at her, and said, "No, Valentina. You know that the climate here makes me sick." She smiled, clearly annoyed, and Valentina felt suddenly guilty for even daring to ask such a question. "I'm leaving the day after tomorrow. Now come, Grandmaman is waiting."

Valentina nodded. She didn't dare reach for her mother's hand again. She had only herself to blame for the fact that a trace of irritation now blemished Maman's clear forehead. Once again Valentina had been thinking only of herself. Maman was better off in Corfu, Ischia, or in the mountains—anywhere that Valentina was not.

No. Valentina looked steadily at her grandmother. She didn't want to go to a cure. She wanted to stay in Antwerp. She just wanted to sit and listen to the silence. There she would wait for the day to follow the night and for the night to follow the day. She would wait, until finally Charles's laugh would penetrate the infinite silence within her. Images would surface in her memory of Charles snuggling up to her, sitting on her lap, and taking his first steps, first away from her, then back into her outstretched arms. But the memory was blotted out. Everything beautiful had been wiped out.

Although Dr. Koch and Grandmaman had different motives, they didn't give up. Dr. Koch was afraid for Valentina's physical health; Mathilde for her soul. Viktor's increasingly cold manner toward his wife also concerned Mathilde. She had always been against this marriage, having hoped for a younger, more communicative husband for her granddaughter.

Finally, worn down by all the discussions, Valentina relented and allowed Dr. Koch to make arrangements for her to lodge at a health resort in St. Moritz-Bad in Switzerland.

As Valentina drifted in and out of sleep in her stateroom, she remembered the long trip to Switzerland, during which she had experienced a similar dawning realization. Viktor and Dr. Koch had brought her from Antwerp to Paris and helped her transfer her luggage to a train from Paris to Chur. An older woman, Madame Adeline Brochet, an acquaintance of Dr. Koch, had accompanied her the rest of the way. After the trains, she boarded a stagecoach, which, harnessed by four strong brown horses, the roof heavy with luggage, carried her over the Julier Pass to St. Moritz, an arduous thirteen-hour journey.

Richard Livingston, an American from New York, had traveled with her in the same coach.

Porridge
Omelet with Ham and Parsley
Mackerel à la Maison
Sirloin Steak Bordelaise, Lamb Chops
Sautéed Calves Liver, Hamburger Steaks
Potatoes, Buckwheat Pancakes
Marmalade, Honey, Toast
Fruit

The considerable choice of items for breakfast was quite different from Henri's usual breakfast fare. Sunlight filtered through the elegant glass skylight that arched over the dining room, brightening the painted woodwork on the walls and the graceful wooden pillars with their ornate capitals.

It was already almost noon and Henri was the only guest in the dining room except for five gentlemen traveling together. They were the Russians whom Henri had heard boarding the ship in Dover. The remains of an abundant breakfast lay before them; their expansive laughter could be heard throughout the room. They were of varying ages, but it seemed that they shared the same memories. To Henri, it sounded like they were regaling each other with old stories, the kind that are told and retold, embellished each time, in order to affirm and refresh old friendships.

Henri generally felt uncomfortable in the company of men. He hadn't ever embraced the boisterous rituals through which men swear fellowship. All the backslapping and swaggering was awkward for him.

Nevertheless, he couldn't help but ask himself what had induced these five men to take a trip together. As he left the dining room, he passed the group and greeted them. One of the older Russians answered jovially, "Bonjour, Monsieur! God doesn't want anyone to eat alone or sleep alone. Why don't you join us at our table…" He stood up, extended his hand to Henri in an inviting gesture, and introduced himself, "Ostrowskij, Andrej. My pleasure."

The man had thick, dark hair with a bit of gray at the temples; he had a small round mole in the middle of his chin, where other people had a dimple, and full lips. He swept his hair from his forehead in a distinctive manner, with the back of the hand instead of his palm.

The other four introduced themselves as well, but Henri didn't even bother to try to remember their names. Ostrowskij, however, stuck in his mind because of the unusual mole and the man's catlike elegance. He made him think of the numerous cats in his studio that Lisette had always insisted on feeding when she was over.

"I always think of you when I see cats," she had told him once, digging her arm into his side. "You can only be enticed with meat. But when you are full, you go out again and stroll through the city, drawn by the smell of the streets wet from rain, the damp walls of houses, and muggy summer afternoons. Then you sit down in the unmowed grass of strangers' front yards and soak up the fragrance of the lilacs and roses…" She let her arm drop from his hip and turned away. "I hate that, I hate that about you, the strolling." Tears formed in her eyes. "Sometimes I hate you. That's why I'm nice to these cats," she explained softly. Henri didn't like the resigned tone in her voice, so he didn't answer.

Henri stood indecisively in front of Andrej.

"We ordered caviar for the pancakes," said one of the Russians and pointed to a younger blond man who sat directly across from him. "It's Nicolai's birthday. His thirtieth. Would you like to drink a toast with us?"

"Here comes the champagne!" Andrej called, and Henri sat down, even though he had no connection to Nicolai.

"Another glass for the gentleman here," called the Russian to the steward, a good-looking blond lad with blue eyes, whom the ladies had eyed surreptitiously the day before.

Henri wasn't sure that champagne before noon was a good idea, but the man sitting next to Henri, a blue-eyed giant with a smooth, broad baby face and thin ash-blond hair, had already filled the glasses.

"To Nicolai!" he called. Explaining, he turned toward Henri, "To Nicolai who is not only thirty, but who will also get married when we arrive in New York. To Nicolai!" he repeated and raised his glass.

Young Nicolai made a face and drew his index finger across his throat to indicate that he thought marriage might be the end of him.

"Old age draws near and freedom is coming to an end. This has been a beautiful farewell to my old life with you," he said and raised his glass. "To Paris, to London, and the most beautiful bordellos of old Europe. To our friendship and to the hidden joys of the future!" He laughed and clinked glasses with everyone, including Henri.

How true, thought Henri.

He could picture it all. Nicolai would get married in New York and then take a lover soon afterward, a saleslady or a girl from the telegraph office. He would pay for her apartment because the money she earned, as everyone knew, wasn't enough to live on. He would start a business, raise children, and get together with his friends here and there for a drinking spree and a trip to a whorehouse.

He wouldn't be making any more trips like this; the next time, his wife and children would be on board. He would show them London and the Eiffel Tower in Paris and not mention all that he had done and seen in these cities. He would stroll with a walking stick and his family beside him in Hyde Park, half-bald at that point. He would be proud of everything he had achieved and would buy his wife a new hat and an elegant coat to mark this beautiful day in Paris. He would secretly send his switchboard operator a postcard and maybe even a telegram saying that he missed her. He would tell them a few suggestive stories about his earlier trips. His children would laugh and believe everything; his wife would fill in a few omissions in her head with her imagination, but then discard them again as nonsense; and his lover would try not to think about anything or feel anything.

These six men knew all this, drank toasts to it, and accepted things as they were. Henri, however, just felt relief that he had never married. This phony, bourgeois world turned his stomach.

He looked at an oil painting, a placid landscape that hung across from him on the wall. The picture calmed him. He thought of his studio, of the wooden crates in which the clay lay wrapped in damp towels. He thought of the stone that he had looked at in St. Triphon. It had been delivered to him a few days earlier in Antwerp. He thought of his old studio in Paris, the tall, filthy windowpanes that looked out onto the garden; it seemed unlikely that they had ever been cleaned. And he remembered Lisette, who had written in the grimy dust, "Go away. Don't ever come back." Then she had left.

The Russians wanted to order another bottle of champagne, but the stewards needed to set the tables for lunch and asked the group to move to the smoking lounge. Henri accompanied them to the door of the men's lounge and said good-bye.

The baby-faced giant shoved the younger ones through the door to the smoking lounge. Nicolai followed dutifully. The last one to enter blinked at Henri with his watery eyes and said, "Until later, then. We will be drinking lots more champagne this week."

And with a slight bow and a graceful wave, he closed the door of the lounge behind him, waving once more to Henri.

As he stood before her, he couldn't get over his good fortune at getting to see her like that: with her hair loose, like when she was a young girl and they were allowed to be together without any formalities. She had written to him. She had asked him to help her. He was the only person she could trust. He was her savior. When Babette, Valentina's maid, had asked for him at the harbor and slipped him the letter, he hadn't hesitated. After scanning it, he had only nodded to Babette and said, "Hurry back and tell Madame that everything's all right. I have gotten the message."

Now here he was with Valentina on his ship, like a knight with his beloved queen on the run.

"Jan, come here! Sit by me!" Valentina pulled him closer to her with both hands. "What are you thinking about? Sit…"

She didn't let go of his hands.

"How can I thank you," she said. "You are the only person, the most trustworthy friend that I have. I knew what I was asking of you even when I wrote the message to you, without being able to give any kind of an explanation. I knew that you would be taking on something that you could be punished for, even if I never ever betrayed you. Forgive me that I asked you to break the regulations."

How beseechingly she looked at him!

"But don't worry," Valentina continued. "No one will ever find out that you know me, that you smuggled me onto the ship, and tucked me away in an empty stateroom…"

Valentina's eyes filled with tears. Jan watched how a teardrop formed in the corner of her eye, quivering for a moment before finally rolling down Valentina's cheek. Jan bent toward her, hesitated, and brought his face closer to hers, his lips almost touching the trail of the tear. But then she let go of his hands and wiped her cheek before he could come any closer.

He wanted to say something, but Valentina continued:

"No one can be allowed to figure out that we know one another. Otherwise you will be drawn into things. Starting now, this is my problem, and mine alone, do you hear me? I won't let you have anything to do with it, no matter what happens!"

He shook his head, wanting to interject, but Valentina put her finger on his mouth.

"No. Don't say anything. I will never forget what you have done for me, but from now on, this is my affair."

What was she talking about? She had linked her fate with his, and now she wanted to throw him out of the boat again?

Supposedly because she wanted to protect him? It was smart to conceal his involvement, yes; he could do more for her if he wasn't arrested. But he wasn't a coward. He had offered her his help. But he hadn't done that just to be banned from her life again.

"Your affair is also my affair," he said and turned angrily away from her. "Have you forgotten that we spent our childhood together, that we told each other everything, that we swore eternal friendship? Didn't you notice my feelings for you back then? Of course you didn't. We weren't allowed to be friends anymore..." He stopped, too proud to continue speaking.

Valentina bit her lip and stroked his hand.

"Jan, Jan...calm down. Calm down. How could I forget our childhood? I just said that you are my best friend. I took terrible offense when Griet didn't bring you to me yesterday morning. Of course I wanted to see you. I scolded her for that, believe me. Then she made excuses, said that you had to leave right away, that there were problems with the *Kroonland* and it wouldn't set sail until later in the evening..."

She tried to take his face in her hands, to force him to look into her eyes. But he didn't want to. He turned his head stubbornly away.

"We're talking about different things," he said. When she didn't contradict him, he felt a rage start to grow inside him.

"Jan, I want to ask you something else, even though you are mad at me. Just to be clear, I don't want you to be involved in my affairs in any way, not now and not later. But I would like to ask you if you can do one more thing for me. The doctor told me that there is a radio station on the ship and that it is possible to transmit messages to the mainland. I am not allowed to move freely on board. But I would like to send my grandmother a telegram. She will be terribly worried about me, but she won't betray me. And so you know: I am using her name instead of mine…So would you do me a favor and give this message to the radio operator with the request to pass it on?"

"Oh, so now I am supposed to help you again?" he answered fiercely.

"It is just a request. You can refuse."

"Sure, I can refuse," he retorted.

"So? You'll do it?"

"What? Pass on the message?"

"Yes."

He was silent.

Valentina stood up and came back with two envelopes.

Despite himself, he reached for them.

Valentina breathed a sigh of relief. "And this message…please give this message to the radio operator too."

She didn't let him answer. She just pulled him to the door and said, "Thank you, Jan. As soon as things have calmed down, I'll let you know. Here on this ship we can't betray ourselves. But I promise you, I'll get in touch. I'll tell you everything. Believe me, we will never lose each other. Never."

Then she pushed him out the door.

"I'm not interested in the case. I don't have anything more to say. I also haven't set eyes on this woman like the others.

"I have been the ship's engineer on the *Kroonland* since early 1903. The *Kroonland* was built in Philadelphia in 1901 up to the latest technical standards: two chimneys, twin propellers, twelve thousand horsepower with electrical lighting, heating, and ventilation in every passenger area.

"We were delayed this time, which is unusual. There was a problem with the Marconi station. The wireless telegraphy is still in its infancy, you see. We fixed the problem quickly, but we had to wait for the next tide before we could put out to sea.

"I didn't hear about the woman until the next day when the captain informed the officers that there was a stowaway on board, a lady, without money or luggage. He said that she didn't have proper daytime attire and therefore wouldn't be allowed to move about on board during the day. He said she wasn't your typical stowaway; she looked like a high-society type.

"I don't know who will eventually pay for the expenses she has incurred.

"I don't like stowaways. The fact that we were delayed is already a blemish on our reputation. The Red Star Line is very proud of their reliability and precision. On a large ship, everything has to function smoothly, and I am responsible for making sure the machinery is running properly. If all the cogs don't mesh, there is chaos.

"We have a four-hundred-man crew and take up to fifteen hundred passengers on board. You can't imagine the discipline and order that are required.

"As an employee of one of the leading shipping companies in the world, I can only imagine how incidents like this one will affect our reputation.

"I don't know what is going on in this woman's head. I don't want to know, either. She must be sick or possibly crazy. I'm assuming she left her husband and children. She isn't exactly a young girl anymore.

"As for this new trend of women traveling alone, I know there are times when it can't be avoided; not all widows have someone who can accompany them. But that has to remain the exception.

These suffragettes who are popping up everywhere are putting bees in women's bonnets. I wouldn't have become an engineer if I didn't believe in progress. Technology is moving the world forward. But that doesn't mean that the basic social structure can come unhinged. We men don't want to start having babies all of a sudden.

"Everything has its proper place, and that is for the best."

Albert Hiller, ship's engineer on the Kroonland

The passengers on the *Kroonland* had taken over the promenade decks, and the weather was downright boring in its beauty: blue sky, blue sea in every direction, as far as the eye could see.

Not that anyone wanted a storm, but a white cloud or two in the sky would have enlivened the view. The shadowless noon light didn't allow for the trace of a secret. Henri thought of his mysterious neighbor, but hard as he tried to find her, she seemed to have vanished without a trace. Henri didn't dislike the fact that she preferred the moonlight and a sparkling night sky to the summery goings-on on deck. However, he felt that she had some significance in his life that he hadn't yet figured out.

"Monsieur Sauvignac!" called a bright voice that suited the daylight and blew over him like a soft summer breeze. "Hello, Monsieur Sauvignac…Here!" Mrs. Henderson was waving to him. She leaned over the railing next to Mr. Brown, looking enchanting in a blue- and white-striped summer dress with a wide blue waistband and long sleeves that billowed at the shoulders. The white stand-up collar was cut like a man's, and Henri grinned when he saw that she was wearing a tie too. She wore a matching bow in her hair that was reminiscent of a dove's spread wings. A white ruffled parasol shaded the upper half of her face. She appeared refreshed, and Henri had to smile involuntarily as she waved at him furiously as though they were old acquaintances.

"Mr. Brown and I are going for a walk on deck and we were just discussing whether we should play a game of shuffleboard. Do you have any interest in playing? Later, in the afternoon, it will certainly be too hot..."

Mr. Brown took Billie Henderson lightly but possessively by the arm and greeted Henri with a nod. He looked rather formal in his elegant brown suit. Though he wasn't especially memorable, his white shirt, brown vest, and plain straw hat suited him.

"Good day, Monsieur Sauvignac. So here we are again. It is hard to lose sight of someone on a ship." He didn't sound especially enthusiastic about having run into Henri. "We would like"—again, he spoke for his companion—"to play a game of shuffleboard with you, but maybe not right now. I told Billie that we should have lunch soon, and it is already twelve thirty. It would be too bad if we had to break up the game."

Billie Henderson looked off into the distance as if she would find answers there, and then pursed her lips as though she wanted to pout or give him a kiss—or both. Before Henri could respond to Mr. Brown, she said, "And I just told William that I am still full from breakfast. I tried way too many delicious things."

"Nevertheless, they are expecting us at lunch, my dear," said Mr. Brown. An awkward pause followed.

Billie's brown curls trembled under her dove bow, and her parasol tipped forward slightly as she motioned with her hands. She looked at Henri, as though silently encouraging him to conspire with her against lunch.

"Lunch may be mandatory," said Henri, "but shuffleboard is not. Nothing is preventing us from stopping before the game is over."

Mr. Brown nodded with a confident willingness to compromise. Dimples appeared on Billie's cheeks as she smiled in agreement, "That's good. But then we won't know who has won!"

"Is that important?" asked Henri.

"Yes," she replied seriously.

She gathered her skirt and, still on Mr. Brown's arm, led the way to the oval court. Her parasol wavered and performed odd pirouettes as she walked. She turned around several times to make sure Henri was following behind.

He did so with a great deal of pleasure. He was looking forward to playing with her.

In steerage, lunch was put out promptly at noon on long, narrow wooden tables. The emigrants huddled on the benches and filled their tin cups with potatoes, beans, and dried cod. The menu would change only slightly over the course of the trip, featuring dried herring, corned beef, or bacon before more dried cod. And tea. The passengers complained endlessly that the food was too salty and caused flatulence.

The separate sleeping quarters for men and women overflowed with baskets and crates, tied up rolls and suitcases. As long as the weather was good, everyone stayed outside, if for no other reason than the noise inside made them half-crazy: the engine rooms lay directly between the women's and men's dormitories.

Meals took place later in the first-class dining room, and the choices were more extensive. Mrs. Henderson, Mr. Brown, and Henri headed in for lunch after their game of shuffleboard broke up early at Mr. Brown's request. Mrs. Henderson picked at a salad and said little. Mr. Brown talked about Philadelphia and his work as a patent attorney. He was kept busy during this period of great inventions, and Henri believed him when he said he earned good money. He refrained from asking Mrs. Henderson about her spouse or whether she worked. Both questions would certainly have embarrassed her.

The family with the three children sat with them at the same table. The father, seated next to Henri, looked sternly across the table away from his family. He introduced himself to Henri as Anselm Vanstraaten. His full, carefully groomed beard gave him a striking appearance, but his steel-blue eyes could make a person uncomfortable. On the other side of the table, Madame Vanstraaten ate quietly, her gaze lowered, as though she didn't want to look her husband or anyone else in the eye. Next to her sat a little girl whose name was Olivia. She wore a white dress with lace trim, white knee-highs, and black patent leather shoes; the large ribbon on her head was slightly askew. She had inherited her mother's thin blond hair, which did little to hold up the heavy ribbon. The mother straightened the headdress, and the little girl moved closer to her mother. The boys were making faces but weren't asked to stop because their mother didn't notice and their father didn't care. He was too busy explaining to Henri that he was a ship's engineer. Safety technology was his specialty, and he went on to explain in detail why the new steel and watertight compartments made the modern ships unsinkable.

As Vanstraaten was extoling the merits of the new steel construction at length, he felt a finger softly tap his sleeve. A delicate floral scent—reminiscent of jasmine—wafted across him. Mrs. Henderson whispered to him, "Excuse me if I'm interrupting your conversation. I just wanted to say good-bye. I am going to lie down for a bit. We'll see each other later."

She stood up, as did Mr. Brown.

"Thank you, William," she said, more loudly so that Henri could hear. "That is very kind of you, but it isn't necessary for you to accompany me. I can find stateroom 27 by myself. Shall we meet for the music program on deck? The ship's band is giving a concert this afternoon at four."

She left an empty seat next to Mr. Brown and left Henri feigning interest in Monsieur Vanstraaten's long-winded technical explanations.

She told me her stateroom number, thought Henri.

A trace of jasmine hung in the air and led straight to stateroom 27, if anyone wanted to follow it. Henri had noticed that Mrs. Henderson had freckles on her face, and while Monsieur Vanstraaten talked, Henri found himself thinking about them—and how much he'd like to see if she had them anywhere else. He pictured her body spread out before him like a starry sky and lost himself in the fantasy of naming her freckles as though they were constellations. How intentional had it been for her to mention her stateroom number?

Wasn't that as good as a direct invitation to follow her? Hadn't she expressly declined Mr. Brown's company and pointed the way for Henri?

There are always women who make the first move, thought Henri. Whether or not she was conscious of it, she had started the game. And we men, he thought, we just follow the trail of jasmine.

Henri was an experienced collector of trails and signals. He didn't do so consciously. His senses simply picked up on all the silent signals: the softening of a voice, the sparkle in the eye, the scent of the skin. He noticed the twitch of the lips before they were pulled into—or suppressed—a smile, the imperceptible tremor in a laugh, the small erratic uncertainties in hand movements, a blush that was gone in a flash. The discrepancy between word and gesture when no really meant yes.

He had spent his life observing people and objects. It was his profession and his passion. After pondering for a few minutes, he came to the conclusion that Billie Henderson had been very direct. Maybe she needed someone, anyone, to take her into his arms.

The sun fell through the glass dome in the dining room and bathed Henri in golden light. When Henri started listening again to Monsieur Vanstraaten, he had lost the thread. Monsieur Vanstraaten didn't seem to notice: He was clearly accustomed to delivering a monologue.

"As the ship's doctor, as any doctor, I am required to be discreet. Therefore, I can't add much to Madame Meyer's story. Stowaways who are discovered have to be examined by a doctor. I can assure you that Madame Meyer is neither mentally confused nor hysterical. She suffers perhaps from a certain melancholy as grips us all when we are faced with difficulties in life and which can throw anybody off course. I cannot and will not say anything more."

Dr. Alfred Kirschbaum, doctor on the Kroonland

It took Henry almost an hour to find stateroom 27.

Henri listened at the door for a moment, but no sound came from the stateroom. He knocked. Silence. He knocked again. Then he heard Mrs. Henderson's voice call out brightly, "Just a moment...one moment...I'm coming, who's there...?"

She opened the stateroom door a few inches. Henri saw the surprise in her face.

"Monsieur Sauvignac!" she exclaimed in a high voice.

Obviously she had really lain down because she now held her dress in front of herself as a protective shield. Her shoulders were bare; with one naked arm, she pressed the dress over her breasts and with the other, she held the stateroom door open. Clothed in nothing but her white stockings, she looked utterly enchanting.

"Mrs. Henderson," Henri said, honestly surprised. "I've obviously come at a bad time. Excuse me."

She looked at him for a moment with a quizzical expression on her face. Her hair, pinned up in a loose bun, was askew, and some tresses had come loose. They rested fetchingly on her naked shoulders. Henri Sauvignac didn't budge.

"Come in," she said. Henri didn't know what was going through her mind, but she opened the stateroom door further and pulled him across the threshold. "My God, you'll compromise me! If anyone sees us like this—you in front of my door and me half undressed behind it...You are impossible, you know that? Sit down, I'll be right back." She pointed sternly at a settee and disappeared into the small dressing room. He could see directly into her bed from the settee. The cover was pulled back, and the pillows were out of place.

Too bad that she's getting dressed, thought Henri. He called quietly over to her, "You don't have to get dressed on my account,

Mrs. Henderson. I find you charming even when you are just holding your dress in your hand."

"What? What did you say, Monsieur Sauvignac? I believe I didn't understand you correctly..." Henri still couldn't tell whether she was outraged or just pretending to be so. Perhaps she really hadn't understood him. He stood up and took a couple of steps toward her. She emerged from the dressing room at the same time. They stood facing each other. Billie had slipped her dress back on and was now cinching the belt in the back.

"What were you trying to say? I have the impression it was something improper, but I'll give you a second chance." She pulled a hand out from behind her back and pushed a curl off her forehead. The motion was a little too slow.

She doesn't know what to do with her hands, that's it, Henri reflected. So he took her hand and gently pulled her arm down, interrupting the pointless gesture. He moved behind her, pulled her arm back gently, and put it back where it had been on the buckle. She stood still, hardly daring to breathe. But before she could do anything, Henri kissed her on the nape of the neck.

It was warm. Henri blew on the fuzz of hairs at the base of her hairline, turned her around, and kissed her throat. He continued on, kissing the delicate blue-veined inside of her wrist, visible through the open cuffs of her sleeves.

She looked at him but didn't say a word.

"I would like to look at your freckles," Henri said softly, "if you'll let me." He was just raising his hand toward her breast when she gave a loud hiccoughing sob and threw her arms around his neck. She started to cry—which wasn't what he'd intended at all. Henri didn't have anything against tears, but he didn't want her to be sad. With her pretty, open face, the nose that didn't sit straight on her face, the scattered freckles, Mrs. Henderson was supposed to be happy and bright. He didn't know her well, but he was intrigued by this spontaneous and unusual girl.

"Mrs. Henderson—Billie—what is it? I can see that it isn't the right time to look at your freckles. Please forgive me…" She only cried louder. At a loss for what to do, he handed her his handkerchief.

"I have no idea why you are so sad. Quite the opposite, in fact. I, I am…surprised."

She pressed her forehead against his chest as if she wanted to bore into him.

"I," she finally said, her head still pressed against his chest so that he could scarcely understand her, "I wanted you to come. You look as though you know how to hold a woman in your arms, and hold her tightly. You look strong." She raised her head and looked at his face with a mixture of uncertainty and confidence.

"I liked you right off when you sat across from me at dinner on Saturday night…" She stopped speaking and looked away pensively.

"Excuse me. I sometimes have to cry. Sometimes it just happens. I have to cry." She paused briefly and said with a small nod, "I like you."

"And, dear Mrs. Henderson, what is a man you like supposed to do?" Henri couldn't suppress a smile.

"Hold me in his arms and look at my freckles…" Then she laughed. His handkerchief was pressed in her fist and she gave it back to him now, like an obedient child. Her nose was a little red from crying, her tresses even more tangled. Henri reached up and fumbled with the comb in her hair, then pulled it out cautiously. He wanted to ask her what the crying was all about, but he didn't. He unbuttoned the bodice of her dress until he saw the top of her breast. She didn't stop him. Instead, she closed her eyes, her damp lashes darkened by her tears, and turned her face up to him. He kissed her lashes, her nose, her upper lip. His massive walrus moustache tickled, and she wrinkled her nose and twitched slightly with closed lids.

Then she opened her eyes, put her arms around his neck, and said breathlessly as she pulled him closer, "More, more."

Henri held Mrs. Henderson very carefully in his arms.

She suddenly seemed very young, as though perhaps her experiences with men had never penetrated her heart. Although she reminded Henri a great deal of Lisette, her body was different. So he held her carefully, even a little stiffly, not wanting to make a false move. The last thing he wanted was to offend her because he had confused her with another woman.

"Billie?" he asked, but she shook her head and kept her eyes closed. She didn't want to talk.

"Billie, you'll have to put on another dress for the concert. This one is too rumpled to wear on deck," he said. She nodded with her eyes closed.

Henri let go of her carefully.

"It is already three thirty and you arranged to meet Mr. Brown."

She nodded again. Then she let him go and turned her head away without saying anything.

He took a pillow and put it in her arm like a doll from her childhood. Then he left. She still hadn't moved. He closed the stateroom door behind him.

As they crossed over Julier Pass, it had begun to snow. Valentina remembered it perfectly. She had barely tolerated the entire trip. Madame Brochet had taken care of everything, the overnight stay in Chur, the luggage, the reservation for two seats in the stagecoach. In Paris they had had the most beautiful fall weather and even when they had climbed into the post chaise harnessed with four horses, a silken blue September sky had arched over the city of Chur.

Valentina was as indifferent to the weather as to everything else. She had pulled the black tulle veil from her hat over her face, as though it might protect her from the world, and exchanged only a few words with her companion. After the train had left Paris and she had waved good-bye indifferently to Viktor and Dr. Koch, she folded her hands in her lap and sat staring listlessly out the window. Madame Brochet had pulled a book out of her traveling bag and immersed herself in Baedeker's *Switzerland*.

They shared the stagecoach from Chur with a white-haired gentleman from Zurich who spoke neither French nor English and a young American with a head of shiny black curls and friendly brown eyes, who bowed gallantly to them when he climbed into the coach. It was obvious that Valentina was in mourning, as she wore a long, black wool suit, from which only a white frilled collar peeked out. Black made her seem even more fragile, and her delicate face looked as white as porcelain under the veil of her hat.

The landscape through which they passed had become a beloved tourist destination in recent years, and with good reason. The rugged alpine scenery, punctuated by steep gorges, sheer rock walls, and picturesque castle ruins inspired awe in just about every visitor. But the gentleman from Zurich knew the route and fell asleep despite the constant bumping, and Valentina appeared not even to notice the beauty right outside her window.

The higher they went, the colder it became. The horses had already been changed a couple of times, and the passengers had stretched their legs and had some warm soup. The sky clouded over, and shortly before they reached the summit, it began to snow.

The shock of seeing snow in early September pulled Valentina out of her lethargic state. She pushed back her veil and looked out the window with genuine interest. The white flakes drifted past the pane. The young American seized the opportunity and said in passable French to the two ladies, "May I offer you my throw? You must be rather cold. Put it across your knees…I'll use my topcoat."

He pulled a rolled-up plaid blanket out of his traveling bag and handed it to Madame Brochet. Then he turned to Valentina, "You don't need to be afraid. September is the most beautiful month in the mountains. In Engadin, it is often sunny and warm. But early snow isn't unusual. It won't last long, I hope."

"You are obviously familiar with this area?" Madame Brochet asked, clearly surprised. Valentina glanced at the traveler.

The young man, who had introduced himself as Richard G. Livingston, laughed delightedly at the prospect of being able to make the long trip pass more quickly with some conversation.

"My mother is originally from Engadin," he nodded. "She moved to America with her family when she was a child. Her father was a confectioner." He laughed again. "He was more successful in New York than he had been at home; the Americans love candy. My middle name is Gion, which sounds like John. It's a name from this region."

Valentina listened attentively but didn't say anything. Her legs warmed up slowly beneath the throw and she remembered what it was like to feel comfortable.

Madame Brochet, who was happy to exchange a few words with someone so good-natured, continued to ask Mr. Livingston questions.

"It seems that you come here often, despite the distance?"

Mr. Livingston answered Madame Brochet cheerfully enough, but his eyes were mostly on Valentina, whose cheeks revealed a touch of pink.

"I love the landscape here. My mother used to talk to me a great deal about her home. I inherited her love of the mountains. I've been here several times to hike in the mountains. Engadin is a wonderful place for mountain climbers." He looked out the coach window and bent closer to Valentina.

"Look! It stopped snowing! We'll have good weather when we arrive in St. Moritz. May I ask where you are getting out? Are you staying in St. Moritz?"

Valentina was surprised to hear herself answer. "Yes, we are staying at Kurhaus in St. Moritz-Bad. The doctor prescribed a cure for me, and Madame Brochet," she laid an arm on her escort, "has been kind enough to offer me her companionship." She paused and then asked, "And where do you live?"

He ran his fingers through his dark curls. "In Pontresina. I'm a little closer to the mountains there. But it isn't very far for a good walker from Pontresina to St. Moritz. If you would allow me, I will pay my respects to you at Kurhaus. Maybe I can talk you into a small excursion."

Madame Brochet appeared to be excited at the idea. Valentina only said, "Maybe. Once we have settled in…?"

"I promise I will be a good tour guide. I know more than what's in Baedeker," answered Richard G. Livingston, smiling.

Henri Sauvignac didn't have any interest in listening to the ship's orchestra play. He hated promenade concerts, even on the deck of a ship. He thought about Mrs. Henderson and how she had looked when he left her, with the white pillow tucked in her arm.

Why had she cried?

Suddenly he thought of Lisette too.

He hadn't thought about her so much in ages. It was almost as though she were on board with him. It wasn't enough that he couldn't leave the ship; he couldn't escape his thoughts either.

Henri lay on his bed and stared at the ceiling until he fell into a restless half-sleep riddled with peculiar dreams in which the ship's band played for a circus performance and the passengers performed tricks. In the middle of the circus stood a lady in a white evening gown, who was staring around in amazement at everything going on around her.

Monday, July 25

Valentina had dined in her stateroom on orders of the captain and then gone to sleep early. In the morning, she rubbed her eyes and stared at the ceiling of the stateroom, taking a minute to remember where she was. She'd slept through the night without waking up once. In fact, she realized, it was the first night in months that she hadn't lain awake or startled awake out of confused dreams. Something was happening to her. She felt as though she was slowly emerging from a long and terrible dream.

Valentina smelled breakfast and was amazed to realize that she had an appetite. The water in the washstand pitcher had grown cold, and she noticed that too. She looked out her window and was struck by the bigger swells. The sky was no longer blue. Most amazing of all, she realized that that she didn't feel the slightest regret at having run away.

The captain had sent word that he'd be stopping by to speak with her at noon. Valentina asked Lotte to help her get dressed.

When he arrived, Captain Palmer presented her with two offers. First, he was willing to permit Valentina to join the other guests in the dining room for dinner, where her formal dress was appropriate. Second, he had discovered that one of the passengers, a certain Madame Klöppler of Berlin, was on her way to New York with a collection of dresses that were going to be displayed at Macy's. Madame Klöppler had agreed to loan some of the gowns to Madame Meyer so that she could leave her stateroom during the day.

"If you agree, I will pick you up this evening and accompany you to the dining room. I will ask the purser to assign you a seat."

"Thank you," answered Valentina. "I do appreciate your offer. You are allowing me to not feel like a criminal. But I don't really care to mingle with the other passengers. I don't want to create any more of a sensation—"

"And I imagine you'd like to pass on any intrusive questions," added the captain.

"Dr. Kirschbaum asked me to do him the favor of visiting Madame Meyer, and naturally, I agreed. The doctor is such a kind man. I liked him instantly. I needed a pill for a headache so we got to talking. When I told him that I designed clothes, he asked about it with some interest. It certainly isn't a profession that many women practice. I design clothes for the modern woman, those who want to free themselves from the old styles and would prefer to wear more comfortable clothes.

"Women today play sports, they ride bicycles, they have careers. The corset isn't suitable anymore. Corsets disfigure the female body. Even though we are constantly being told the opposite, they are actually bad for women's health. But the reform dress is gaining in popularity. The Wertheim department store in Berlin was very successful with its exhibition of reform dresses earlier this year. They even established a department for them, which, incidentally, a friend of mine, Else Oppler, runs. I have arranged for a similar exhibition at Macy's in New York. When I told Dr. Kirschbaum about this, he asked me if I would be willing to loan Madame Meyer a day dress. I believe that women have to help one another and fight together for deliverance from these constricting rules that govern fashion, so I immediately agreed.

"Madame Meyer is an unusually elegant woman. My dresses looked superb on her. She didn't exactly serve up her story to me on a silver platter. On the contrary, I couldn't get a thing out of her. But then, I can't imagine it being otherwise. She clearly belongs to the traditional upper classes. I can't imagine her spending time with our avant-garde artistic crowd.

"That said, what she did—boarding a ship without money or a ticket, subjecting herself to an investigation and perhaps even arrest—is certainly rather unusual. Though it doesn't fit with her outward appearance, there must be something radical about her. I would never have figured her for a criminal.

"Her husband probably took advantage of her and treated her poorly. It wouldn't be the first time a husband denied his wife access to her fortune and defrauded her.

"At least nowadays a wife can try to get a divorce, though as a divorcée she would become an outcast."

Berchthild Klöppler, fashion designer,
passenger on the Kroonland

Henri had spent the morning exploring the ship, skipped lunch, and when he didn't run into either Billie or his mysterious neighbor in his wanderings, he decided to return to his room for a nap. He was awakened from his nap by a gentle rolling motion. The ship must have hit some bigger swells.

Though the rolling was barely perceptible, it upset his stomach, and he decided to head out to the promenade deck to get some fresh air. The sky had filled with gray and white clouds, with only bits of blue visible beyond them, and the water had turned dark and dull. Henri bent over the railing and watched the ship plow through the water, following the waves with his eyes until they joined with other waves and could no longer be distinguished from the rest of the rolling sea all around them.

When he turned his gaze back to the ship, he saw Lily sitting on her own in her wheelchair not far away. He smiled, and she returned his smile and waved. Henri walked over to her to introduce himself.

Her name was Lily Mey. She had relatives in America.

"The sea is beautiful, isn't it?" she asked animatedly. "I would much rather stay out here than be inside. Naturally, Mama won't allow it. But I could look at the sea and the sky forever. The sea is never the same. Have you seen how its color changes with every cloud, with every hour? And now the waves, like carpeting under which a herd of hump-backed camels treks through the wilderness…"

She wrapped a strand of hair around her finger. "A silly thought, I guess." She suddenly remembered what her mother had taught her about conversation and looked embarrassed.

"Not at all," said Henri. "I see the camels very clearly." She laughed. He paused before continuing. "To me, the sea is frightening. If I don't have solid ground beneath me, I feel uneasy. The depths of the water below, the vast amounts of water surging all around. I can't help but think how cold and uncomfortable it must be."

Lily nodded seriously. Henri just now noticed that a notebook and pencil lay in her lap.

"Yes. But when you look at the horizon, the pull of the water disappears. I have seen you bent over the railing, staring down at the water. If you do that, the water exerts a pull, drawing you down. But if you let your eyes wander over the surface, then you will see it differently. You'll see all the colors and light and shadows. Go further and further with your eyes," she raised her head and looked into the distance, "until you arrive at the horizon. And there, where the earth and sky meet, you will see infinity." She stopped. "Naturally, that's nonsense. It isn't infinity, but that's what I call it."

She fidgeted in her wheelchair, uncertain whether she should continue confiding her feelings to a stranger. But then she said, "I think the horizon is the most beautiful line in the world. It's…it's a view into eternity."

Henri listened, astonished, as her voice became increasingly passionate. Her turquoise-colored dress blazed against the silver-gray sea. Henri still felt the rolling of the ship, but it bothered him less. Lily was right; the horizon was a magical line in the distance where that which could never be joined was united.

"Mademoiselle," he said, "may I ask you something else?"

"Yes, of course," she laughed.

"Don't you have the feeling of being imprisoned on this ship and on the water?"

Lily looked at him, startled.

"No," she said and shook her head. "How?" For a moment, her tongue appeared between her lips. A small, pink tongue, like a cat's. She looked very much like a child when she was thinking. Then she said slowly, "No, I don't feel like a prisoner here. I am already trapped in this wheelchair!" She faltered. "It doesn't matter if I am on water or on land. I can't ever run away like other people can."

Henri took her hand and kissed it because no reply came to mind.

As Henri entered the dining room for dinner, he wondered what Billie thought of their afternoon together. He had already sat down when she entered the dining room with Mr. Brown. Mr. Brown wore festive evening attire. Billie wore a soft green dress of lightly rustling silk; her cheeks were pink. He watched as her gaze moved searchingly around the room, stopping when she found Henri. At first she looked surprised that there weren't two more seats at his table. Then she opened her fan and fanned herself vigorously, flashing her eyes at him from the door, sending him the message, You coward! You scoundrel!

Yes, Henri concluded, she was clearly upset that he hadn't tried to meet up with her all day. At least he now had some idea what she was thinking.

When Lisette was angry, Henri thought, a blush of fury climbed like fire from her throat up to her face. She looked like she was standing in flames. Half frightened and half amused, he always wanted to hug her to put out the fire, but he didn't dare. As she got angrier, she balled up her fists and cried from rage. When he looked into her desperate, combative eyes, he knew that in her mind she was throwing daggers at him.

Her father had been in the circus and she had actually learned as a child how to throw knives. She didn't lose her temper often, but Henri didn't doubt for a second that she could hit him right in the heart if she wanted to. In the five years they had known each other, it had only erupted a few times. One time, she didn't think that Henri had taken a strong enough stance toward a neighbor who tortured his dog; another time, she thought he had treated his mother rudely. And once, she wanted to leave him when she found Henri in bed with another woman.

That time, he recalled, she had ripped down the curtains and watched as the fabric had slumped down onto the floor. Then with a broad hand movement, she had sent the plates and cups shattering onto the tile floor. But that still hadn't been enough. Like a tigress, she had finally jumped on the bed, where Henri and the girl, whom Lisette knew well, lay motionless from the shock. Lisette had pulled the blanket from the two of them, and standing over them, tears streaming down her cheeks, her fists balled up, she had screamed, "Go to hell. Both of you go to hell!"

In the end, much later, when Lisette had truly gone and left him, she hadn't raged and there hadn't been a fight. She had simply gathered up a few things from Henri's studio when he wasn't around and disappeared. When he looked for her in the attic room where she had lived for years, she had already moved.

Mr. Brown and Billie were led to a neighboring table by the purser. Billie threw Henri a withering look over her shoulder. Couldn't he have waited in the vestibule outside the dining room for them since he had already chickened out yesterday by not making an appearance at either the concert or at dinner? Henri lowered his gaze guiltily and studied the menu until they were seated.

Across from him sat an unusual couple who had caught his eye on the first day. The mystery was quickly solved. Tall and good-looking, Thomas Witherspoon was accompanying his sister Victoria back to New York after an extensive European trip.

After they had introduced themselves, they all contemplated the enormous menu. Suddenly a whisper arose, and, as if by some unspoken command, everyone turned toward the entrance of the dining room.

There stood the captain. On his arm was the beautiful stranger in the white dress.

Thomas Witherspoon put his hand on his heart.

Victoria put her hand on her brother's arm.

Henri Sauvignac's mind went blank.

Billie Henderson swallowed what she had just been about to say.

All eyes were on Valentina.

Although the captain had accompanied her to protect her from the curious stares of the other passengers, he seemed to bask for a moment in the mysterious splendor that surrounded the lady in white. He exchanged a few words with the purser running by, who nodded eagerly and then asked the new guest to follow him with a gesture. He ushered Madame Meyer to the empty spot at the table where Thomas Witherspoon and Henri Sauvignac appeared already to be expecting her. Witherspoon stood up like a sleepwalker. Henri stood too and bowed formally. Valentina looked at him and smiled. Then she saw Thomas.

Henri noticed her gaze shift down. The minute fluttering of her eyelashes stung Henri since it wasn't for him. She sat down on Henri's right side, and he sat back down as well. As though an enormous spotlight illuminated her, everyone continued to stare. When she raised her eyes again, she looked straight into Thomas Witherspoon's green-gray eyes.

No, thought Valentina, yet she still couldn't turn her gaze away.

Yes, said his eyes.

"No," she said softly.

Henri heard her whispered "No." No conversation between two people meeting for the first time opened with that.

How should he speak to this woman? The beautiful stranger obviously wasn't a regular passenger, and it was clear to him that he couldn't ask any of the questions one would normally ask fellow passengers without being indiscreet. So he said unimaginatively, "Henri Sauvignac. My pleasure, Madame."

She nodded.

"My pleasure," she rejoined, "I am Madame Meyer."

She twisted her mouth slightly. "I imagine there are already quite a few rumors about me that might make it difficult for you to speak with me normally. So let me make it easier and ask you why you are on this ship. I trust that you are a resourceful person and that you won't ask me the same boring questions."

She raised her wineglass and nodded to Henri suggestively.

She isn't wearing any jewelry, thought Victoria Witherspoon, which struck her as a curious contradiction, since she was wearing such an expensive evening gown. She also determined that she wasn't wearing a wedding ring. Both discoveries worried her.

There is a tired expression in her eyes, thought Henri. But the tiredness lies beneath the surface of her eye, at the bottom of the amber sea.

This is the moment that I have waited for my entire life, thirty long years, thought Thomas Witherspoon.

Henri gave Madame Meyer the information for which she had asked.

"I'm traveling to New York and then continuing to St. Louis," he said. He paused as the steward served a first course of shrimp with celery and mayonnaise. He went on to explain about the world's fair and how some of his works were going to be displayed there. Although Valentina listened attentively, he could tell that her thoughts seemed to be elsewhere. Henri was a bit hurt, but forged ahead.

"I was born in Antwerp. I used to work with a stonemason there. Later I went to Paris to study at the Académie des Beaux Arts. I had a studio there for a long time and would still be there if my father hadn't died just a year ago." He paused, but Valentina merely nodded.

"My father had a hauling company. I am an only child and couldn't leave my mother alone to handle the business. I didn't take over the company, but someone had to oversee the transfer of the company to his partner and to arrange my mother's finances. So I gave up my studio in Paris and returned to Antwerp. I would rather have stayed in Paris," he added.

"Did your whole family move to Antwerp?" asked Valentina.

"Oh, I don't have any family," countered Henri. The steward saved him from further explanations by serving the next course, a green turtle soup. Henri changed topics.

"Your dress is sensational," he said, "but you must already know that. It looks marvelous on you."

She didn't smile when she answered, and Henri realized how silly his comment must have sounded. "Thank you for the compliment. My husband was glad that I wore it the evening I got on the ship. We had been invited to a large soirée with my husband's business acquaintances. He deals with Russian diamonds." She touched her ear as though she expected to find diamonds there, but she wasn't wearing any earrings. She revised the movement quickly, but didn't continue speaking.

"There is a large group of Russians among the passengers, have you noticed? They got on board in Dover and I drank some champagne with them yesterday."

Henri pointed across to the table where the five Russians sat, already feasting on the next course, salmon with capers.

Madame Meyer's expression was impenetrable. "I speak only a bit of Russian, even though my husband is Russian. My father is Russian too, but the language was never well liked in our home."

She gesticulated vaguely and stroked her forehead with the back of her hand.

Thomas Witherspoon was normally a polite man, but he'd had enough of the sculptor's conversation.

"Isn't it curious how quickly and unexpectedly the floor begins to sway?" He paused and belatedly introduced himself and his sister with an apology. She followed the movement of his lips with her eyes, but didn't appear to understand what he said. She simply stared at his face.

"How quickly the weather can change," he continued, since she didn't reply. "Above all on the ocean. Earlier, it looked as though there might never be another cloud in the sky. But the sky has turned gray and the sea, too. The officer told me the wind is going to pick up and the swells, too. They aren't counting on a storm, though. On the crossing to Europe, we were tossed mercilessly back and forth for days on end." He looked at Miss Witherspoon, who nodded meaningfully, her bright gray eyes fastened on Madame Meyer as though she wanted to skewer a butterfly with a pin.

"I hope we'll be spared from such a storm on our return journey," Thomas said.

"It was terrible," Miss Witherspoon added, her small figure withdrawing further into itself. "We were all sick. In the dining room, the plates and glasses skidded across the table, but no one could eat anyway. The dining room was completely deserted.

Most people just lay in their staterooms feeling like death; I myself found it more comfortable on deck. But the corridors to the decks were closed. The danger was too great. The wind was very strong, you understand, and the breakers that rolled across the decks... even Thomas was quite weak, weren't you, Thomas?"

Her brother, who had lost himself in gazing at Madame Meyer, recollected himself.

"Yes," he concurred. Then he turned with unexpected cheerfulness to the man across from him.

"Enjoy the beef filet with Périgueux sauce that you have before you; you never know on such a crossing when you will have the desire for it again. We didn't start to feel better until we were out in the fresh air again. Seamen said that it helps to look off into the distance and that you should try to fix your gaze on the horizon. That's supposed to restore your inner balance. A piece of advice I should take to heart, maybe even now."

"Why's that?" asked Valentina. She was smiling, even though her heart began to beat wildly and she understood what he meant more than she cared to admit. "Are you off balance, then?"

"Perhaps you will forgive me for not answering," he responded. After a moment, he added, "Don't I look like I am?"

Valentina didn't answer. Henri poured Madame Meyer some wine, and Miss Witherspoon put the conversation back on course.

"The problem actually lies in the ear, where the organ of equilibrium is, and not in the stomach. Fishermen told us that seamen will eat as much as possible before they head off to sea in their boats. A full stomach helps against seasickness, though it may be difficult to believe." She placed her hand on her brother's and left it there.

"But let's not frighten Madame Meyer, Thomas. Maybe she will be spared from seasickness. She has"—she looked coldly at Madame Meyer—"certainly already been through enough."

Madame Meyer's surprise appearance and the happily bemused expression on her brother's face had put Miss Witherspoon on high alert.

Valentina didn't react to the mention of her suffering and occupied herself instead with her beef filet. Henri steered the discussion to the French kitchen and the preparation of the filets.

Then Valentina turned to Miss Witherspoon.

"Do you always travel together, Miss Witherspoon? Or often?"

"Oh yes," she replied. "We both love to travel. Thomas is a geologist and travels around the world for work. I go with him whenever I can." Thomas Witherspoon looked embarrassed. His sister appeared not to notice. She leaned toward Valentina as though she wanted to tell her something in confidence.

"It would be difficult for Thomas to have a family because one minute he's here and the next minute he's gone. He couldn't expect a wife and children to put up with such a life. He is so thoughtful…" Miss Witherspoon looked at her brother tenderly and then continued on valiantly, ignoring his silent plea not to say anything more. "At least he has me. I didn't get married, even though Thomas has always reproached me. But a man who doesn't marry because he is completely dedicated to his work struggles now and then with loneliness. So I am there for him whenever he needs me."

She looked at Valentina sharply as she spoke, as though she wanted to decode the hieroglyphs of Valentina's loneliness too. Then she continued, "It is so important to have someone who understands you, don't you think? It is hard to be alone…" Her small eyes studied Valentina's well-proportioned features, but she could extract no answer, much less any agreement, from her.

Henri, who had been following the conversation with interest, noticed that Madame Meyer's skin, which had looked like marble when she arrived, now resembled the velvety petals of apple blossoms. He couldn't help but imagine pressing his lips to her skin.

He had to smile as a picture formed in his mind.

My God, yes. It had been spring. The sun shone. There was a cherry tree. A gust of wind blew a snow shower of white petals across the green meadow. Lisette stood on a garden table with her arms spread out and petals blowing over her and coming to rest on the grass. Lisette just stood there, her face turned toward the sky, her naked arms outstretched. Her wool cape slipped off her shoulders and fell to the ground. "I love you!" she cried, meaning the wind, the sky, the tree, the grass. She turned to Henri and said, "Spread out your arms and catch me!" When she jumped into his arms, she asked, "Do you love me too?"

Madame Meyer's flawless skin isn't at all like marble, Henri thought once again. Blood flows in her veins. In her clear, soft voice, she had just said to Thomas Witherspoon, with the echo of a question, "That is lovely for you, that you have such a sister who is always there for you..."

Thomas returned her look, while his sister considered what Valentina meant. But there hadn't been any irony in it; Valentina had only repeated what Miss Witherspoon herself had said. Nevertheless, Miss Witherspoon was wary.

"Yes, that's true," Thomas said cautiously. He reached for the crystal glass, in which red wine sloshed gently back and forth. Valentina looked at him and waited patiently for him to elaborate. There isn't any hurry if you have found what you have spent your life looking for. His clean-shaven face was boyish, but he looked like an adult, someone who wouldn't shy away from life's responsibilities.

His eyes, thought Valentina, are more green than gray. He seems to be the opposite of his sister. His well-proportioned body looked relaxed, which gave him an amiable, open quality. When he smiled, her impression only grew stronger.

Henri, too, was eager to see what Witherspoon would say next.

"My sister and I were inseparable as children," said Thomas, gazing straight into Valentina's amber-colored eyes without so much as a glance at his sister, who sat back slightly in her armchair.

"But," he continued, "I would have been very happy to have had a family. I always wanted children."

Miss Witherspoon's body shot forward then, but she said nothing. Thomas continued to ignore her.

"But Victoria is right. My lifestyle wouldn't be easy for a wife to handle. I travel for weeks, sometimes months, at a time if I have to take soil samples for a company or a country in an area where they hope to find raw materials or resources." Miss Witherspoon relaxed again.

Her brother smiled at Madame Meyer, as though he wanted to ask her, "Could *you* imagine living with me? Despite my profession and despite my sister?"

Valentina didn't say anything. Confused, she forbade herself from thinking how much she wanted to run her fingers over his lips and brows to memorize his face. She couldn't help but think how bushy those brows would become over the years.

In the meantime, Billie had left the dining room with Mr. Brown, casting a cold glance in Henri's direction as they left. She examined Madame Meyer briefly on her way out. While Henri peeked at Billie, Mr. Witherspoon saw that Madame Meyer had finished her éclair. Since coffee had already been served, he suggested drinking another glass of wine in the lounge. His sister, however, had other ideas about the remainder of the evening.

"Thomas, I know how much you like to smoke a cigar after dinner. Monsieur Sauvignac, do you smoke too?"

Henri nodded.

"See, my dear," said Victoria to her brother, "you two should go smoke in the men's lounge while I drink a cup of tea with Madame Meyer in the library." She turned to Valentina, "What do you think of that, my dear? Do you play cards? We could play a game of bridge. I'm sure we could find a couple of ladies who would like to play with us…"

Valentina raised her beautifully arched eyebrows slightly.

"I don't want to offend Miss Witherspoon," Henri interjected before she could answer, "but I think it is too early to separate the men and the ladies. It isn't even ten o'clock yet. I would enjoy your company and gladly abandon my cigar," he continued, turning to Valentina, "if you would give us the pleasure of accompanying us to the drawing room."

"Yes, please give us the pleasure," Thomas said. "I am sure, Victoria, that there will be many more opportunities to play cards…"

"I don't want to upset you, Thomas." Victoria stood up energetically. "You can do as you please. I plan to retire for the evening. We'll see each other tomorrow." She grabbed her evening bag, a black velvet puff, smoothed her skirt, and said good night to the group.

They all stood. Thomas, who towered over everyone, bent down to give his little sister a peck on the cheek. As sorry as he was to disappoint her, this time she wouldn't win.

Meanwhile, Henri said to Valentina, "By the way, did you know that we are stateroom neighbors?"

Valentina laughed. "No, I didn't know that."

Henri noticed, amazed, how her face changed when she laughed, becoming playful, even carefree. It was as though she had divined his thoughts, however, as her expression closed up a moment later.

Before Thomas could say anything to draw Valentina's attention back to him, Captain Palmer arrived at Valentina's side, offered her his arm, and asked, "Madame, may I accompany you to your stateroom?"

Valentina agreed, and Thomas had to make do with an apologetic glance heavy with regret.

"I'll do what I can to make your stay comfortable," said Captain Palmer, kissing Valentina's hand. "I've even found you a tea dress so that you will be able to move about freely during the day, if you like, that is…" He still held her hand, as though he wanted to bring it to his lips once again.

Wasn't it the doctor who had sent Madame Klöppler to her? The way the captain spoke to her confused Valentina. What did he mean? She thought it better not to ask and simply replied, "You really are a gentleman, Captain, just as I expected…"

"Therefore, permit me also…," said the captain, pulling Valentina's evening bag from under her arm. He opened it and took out the key to her stateroom.

"I hope," he continued, "you are satisfied with your accommodations. We don't have anything other than first class. But I would like you to be as comfortable as possible."

Palmer opened her door and held it open, gesturing to her to enter.

"Make yourself at home on my ship!"

Hesitantly, Valentina entered the stateroom. She stood by the door to thank him once again, but before she could utter a word, Palmer had entered the room.

"Thank you for all your trouble," Valentina said nervously. "I appreciate all you have done for me. But now I can manage alone. I wish you a good evening. Maybe we'll see each other tomorrow…" She took a step forward to signal that it was time for him to make his exit, but Palmer wasn't dismissed so easily.

"Madame," he began again. "If you remember, you offered me your earrings, an offer that I would describe as being complicit, if I were so inclined. You know of course that I can do things for you—or not. Because you are so attractive, we should examine what exactly I can do for you. Of course, this will remain just between the two of us. That would be most convenient for both of us, though perhaps more so for you than for me?"

He had gently closed the stateroom door and leaned against it. He reached for her hand. As he tried to pull Valentina to him, he continued, "You are the most exciting stowaway that I have ever had on board. Why shouldn't we take advantage of the situation…?"

Valentina panicked. He was obstructing the door with his body. She had to get him to leave of his own free will—and she had to buy time.

They stood in the dark because he hadn't turned on the light. He covered the switch with his arm.

"Captain," said Valentina without so much as a tremor in her voice, "your suggestion is somewhat surprising. I relinquished my earrings to you as collateral for the expenses of the trip, not as collateral for me. You obviously understood my proposition completely differently. I can tell you I'll consider it. But please take into consideration that I am tired. I know that I am indebted to you, but I must ask that you accept my excuses for this evening. Now if you'll allow me…"

She moved him aside, opened the stateroom door, and pushed him out before he had a chance to protest.

"I will await your answer eagerly," said Captain Palmer to cover his retreat. "I wish you a good night."

Disappointed by the unexpected turn of events, Thomas Witherspoon had retreated to the smoking lounge and was now wondering how Palmer had been able to lead Valentina away like that, as though she were under his supervision. And why had she followed him? Normally he loved to wrap up the evening with a fine glass of French red wine and a good cigar, but this evening, no Bordeaux could excite or console him. He had been awkward and slow. He berated himself for not interrupting the captain and politely pointing out that he was about to go into the lounge with Madame Meyer. He asked himself again why she had followed Palmer, when her look had given him to understand that she was sorry to leave him. He couldn't delude himself into believing that captivating, beautiful, mysterious Madame Meyer felt the same way about him as he did about her. A single moment had been enough to unhinge his life. Now it was about to start anew: with her, whoever she was.

The rumors were wide-ranging: Some said she was a stowaway, others a jewel thief who had been caught on board, while still others insisted she was a courtesan who was after rich men.

He didn't believe any of it. It didn't mean anything that she hadn't been seen the first couple of days in the dining room. Maybe she hadn't been feeling well and had stayed in her stateroom. Yet it was odd how the captain had arrived with her.

Thomas was determined to find out the truth. There was no doubt in his mind that their fates were linked, whether he liked it or not. Whether she liked it or not. Regardless of whether their future held happiness or sorrow, misfortune or death, he didn't have the power to resist her. Their future was unknown, but he was certain of one thing: for the first time in their life together, his happiness would be his sister's misfortune.

He had to talk to Victoria.

Thomas loved his sister, but he loved her differently than she loved him. He was grateful to her, and they had been closer than most siblings ever since childhood. But she needed him to live in the same way that she needed air—and she would fight to make sure she didn't lose him.

He had to speak with her first thing the next day. He also knew he had to bring the ship's doctor into his confidence regarding Victoria.

My dear Charles,

Forgive me that I am just now with you, thinking of you. You have to believe I haven't forgotten you. But how could that ever happen? In my heart I will always be with you.

And yet the world isn't at all what it was like when you left. I have come to a decision. I have left my life behind. I am now on an ocean liner that will reach the shores of the New World in a few days.

Suddenly I am part of the world again, a world I had turned my back on after you died. I don't know where this path will lead me. There may be a man I met after your death standing at the harbor in New York; he always said that he would wait for me.

But that doesn't concern me as much as what I have to say to you: Today, when I went to dinner, I stood in the door and looked into the festively lit dining room. Suddenly my eyes fell on one of the guests. I believe I only looked in his direction because he called to me with his eyes. It was as though he recognized someone in me, and I was just as surprised at what he saw in me. I wanted to clutch my heart to hold onto that sensation of being recognized. My heart, which had been numb for so long, suddenly beat in anticipation, in longing, in hope. His look caused life to flow back into my veins.

I am ashamed that after you left, I died with you. My soul didn't want to live without you. You know that. If you are still somewhere, then you know it.

Then I was led to a table, which happened to be where he was sitting. I was seated across from him.

We looked at each other. I ate and drank and talked like I hadn't done in years, simply and without pain.

My dear Charles, I don't know if you can understand me, if you can forgive me. But that's how it was.

Valentina put the quill down. She closed the ink bottle with a round silver top and put the page aside. Then she stood in front of the mirror on her vanity and looked at her face. She pulled out her hairpins and let her hair fall loosely to her shoulders. She took the brush from the dresser and brushed her hair with practiced movements. Suddenly she laughed softly. She suddenly had an image of little Charles, how he liked to watch her in front of her vanity, his small hands combing her hair, attentive and doting.

Most people on these steamships have nothing and wager everything to begin a new life. She too didn't want to wait for the hereafter. She wanted to live now.

They all have hope, thought Valentina. This entire ship is full of people who don't have anything to lose. However, in contrast to her, they believe in the future, that happiness is possible, despite everything they have suffered. They not only have given up their homes but are willing to start again, to create a new home with their own hands, even with the prospect of new hardships.

Valentina looked at herself thoughtfully in the mirror.

Viktor had forced her to wear the white dress. He wanted her to be as she was before their world changed. Now she slipped it off cautiously. "My captivating, innocent Valentina," Viktor had exclaimed when he first saw her in the shimmering dress two years earlier. He had wrapped his large hands admiringly around her waist.

"Valentina, my little dove, look at you," he said, "look in the mirror at how beautiful and fragile you are."

Yes, she had been flawless back then, her only concern whether she would be able to sing in such a tightly laced dress. Viktor had taken her to a summer ball at the Grand Hôtel Cabourg that evening after she had put Charles to bed and given the nanny the necessary instructions.

Yes, it was true, she was fragile. Life itself was fragile, she had discovered. Nothing would ever be the same again.

But perhaps there could be another tomorrow.

Henri wasn't tired yet. The evening had ended too abruptly when the captain kidnapped the beautiful Madame Meyer and

Thomas Witherspoon had excused himself. He decided to visit the lounge.

There the Russians had settled themselves in comfortably. The room shimmered in plush red tones; the guests' footsteps were muted by the thick carpeting. People tapped their cigarette ashes into the potted palms, encased inside expensive Chinese planters. Out of consideration for the ladies, the gentlemen only smoked cigars in the men's lounge.

Henri was surprised that the Russians weren't sitting in the smoking lounge, but he soon understood why they had chosen the public lounge—there was caviar here.

They recognized Henri and waved him over.

The Borgs were playing cards with another couple; Monsieur Vanstraaten, the father of three, sat alone with a whiskey before him. Every now and then, he raised his glass, looked at it, and held it out toward the bartender for a refill.

Soon the Russians began to sing. One of them, Wanja, sat down at the piano and began to play. The others joined in. Andrej Ostrowskij's voice was extraordinary, and Henri thought he must have had some training.

Tears welled up in his eyes as Henri listened to Andrej sing Russian folk songs, an emotional trait he'd likely inherited from his Armenian grandmother. The vodka flowed. The Russians encouraged him. Henri kept up. But the melancholy music, the steady stream of alcohol, and the gentle rolling of the ship on the vast sea depressed him; despite the cheerful company around him, he suddenly felt lonely and forlorn.

He excused himself to get some fresh air. He felt ill, but it wasn't the vodka so much as his misery that propelled him outside.

He leaned against the railing and looked up at the sky; it had filled with clouds that obscured the moon. A few stars twinkled dimly, flickering out when the clouds slid over them.

Henri suddenly found himself thinking about the day he first saw Lisette. She earned her money by posing as a model at the Académie, and one day he asked her if she would work for him privately. Although he had little money at the time and couldn't really afford his own model, he knew he'd found his muse. Every painter or sculptor will agree that they prefer some models to others. While they all assume the position that is demanded of them, not every model inspires in the artist the same desire to draw.

When he saw Lisette for the first time, Henri knew that she must become his. She never struck any of the standard poses. He could see that her body was different, that it held within it commitment and passion, resistance and understanding, intelligence and sensuality.

She held whatever stance was asked of her, as a model, and in life. She became what Henri saw in his mind's eye. First, she embodied what he thought and felt. Later, she inspired his drawings.

Henri looked out to sea and longed for a world with Lisette.

Tuesday, July 26

"She was a stowaway. Everyone knew about her. I tried not to imagine what she must have done to persuade the captain to escort her to the formal dinner in first class. In any case, when she arrived, she received our stares as though she were the queen herself. Brazen is all I can say. Stowaways are normally thrown into prison when they are discovered. But she obviously has quite an effect on the opposite sex. The men all gaped at her open-mouthed. If you ask me, she isn't all that beautiful.

"I find the whole matter unsettling because of the young girls on board. Although she behaved as though she were better than us, there was something indecent about her demeanor.

"Anyhow, I forbade my daughter, Lily, to speak with her. Young women are so romantic and immature and are inclined to marvel at such people.

"Perhaps too much credit was given to her story. Just look at the pack of journalists here! She is thriving on the attention that she received on board.

"But there you have it. There will always be people who simply have to be at the center of attention."

Hermine Mey, passenger on the Kroonland

Victoria Witherspoon hadn't slept so poorly in a long time. When her brother knocked on her door in the morning, she told him, "Go to breakfast, Thomas. I'm not hungry. I'll have the chambermaid bring me some tea." When she saw his concerned expression, she added, "Don't worry. I just slept poorly." She pressed her fingers to her temple and gently pushed him out the door.

"But you should eat something anyway, Victoria," pressed Thomas. "Did you have your nightmare again? Of course I'm worried when I see you looking like this." He was afraid that his sister might be getting one of her migraines. "Maybe I should send Dr. Kirschbaum around…?"

"Nonsense," Victoria replied firmly. She was glad to see that Thomas was worried about her. "Come by after breakfast. That will give me time to get dressed and drink some tea. Then we'll see."

She grasped his arm and this time really did push him out of the door. "Maybe you'll find some pleasant company…" Her voice tightened as she uttered those words. Thomas responded sharply, "Sure. After breakfast I have to talk to you. It's important."

And with that, he left.

Thomas was right. Victoria had had a nightmare, or rather, the same nightmare that had haunted her since she was twelve years old: a dream of a burning house. It was always the same house and the dream always unfolded the same way. All the rooms were engulfed in flames and people were screaming. Victoria knew that she had to go back into the flames. She had to save some-one, though she never knew whom it was that she had to save. She coughed, almost choking from the smoke; then her clothes caught fire. She always woke up before finding out whether her rescue had been successful and whether she herself had survived.

Often the nightmare (Thomas had been right about that) was a precursor to a severe migraine that rendered Victoria entirely helpless. She could only lie down and wait as the world descended into a tailspin of darkness and pain.

Thomas. He knew her so well, almost better than she knew her-self. Victoria sipped her tea. The taste of peppermint was soothing.

She thought of the night before, how Thomas had been para-lyzed by the sight of that woman. She had to help him keep a clear head. It was all too clear that he might lose his head over her. It was obviously up to her to make it clear to Thomas that this woman couldn't be his future. But how? Maybe the woman wanted money. Everything about her seemed to contradict the rules of decency. No one knew what she had done in the past and what she might be capable of in the future. Perhaps she saw Thomas as an anchor, someone to whom she could tie her des-tiny. Perhaps she hoped he could help her gain entry to Amer-ica. Regardless of how he felt, Victoria knew that Thomas would never be happy with her.

Feeling somewhat guilty about his ailing sister, Thomas rushed over to the dining room. He was bitterly disappointed to discover that Valentina was not at breakfast. Since he didn't feel inclined to chat with anyone else, he went to visit the ship's doctor to ask him to look after his sister. However, the doctor wasn't in his office.

Thomas eventually ran into the doctor on the promenade deck, where he was speaking with a corpulent woman with a great deal of urgency. Thomas didn't want to interrupt him.

"Believe me, I was quite happy to do you the favor," Thomas heard the woman say firmly to Dr. Kirschbaum. "She should be grateful to you for suggesting it. I will say that she looked at my dresses with a certain degree of skepticism."

The lady seemed disappointed. "I don't know whether Madame Meyer will wear any of them or not, but there's nothing more I can do for her."

The two sat down on a bench. At the mention of Madame Meyer, Thomas became more attentive, eavesdropping from the railing.

"Please," he heard the doctor say, "do not give it another thought! It was only an idea and I am very grateful to you."

The corpulent woman nodded. Until that moment, her round face, distinguished by a powerful chin, had looked belligerent, but now it softened. Thomas was struck by her appearance—it was unusual to see a woman not wearing a corset. She wore a purple velvet dress that draped over her full figure and an ornate green bolero.

"But I felt something disapproving in her," she said, looking hurt. "As though my dresses would give her some kind of skin disease. But there are many women who are not yet ready to join the reform movement." She paused.

"Anyhow, I have to rework the dresses before I can show them in New York..."

"You have shown yourself to be exceedingly generous," Dr. Kirschbaum said. "And if Madame Meyer should in fact decide not to take you up on your offer, I am sure that it has nothing to do with you and your dresses. She may have personal reasons that neither of us knows about." He suggested they order a cup of tea or hot chocolate.

Madame Klöppler nodded briefly and continued, "In many places, our reform movement is still being met with a lack of understanding, sometimes even flat-out rejection."

She glanced warmly at the ship's doctor, "You already said yourself that it is difficult to make new ideas take hold, even in medicine. It's an experience that we share." She sounded appeased, though her displeasure flared up one last time. "I cannot begin to imagine why someone would prefer to spend the entire day and evening in the same tightly laced dress…"

The sentence died away. She turned once again toward Dr. Kirschbaum and invited him to expand on his views concerning body and soul; above all, the soul.

Thomas didn't dare interrupt the conversation. He would go look in on his sister to see if she had been spared from a migraine.

Billie, thought Henri, as he stood in front of the mirror and tied his tie. Right after breakfast, I will go look for you and ask you to take a walk with me on the promenade deck. I will apologize for being cowardly at dinner last night. You are right that I don't want any conflict or tension. After all, you have Mr. Brown in your life.

Henri was about to head out the door when he heard a knock.

"Good morning, Monsieur. A card for you…" A deckhand held out a silver tray with a letter on it.

It was from Billie.

Henri, could you come to the promenade deck, right now?
                                                    Billie Henderson

It looked as though she had written the few lines hastily.

Henri grabbed his overcoat and went to look for her.

It was chilly on deck. He spotted her right away; she was shivering in a salmon-colored dress and a short black overcoat. She had affixed a small black hat to her head with a ribbon under her chin so that the wind wouldn't blow it away.

"Good morning, Mrs. Henderson. You called for me, and here I am, your obedient servant." Henri kissed her black-gloved hand. She looked at him angrily. A stern crease had formed between her eyes.

"Good morning, Henri. You shouldn't suggest you are a servant after you were almost my lover. You should be ashamed of yourself, disappearing from my life to devote yourself to that lady in the white evening gown. I saw that you saved her a seat beside you at dinner even though we had already been together."

"I did not save a seat for Madame Meyer. It was a coincidence that she sat next to me."

"So her name is Madame Meyer," Billie interrupted, "and her skin is as white as snow. A little change from the freckles that had captivated you earlier in the voyage."

Her sarcasm hurt her more than Henri, and he saw tears quivering helplessly in her eyelashes. Henri took her by the arm and led her to a deck chair. Once she was seated, he turned to her and said, "Billie. You must listen to me. Madame Meyer sat next to me by coincidence. You do believe me, don't you?"

"I don't have much time," she answered reluctantly as he pulled up a second chair and sat down by her. "We already had breakfast and William is in the men's lounge. He is going to pick me up soon. I want to know why you avoided me last night."

Henri nodded.

"You'd better have a good excuse."

He shook his head. "I don't have any regrets and I don't want to behave as if nothing happened. But I didn't expect you to burst into tears. I didn't know that you weren't well. I wanted to look at your freckles and see you smile. When you mentioned your stateroom number at dinner, I understood it to be an invitation to come to you. But I was looking for a good time, not melodrama, when I knocked on your door. I know that isn't very ethical of me, but that is the truth. I assume that you and Mr. Brown are together—excuse me for this assumption, but since I have to make this short, I am being direct—and I didn't want to…I didn't want to shake up your liaison. We don't even know each other. And I don't know about your relationship with Mr. Brown. And I didn't want to ruin anything."

She looked at Henri with huge eyes.

"No," she said, "it's true. We don't know each other. But what I understand now is that you don't want to get to know me either; that you actually never had that in mind. It would be convenient for you if I were in a relationship with Mr. Brown because then you would simply be able to have some fun without getting committed. This was to be a small summer fling, so to speak, from which, shall we say, you have run away…"

Henri was quiet. He didn't want to lie to her. He found her remarkable and charming. And he desired her. And didn't want to offend her.

Billie got up from her chair. Her face was blank. She reached for her small umbrella as a child reaches for his teddy bear.

Before she could run away, Henri grabbed her arm. "I wasn't avoiding you last night. But I didn't want to be with you and Mr. Brown together, without knowing why you had cried." It wasn't a lie. "It's true—I am afraid of being pulled into your story. However, I would like to know what brought you to tears. I like you. Really, I do…"

She withdrew her hand, turned away, and said as she was leaving, "Don't trouble yourself. Use your efforts on Madame Meyer. There's no need for you to get to know me."

"Some people attract attention while others do not. She is someone to whom all eyes are drawn. She probably doesn't even do it on purpose. Presumably the captain escorted her into the dining room to protect her from curious glances.

"I have children; no one looks at me anymore. I am only the mother of these children. I could have been jealous when I saw how all eyes turned toward her, full of curiosity, full of admiration, but I could only see what she had left behind—her family, her home, her possessions, her city, her country. She left behind everything that she had.

"Now she is free.

"She stood there in her white dress and she didn't have anything more, just herself and her dress.

"We knew that she had come on board without luggage. Such things get around.

"All I could think was: she is free. She has cast off all of her burdens. I suppose I did envy her, but it wasn't mean-spirited. I envied her courage, but I felt, too, how sad it was that she had to leave everything behind to be able to be herself.

"It's hard to imagine paying such a price for freedom. But look at me. You always have to pay. I am not who I would like to be. I am a wife and the mother of three children, nothing more.

You don't say that every day, of course. Otherwise you couldn't live. But she reminded me once again of the truth.

"I wouldn't change places with her. I love my children and I would never leave them. But right now, I also wish that I wasn't so unhappy."

Maria Vanstraaten, passenger on the Kroonland

The ship continued to plow forward through an infinite gray-blue desert of water. Henri's discontent grew as he watched it. I hope that the captain knows where we are, he thought grimly.

He couldn't remember why he had let himself be persuaded to get on this damned ship. He quarreled incessantly with himself. What did he care about Billie and Mr. Brown? Or whether the shy Madame Meyer, whom no one seemed to like, for some reason, had lost her head? What could he do for Lily, stuck in her wheelchair? And why should he be interested in a clan of men like the Russians or in families whose problems he didn't share?

He was suddenly seized by an overwhelming desire to get off the ship. Now. Immediately. He had had enough of its strange social life. He wanted to be back in his studio. He wanted to get back to work. He wanted nothing from his fellow passengers other than to know he would never see them again. They would all carry on with their lives, just as he would. Mrs. Mey would teach her daughter how to behave and tuck her out of the way somewhere. Mr. Witherspoon would continue to go on trips with his sister until they looked like two dried up old prunes. The children in the Vanstraaten family would turn out well and badly. Madame Borg would correct Monsieur Borg at all times. As for what Billie and Madame Meyer did with their lives, for heaven's sake, it was all the same to him.

"You can only take care of your own life," he heard Lisette say from behind him, "I know."

Henri's discontent suddenly turned to anger. He whirled around, but there wasn't anyone he could hit.

How stupid he was. Of course Lisette wasn't there. Yet he had been sure it had been her voice. Henri sat on a bench on the deck, feeling uneasy.

Billie.

Lisette.

Suddenly he remembered her dress.

Memories were flooding back to him. Suddenly he saw it in his mind's eye: a champagne-colored dress of filmy taffeta, with a broad skirt like a ball dress and a closely fitted embroidered waist. It had been a beautiful dress. Lisette didn't have any money and had never owned anything like it. Henri had only ever seen Lisette in her black skirt and white blouse with the stand-up collar.

And this dress.

One afternoon she ran into the studio excitedly. Her brown tresses had come loose, as usual. She wiped her forehead, wiping away perspiration. She had run across the city in the oppressive summer heat with a large package under her arm. She turned to Henri and said, "I'm going to show you something. Right now. Wait a minute!" Then she had disappeared into the kitchen.

When she emerged from the kitchen, she had been transformed into the most beautiful girl he had ever seen. The soft color of the dress gave her face a sweet glow, illuminating her brown eyes. She had even put some rouge on her lips. For the first time he noticed how small and delicate she was despite her sizeable zest for life. She stood before him, beaming; spread out her arms, turned around three times, and asked, "Well, what do you think?"

"You look ravishing," he had answered.

"Really?"

"Yes, really."

"Then take me in your arms." He did so, though with a certain impatience because he was in the middle of finishing a piece.

"Giselle made it for me. I sold a drawing. Imagine! Sold! To Monsieur Moreau-Nélaton! For a great deal of money! And with the money, Giselle made this dress for me."

She looked around and pulled the taffeta of the skirt wide. "Do you know why I wanted it? Why I put it on?"

"No," he answered, his thoughts already drifting back to his work. "What do you think of going out on Sunday evening?" he said, trying to cut the conversation short. "We could try to go to the opera so that you can parade around in your dress. I have to deliver the bust for Madame Latour this weekend, but I will keep Sunday evening free for us."

"But I…," she said despondently. "I put it on because—"

"Lisette," he said irritably, "can we talk about it another time?"

"But I have something very important to tell you. I…wanted to ask you something. If you, I…If we…"

"Lisette, listen. I really must get back to work. On Sunday you can tell me anything you like…"

"OK," she answered, laying the flowers she had brought on his workbench. She left the studio without a word.

On the upper deck, the two Vanstraaten boys were engaged in an intense duel at the Ping-Pong table.

Their father was reading in the lounge but invited Henri to join him when he entered. Since Henri couldn't come up with an excuse, he sat down and ordered some coffee.

Although Monsieur Vanstraaten led people to believe publicly that he wasn't concerned about his wife and children, it became quickly apparent that he had some very specific ideas about his sons' futures.

"Willem takes after me," Monsieur Vanstraaten said happily. "I see the engineer in him. He is a serious boy and doesn't give me any grief. At thirteen, he already understands what his future holds."

"What does his future hold?" Henri asked, surprised and genuinely curious.

"Well," Vanstraaten hesitated, "he knows that he has to embrace a proper profession to create and support a family, and I believe he will take his work seriously enough to be successful. I have made it clear to him since he was little that life isn't a game." He paused. "We all have dreams, but we're better off burying them."

He stopped speaking then, almost as though he hoped that Henri would contradict him. When that didn't happen, he cleared his throat and continued, his hands gripping the arm of the chair. "Yes. We have to bury our dreams. Dreams are but shadows. Such is life." He lightly slapped the upholstered armrest with the palms of his hands. "I don't want my children to be surprised by this insight. I want to prepare them for life, which means assuming your obligations and fulfilling them. Anselm, my second son, has trouble accepting this notion. He needs a strong hand to keep him on the right path. He is easily distracted, and, at eleven, he is still very childish."

Monsieur's countenance expressed discomfort, as though everything childish was suspect, a subversive power with potential for interference.

"He dawdles, is interested in everything and nothing, and has a hard time behaving at school. I have to tell his teacher repeatedly to discipline him, severely if necessary." Vanstraaten looked Henri straight in the eyes. "I have to do that at home too. The boy is immature and still needs to learn a great deal if he is to have what it takes to study law." He stroked his groomed beard, seemingly content that his own childhood was behind him.

"He already knows that he wants to study law?" asked Henri with increasing amazement.

"I'm assuming that he will study the law. Parents should know which subjects to encourage their children to pursue. Do you have children?"

"No," responded Henri reluctantly and sheepishly brushed an unseen fleck from his pant leg. "But by all means continue. I'm very interested in hearing what you think of being a father."

Monsieur Vanstraaten nodded approvingly and continued, "It isn't easy. You want the best for your children and at the same time to make them productive members of society. Perhaps I am too strict, but I got the boys corsets. Between us men, both boys are at an age when boys are inclined to waste their strength and hurt themselves. These corsets were recommended by many doctors. They prevent the boys from…well, from hurting themselves…" He looked distressed now, and Henri didn't know whether he was thinking of his own youth or whether he felt a sudden empathy for his sons.

Eventually the conversation came around to the lady in white.

"And," asked Henri, "what do you think of the beautiful stow-away, Madame Meyer?"

"I don't know what to think of her," said Monsieur Vanstraaten. "White as snow, red as blood, black as ebony..." His laugh came out as a dry cough. "Or something like that. She is quite romantic, like a dream that I have buried. I used to think that is what women were like—a fairy tale, a dream. But they're not. Women's hearts are deceptive. The beautiful ones have it easier because men will spend money on them, but they are all deceptive. Life demands discipline, and we would do well to keep women on a short leash. And our own flesh too." He took a sip of water and pursed his lips.

"It is true that when I first saw her I remembered my old dreams, my lost dreams. It was a nostalgic moment. But you have to live with that. Today's dreams belong to technology, science, the future. Human happiness is only an illusion, and the pursuit of it only preys on our weaknesses." Carefully he folded the napkin that the waiter had brought with Henri's coffee.

Monsieur Vanstraaten hadn't once mentioned his young daughter, and Henri considered asking Vanstraaten about his plans for her. Instead he pulled his watch from his vest pocket, opened it, glanced at it, and excused himself. He got up and bowed slightly. "I believe I'll take a walk on the deck before lunch is served. My regards to your wife."

Henri felt as though he had been run over by a mill wheel. He took a deep breath and then slowly exhaled.

He felt a sudden swelling of gratitude and tenderness toward his own father. That he had permitted Henri to apprentice with the stonemason, despite having had other plans for Henri, was a sign of greatness. Nor had he systematically beaten his son or probably spent much time considering the dire consequences of masturbation.

Although Henri was an atheist, he crossed himself three times in honor of his grandmother, whether she was responsible for his father's character or not.

Dr. Kirschbaum closed the stateroom door and nodded when Thomas Witherspoon asked him if he could speak with him for a moment. "It would be better if we went into the treatment room," he said, leading the way. "Your sister needs her rest."

He didn't beat around the bush.

"Mr. Witherspoon, I have given your sister a shot of morphine. She will probably sleep for a while. There isn't any other drug that I can give her for her migraines. The pain is obviously unbearable, and morphine is the only thing that helps."

"I know," said Thomas. "My sister has suffered from migraines for years, almost as long as I can remember. I have learned the signs now. First she has a nightmare and sleeps poorly. By then, it's too late to stop it. She gets morphine at home too."

Thomas laced his fingers and walked restlessly back and forth in front of the ship doctor's desk.

"Do you worry that your sister is addicted to morphine?" asked Dr. Kirschbaum so directly that Thomas briefly sat down.

"Yes, I do. Morphine is really the only drug that helps her. And she has been taking it for years. I can see that it helps her, but it's also the only thing that assuages her fear that I might leave her. Sometimes I think I am the trigger for the attacks. If I do anything that causes her to be afraid, the thought that I might travel without her, or…"

"Are you married?" interrupted Dr. Kirschbaum pleasantly.

"No. I am not married. I...I have a job that requires me to travel a great deal. It would be difficult with a family, if I had one." He stood up and began to pace restlessly again.

"And your sister goes with you on your trips?" asked the doctor without expecting an answer. "And makes sure that you don't get to know any women that you might like." He leaned back in his chair and regarded Thomas attentively.

Thomas pushed a blond strand off his forehead, sat down, and smiled disarmingly at Dr. Kirschbaum. Charming laugh lines formed around his eyes.

The doctor looked at him quizzically and continued, "And now and then, it happens that you fall in love with a beautiful woman, which is very difficult for your sister, who has obviously made it her business to protect you."

Thomas nodded. "Yes. She feels that she has to protect me. That's how it's always been. She's ten years older than I am. Although we always had a nanny, she took care of me like a mother."

Thomas noticed the doctor's questioning look.

"Our mother died when Victoria was twelve and I was two. My father never married again."

Dr. Kirschbaum wanted to inquire how his mother had died, but Thomas, acting as though he had just been set free, continued.

"As children, we were always well cared for; my father was wonderful. He took care of us himself when he could. But more than anything, Victoria was always there. She never let me out of her sight. We were inseparable, which was odd given the huge difference in our ages."

"When did the migraines begin? Can you remember?"

"I don't know exactly," responded Thomas. "When she was a young girl. Maybe she was fifteen at the time. Or sixteen. I can't say exactly."

"And because of her migraines, she couldn't go to balls like other society girls, right? Or fall in love and get engaged and marry like her girlfriends…"

Thomas didn't answer. Dr. Kirschbaum knew that he was right. Once again he'd reached the limit of his understanding. He only knew that morphine wasn't the solution.

"Thomas, how lovely that you are checking up on me!"

The morphine brought Victoria almost immediate relief, and once the raging headaches and nausea had subsided, she generally fell asleep. When Thomas went to check on her, she was awake and looked relaxed. So he decided to speak with her about what had been on his mind that morning. He sat down next to her on her bed and took her hand.

"Victoria," he said, "I'm so glad that you're feeling better. I spoke to the doctor and would like to talk to you about that." He sensed that she wasn't happy to hear that but didn't let that deter him.

"I have been worried about your use of morphine for quite some time. There isn't any other drug for the migraines and I know it helps you. All I want is for you to be fine. But everyone knows that morphine is addictive. Dr. Kirschbaum agrees with me that you've gotten hooked…"

"Thomas, I didn't give you permission to raise such a personal subject," Victoria cut in, upset, "and certainly not permission to speak to the ship's doctor about me. My afflictions are my own business—"

"You're wrong," interrupted Thomas. "Your life concerns me just as my life concerns you. Morphine addiction can be treated; it is possible to overcome it, but only with support. I want you to know I love you, and I am on your side. But that is only half of it. You have a great influence on my life, and I need to talk to you about that too."

Victoria sat up in bed. She was not used to her brother speaking to her like this, and she didn't have any desire to continue the discussion. "Please get me a glass of water, and once again, you have gone too far. It is my business to take a doctor into my confidence if I should feel that it is necessary. As for your life, I have always tried to be there for you, but you must do what you like."

She had stood up and begun pacing back and forth.

"Calm down!" Thomas cried. "I know that you are always there for me and only want what's best for me. But listen to me a minute!" He pulled her back onto the bed and tried to take her hand again, but she wouldn't allow it.

"Victoria, for me, because of me, but perhaps for other reasons I don't understand, you have never had a relationship, have never married. Whether or not it's clear to you, you expect the same from me and you are always finding reasons why not marrying is good for me."

Victoria wanted to interrupt him, but he continued. "You have probably noticed I have fallen in love. From the first time I set eyes on Madame Meyer, I was in love with her. I have fallen in love like never before in my life. And I won't let you ruin my life, even when you only want what's best for me.

"I owe you my life." He tried again to take her hand, to take her into his arms. "And I know what I owe you. But I cannot allow you to take from me a woman that I love; my debt to you can't go that far."

His voice had gotten louder with each sentence. Victoria had stopped trying to interrupt him. She stood up and went to the door.

"I know I am only a burden to you," she said bitterly, "an ugly, obstructive leech that you have not dared to remove because you feel obligated to support, to tolerate me. Because you are decent. Do you know what it feels like to be in your shadow? An old maid who hinders you, the beautiful, bright, successful Thomas Witherspoon, from the joys of life?" She opened the door and gestured for him to go. "Go, leave me alone. I understand what you are saying."

Never before had they spoken to one another like that. Yet they both knew that there was no more to say for the time being.

"As you wish," answered Thomas. "You know perfectly well that I don't think of you that way…"

"Oh, sure," Victoria threw back. "It's good that the truth is finally coming out."

With that, Thomas left the stateroom without another word.

When Henri returned to his stateroom, he could hear the couple in the room next to his having a fierce argument. Fragments of Clothilde's high voice, punctuated by her husband's lower, more muffled voice, penetrated the stateroom walls. Although he couldn't hear everything, he pieced together enough words— "always," "indifferent," "irritable," "discontented," "exaggerate"— to guess that it was about the usual suspects: unmet expectations, lack of attention, and remoteness. Suddenly the voices reached a crescendo—he heard the name Madame Meyer—and the door flew shut. One of them had stormed out.

Henri took off his shoes and his jacket and lay on the bed, unsure what to do with the afternoon, which stretched out interminably before him. He loosened his tie, unbuttoned his vest, and stared at the lightbulbs on the stateroom ceiling, a recent invention. Although he could see in the unaccustomed brightness of the electrical lights that his shoes weren't well polished, he realized that he could only see dimly what lay ahead for him. He had little idea what to do next with his life. He couldn't seem to shed the memories of Lisette, which followed him wherever he went. If he didn't do something, she'd continue to plague him forever.

Yes, he had trouble with the idea of marriage. He hadn't wanted Lisette to become like the women he saw all around him on the ship. He hadn't wanted to spend the rest of his days having small, spiteful quarrels. He hadn't wanted the day to come when she would weigh and evaluate each of his words and shake his hand impatiently off her arm, a day when she would rather buy clothes and hats than lie skin to skin with him.

He had wanted her to remain the Lisette who sketched better than he did, who threw her arms up in delight when she saw something that excited her, who called him a monster. He wanted her to be the woman who gave herself to him with the same passion with which she ate and drank and talked and fed strange cats; who balled her fists when she was furious, who let the studio door crash shut instead of properly closing it when she left abruptly. He had wanted her to tiptoe softly behind him forever, to nestle up against him, put her hands over his eyes and say, "Guess who!" And he wanted to reply, once again, "I have no idea." She would then have pressed against him, her hand moving beneath his smock in search of his naked chest. He wanted her to lick his throat tenderly and sit astride him on his knees. He wanted to fall asleep with her arm in arm yet let her go the next morning if she wanted to leave.

One evening she had visited him in his studio after they hadn't seen each other for several days. She was wearing her usual black skirt and white blouse and had wrapped herself up in a wool shawl. It was fall, and the weather had turned brisk. It was cold in the studio, but Henri hadn't put any more coal in the stove because he had already finished for the day. He had wrapped a thick wool scarf around his neck; he had gathered up his tools, writing on an old piece of wrapping paper with a stump of pencil which chisels he had to replace. In the adjoining room where he slept, he had heated the small pot-bellied stove. As a surprise for Lisette, he had put a pillow filled with heated cherry pits in the bed. She was always cold and asked him to rub her cold feet. He preferred rubbing her cold bottom.

She had wanted to eat around the corner at Chez Martine, ordering *boeuf à la mode*, a tradition whenever they went there. However, if they hadn't seen each other in a few days, they usually started kissing and kept kissing until she had undressed him or he had undressed her. Once they started, they couldn't stop. It took a while for them to make it to Martine; Lisette arriving with mussed hair and pink cheeks, Henri with unwashed hair still covered with dust.

On this particular evening, she had opened the door with unusual care, a bottle of red burgundy under her arm and a mysterious look on her face. After a quick kiss, she disappeared into the adjoining room.

"Don't come in here for ten minutes and wash your hair," she called to him. It was an unusual request, even if justified after a day in the studio.

In the adjoining room, Lisette had lit every candle she could find, opened the wine, and put out two glasses and a red rose she had picked, most likely from the garden in front of the house.

Henri wasn't sure if he had missed an important date; if it might be the anniversary of the day they had met. He wasn't particularly attentive to such things. But he did as he was told. As a precaution, he put on a white shirt, with tie and collar, and then he entered the room. Lisette beamed. She sat at the table with her arms crossed behind her head. He would have liked to swoop down on her then and there. Her breasts had always excited him. He would have liked to open her blouse, reach inside, and gently stroke her nipples with his rough thumb until they grew taut and swollen, teasing them lightly until she moaned. With his other hand, he would have pushed up her skirt, threading his fingers up through her garter belt and panties to feel whether she was damp between her thighs.

But she had seen through him and shaken her head, laughing. "Sit down. I want to talk to you about something serious." Her eyes gleamed more darkly than usual. He could tell she was excited.

"OK," she said, "if I had stayed with my father in the circus and become a proper knife thrower"—she laughed—"I would throw a whole circle of knives around you right now so you wouldn't be able to leave."

With this notion of encircling Henri with knives, her face lit up. She bobbed up and down on the chair, tilted her head back, and threw her arms over the back of the chair with as little modesty as a longshoreman. She was stunning. He had seldom seen her so radiant. Her breasts appeared fuller than usual to him, and her small, sleek, elongated body excited him.

"Go ahead, Lisette, keep talking. You are terrible. Go on, or I'll be terrible to you."

He had become impatient and wanted to take her to bed. "You," she sometimes panted, when they clung to each other, bathed in sweat, "kindly be careful. I am as fragile as your stones!" He pictured her sitting on his back, holding his arms triumphantly, and biting him on the neck, tenderly, but hard enough that the teeth marks were still visible the next day.

"You are strong. You have a bull's neck. You can handle that," she told him, laughing when he cried out.

But this time she didn't want him to hold her.

"Henri," she had said gravely, "don't move. I have something to say. I am already twenty-three years old. We have already been together a long time and I am gradually getting older. So I have a request."

Her warm, dark voice faltered nervously. She now sat straight as a poker and coiled her arms around her own waist, as though she wanted to stabilize herself. Then she continued, "This time I didn't put on my beautiful dress. You know I am superstitious, and it didn't bring me any luck on my first attempt. But this time you must listen to me." She had looked him in the eye, her upper lip suddenly quivering.

"Henri. Will you marry me?" she had asked.

He was paralyzed. He couldn't say a word. He just stared at her, stunned.

"Will you marry me?"

"No," he had answered. "What makes you think that I would?"

Her face had screwed up in pain. She looked surprised, as though shocked at the violence of her own emotions.

He had stared at her, petrified. Then, after a moment, he tried to reason with her. "Lisette. You are the daughter of a knife-thrower and a fire-eater! You aren't some middle-class girl. You paint, you draw, you study at the Académie. You are an artist. You sell your drawings! How is it that you want to marry? Besides, you have always known that I don't think much of marriage, that it goes against my beliefs. And yours too. Or have I somehow let you think otherwise?"

As he spoke, she slowly buttoned the top two buttons of her blouse.

She shook her head. "No, you haven't," she said.

They both stood up. The old wooden table stood between them; the wine glasses were untouched. The candles burned, no longer festive, but instead gloomy and surreal.

He didn't understand what had just happened.

They were going to go to Martine. They were, as always, going to make love and then eat Martine's *boeuf à la mode.* Why were they standing here now with the table between them, not moving? The cherry-pit pillow meant to elicit a soft, blissful sigh from Lisette when she snuggled under the covers lay untouched.

"Lisette!" he said, confused. "Lisette! Nothing has to change!" He had taken a step toward her to take her in his arms, but she had shaken her head vigorously, not saying a word.

He had tried again to take her in his arms, but her body, usually so soft and warm, was rigid and cold. She extricated herself from his arms, took her shawl, and was gone.

A few days later, the few possessions that she had kept at his place disappeared.

Valentina slid into the warm water. Lotte had drawn a bath for her and had added a few drops of rose oil to the water. Hot steam rose from the tub, condensed on the walls, and cloaked the light-bulb in a damp fog. Valentina could hear the even chugging of the engines and feel the vibration of the ship.

Her hand moved though the water, coating her long, thin limbs. She moistened her shoulders and watched as the water flowed gently between her breasts. As the steam filled the bathroom, she was enveloped in the scent of roses, reminding her of the day little Charles was born. It had taken twelve long hours for him to arrive. The midwife had bathed the child and wrapped him in a warm towel, then placed him on her breast, commenting that that wasn't too long for a firstborn. Little Charles had cried, just as he should. Although she was shaken from the pain, the excitement, the fear, and the joy of delivering a healthy child, everything had gone smoothly.

Her grandmother had lived with the Gruschkins in the days before and after the birth and took over the running of the household during that time. Once again, she replaced Valentina's mother, who was ailing in Carlsbad and had telegraphed how much she regretted not being able to witness the arrival of her grandchild.

My God, the small Charles. How happy he had made her! Viktor was proud of his son. Although Grandmaman remained skeptical about their marriage, Viktor and Valentina had been happy together back then. Valentina was suspicious when her husband occasionally disappeared in the evenings, but chose to turn a blind eye to his wanderings.

It was all so long ago.

Valentina breathed in the rose scent deeply. She felt as though she were slowly waking up from the rigor mortis that she had shared with her child. For two long years, she had not looked at her body. Yet now, as though by some miracle, visions from her past were surfacing in her mind—and, for the first time, it made her happy to think of them. Until the day before, only painful images were seared in her memory, eclipsing all her beautiful memories from before. Death had taken not only her child, but also all of the joy that she had shared with him during his fleeting two years of childhood. Her ability to feel anything other than sadness, despair, and guilt had died with her child.

Valentina began to cry. The tears streamed down her face, mixing with the bathwater. In a world that had gone dark, the possibility of happiness had returned. Her world had gone dark, but a glimmer of hope had surfaced within her. For the first time, she felt open to the possibility of happiness.

Henri had dozed off, but woke to a melody of some kind. At first Henri couldn't identify the sound, but after a moment, he recognized it as a voice. Yes, it was a French nursery rhyme, a lullaby. Henri got out of bed and, stumbling slightly, put his ear to the wall. The sound came from Madame Meyer's stateroom.

Henri went out into the corridor, but was met with silence. He must have been mistaken. No, there it was again, quite clearly, the beginning of a song that his mother had occasionally sung to him as a child.

Henri returned to his room and freshened up, combing his stubborn hair and walrus moustache, which his friends had mockingly referred to it as his Nietzsche moustache. He wiped his black shoes with a white handkerchief, chose a white bow tie for his white vest, and a white shirt with a high collar for his tails. Once he was ready for dinner, he knocked on Madame Meyer's stateroom door. After knocking a second time, he heard someone call from inside, "Who's there?"

"Madame Meyer," said Henri, clearing his throat. "Excuse me for disturbing you. It is Henri Sauvignac, your stateroom neighbor and your tablemate at dinner last night."

The key turned in the lock.

The door opened. She stood in the door, looking just as beautiful as she had the previous evening. Her hair looked different; it was now in a heavy, braided bun. Instead of the white evening gown, she wore a lilac housecoat of velvet, which made her skin look like milk and her hair like honey. Her amber eyes looked darker.

"Good day," Valentina said, surprised.

"Good day," responded Henri. "I wanted to ask whether I could escort you to dinner."

She looked at him in amazement, somewhat warily. But then she smiled.

"Yes, I'd love it. You beat the captain to it." She smiled again. "That suits me quite well. Shall we say in an hour?"

Henri bowed and said, "In an hour. I'll knock on your door."

Henri couldn't have explained what compelled him to approach Madame Meyer other than the fact that he was drawn to feminine beauty. Besides, he, like all the passengers who had heard of the stowaway, was curious about her. He knew that few were interested beyond a superficial interest in gossip and scandal. Henri, however, was convinced that her story might have some meaning for him and wanted to learn more about her.

His curiosity was even greater than his desire to seduce her—which was new to Henri. He had always lived independently. Even though his romantic relationships had created a temporary dependence on others, they had always disintegrated, leaving him alone once again.

However, ever since he had observed Madame Meyer climb out of the hackney cab in Antwerp, something had changed. He couldn't help but think that, even as she left her own life behind, she brought with her some part of his past that he wanted to leave behind.

His recollections of Lisette had become more urgent. Although he would have liked to deny it, he sensed that Lisette was still in his life. She would not leave him in peace, surfacing in his memories as though there were still a score to settle between them.

Reluctant though he was to admit it, he found he was still preoccupied with Billie. He could not deny that he was moved by her. He was also worried about her and, surprisingly, felt a certain responsibility for her—an idea that disconcerted him, since it ran counter to his solitary nature. It was little comfort that she was traveling with Mr. Brown. Even when he told himself that Mr. Brown was the one truly responsible for her fate, he didn't really believe it.

It felt peculiar to escort Madame Meyer to dinner, not only because Henri was wearing rather old tails that were tight around the arms and a bit shiny in spots, but above all because, on land, he never would have been allowed to take a lady of her class to dinner.

However, here, on the ocean, on this gently rolling ship where fifteen hundred passengers were penned up together for better or worse, the normal rules of society had been temporarily cast aside. Although no one mentioned it, everyone felt it.

It was as though the passengers, knowing the ship could go down, felt death more closely and therefore yearned more than ever for life. Their doubts, anxieties, and desires were clearer to them on the ship than on shore. Although they couldn't run away, they also found that they were freer than at home. Once they arrived in America, they assumed they wouldn't meet again.

And so, just as the weather and the sea changed, the cards had been subtly reshuffled.

Valentina's elegance and beauty enhanced Henri's own image, which assumed an unprecedented aura of grandeur. Unaccustomed to entering a room with a gorgeous woman by his side, Henri felt like a bear beside a princess. The shimmering white of her gown and the long train gave their arrival a fairy-tale quality. She was the young mermaid who assumed a human form in the evening, the fairy who combed her long hair in the moonlight. She was a creature of the night, a star that shone brightly in the black sky before dimming at dawn.

As they walked toward the dining room, Henri was aware of a barely audible buzz—of whispering, of mouths being pressed to their neighbors' ears, of elbows being jabbed into companions' sides, of eyes turning toward them and scrutinizing them from head to toe. Valentina handled it all with grace.

The businessman whom Henri recognized from the newspaper turned to assess them. He studied the beautiful Madame Meyer as though he wanted to buy her, appraising her slender body down to the tips of her white evening shoes, barely visible beneath the hem of her dress. His eyes lingered on the slender circle of naked skin that was visible between the end of her short lace sleeve and the top of her long, white, sateen gloves. Henri tried to put his arm around Madame Meyer to protect her, but there was little he could do to shield her from their fellow passengers' prying eyes.

Henri saw Madame Vanstraaten watching them inconspicuously. Though her eyes rested on Madame Meyer, she seemed lost in her own thoughts, which, judging from the look on her face, were probably melancholy. With a resigned gesture, she directed her children down the stairs in their usual age-based sequence. The youngest held her hand.

Her husband observed Madame Meyer and Henri with a certain displeasure. Although Valentina had made quite an impression on him, it seemed that he didn't trust her. She offended his principles, even if he couldn't explain exactly how. The light blond tresses of the Belgian businessman's companion were more appealing to him. The scent of her sweet, flowery perfume wafted in his direction, and he switched to the other of the stairs, where the businessman and his beauty descended the steps.

The blonde, sensing that he was tracking her, turned toward him for a moment, looked him in the eye, smiled provocatively, then turned back and continued down the stairs as though nothing had happened. Monsieur Vanstraaten stumbled on a step and switched back to the other side of the staircase, following his family, who had made their way into the dining room without him.

Henri observed all of this while keeping an eye out for Billie. Valentina, on the other hand, had only one thought: She hoped that the tall, lanky American would appear now, so that she could sit near him. She repeated his name to herself like a mantra, as though that alone would be enough to summon him.

Henri and Valentina had just been seated at one of the long tables when Billie arrived. She wore a deep red evening gown that looked lovely on her. With her head held high, she paused at the entrance. Although she wasn't especially tall, her natural vitality gave her an outsized presence. The good-looking blond steward hurried up to her to accompany her to a table.

Billie greeted the steward with what Henri considered excessive enthusiasm, acting as though she had known him forever. She let her gaze roam around the dining room, but she already knew where she wanted to sit and headed directly for Henri and Valentina's table. With a brief nod, she sat down across from them.

Lily smiled from the neighboring table. She looked at Henri and shook her head slightly. He couldn't figure out whether the gesture was an attempt to shake her hair out of her eyes or intended to convey something to Henri. Henri returned her greeting; he was sure that she would be paying close attention to his table throughout the evening.

A few minutes later, Thomas Witherspoon appeared alone. He spotted Valentina immediately and approached her with giant strides, without even waiting for the maître d' to receive him. However, there weren't any seats left in Valentina's immediate vicinity, so, after greeting her, he had to content himself with gazing at her from another table a short distance away. He tried to follow her conversation with Henri and Billie without snubbing his table companions. Valentina, too, looked over at him repeatedly, happy that he was there and unhappy that he wasn't beside her.

Billie greeted Henri perfunctorily. Then she slipped off her gloves and turned to Valentina.

"Good evening," she said. "I take it that Monsieur Sauvignac hasn't mentioned me. I am Billie Henderson." She looked provocatively over at Henri. Her freckles were barely visible in the lamplight. Maybe she had covered them with powder. Henri stared at her, realizing the volatile mood she was in. He had no idea what she would say next.

"But Monsieur Sauvignac has told me about you," Billie continued.

Henri was surprised at her lie and shuddered at the thought of what would follow. Valentina appeared surprised, but only said, "My pleasure, Mrs.—or Miss—Henderson…But you already know my name. Valentina—"

"Meyer," finished Billie. She didn't respond to the implied question about her marital status. Instead, she turned earnestly to the consommé that had just been served and began to stir it violently with her spoon.

"Madame Meyer, you are a celebrity on this ship. Everyone is talking about you." She took a spoonful of the broth and made a face. "Hot! Be careful!"

"Well, I hope people won't burn their tongues with my name," replied Valentina with a polite smile. "By the way, you look bewitching in that dress," she added amiably. "Let's talk about you instead."

Henri had rarely, if ever, been as squeamish as he was at this moment. Valentina pushed her soup bowl to the side. "Are you an American? Do you live in New York?"

"No, in Philadelphia," Billie smiled uncertainly. Maybe she was preparing herself for her next attack.

"Are you traveling alone?" Valentina looked at Billie attentively.

"Yes." Billie lowered her head and blushed slightly. "Sort of."

"Oh, I thought I saw you yesterday escorted by a gentleman," Valentina said casually. Billie blushed deeper, and Henri answered quickly in her place, "She met Mr. Brown in Antwerp; they know each other from Philadelphia. Sometimes you have to travel far to meet someone who lives close by."

The steward brought the next course, ham in a Madeira sauce. Mr. Brown had still not appeared.

"Where is Mr. Brown, actually?" Henri asked, turning to Billie. "It's too bad he's not here."

"Why do you think I would know?"

"Well, you seem to know him better than the rest of us," Henri explained. Billie looked at him, clearly distressed, and Henri realized the cruelty of his comment.

"He wasn't hungry," Billie said and sat up straighter. "And I wanted to get to know Madame Meyer."

Henri didn't care for the ham. The rind was tough and the ham itself was too salty. The carrots were overcooked as well.

"You are very honest," Valentina said to Billie. "I like that. Most of the people here would like to find out something about me, but don't place much value on getting to know me. A person in my situation must be creating quite a disturbance, don't you think?"

Valentina turned to Henri, looked at his plate, and asked, "Don't you like it? I don't find it too bad. If you'd like to go find Mr. Brown," she looked across at Thomas Witherspoon, "you could go smoke a cigar with him in the men's lounge while I drink a cup of tea with Miss Henderson in the drawing room."

She tilted her head back, clearly amused. Henri hated both of them at that moment.

Billie laughed, revealing her small white teeth, and pressed her finger against her nose. She looked happy at that moment.

Henri knew that her face could change in an instant, but no matter how often her expression changed—and it did often—it was all genuine.

"I doubt," Henri said to Valentina, "whether Miss Witherspoon should become our model, given how she feels about the separation of the sexes." He glanced apologetically at Thomas Witherspoon. "We could all go for a walk on deck after dinner, assuming Mrs. Henderson doesn't have to get back to Mr. Brown..."

"Mr. Brown and I haven't arranged to meet," Billie interjected indignantly, wanting to make that clear once and for all. Henri caught a faint whiff of her jasmine perfume.

Valentina nodded. "A walk on the deck is a great idea, especially after spending the entire day in my stateroom."

Billie stared at her. "You mean that you spent the *entire* day in your stateroom?" Billie couldn't imagine being shut up for so long in such a small space.

Valentina smiled. "Yes, the dress code forbids evening wear during the day, at least in public. Besides, I'm a stowaway, as everyone on the entire ship knows by now."

Billie inhaled as though she planned to say something; her face was full of pity.

"There's no need to pity me. The captain was very courteous, as was Dr. Kirschbaum. A woman who is traveling to New York with her dress collection has even put daytime dresses at my disposal. But the dresses and the permission to move about on the ship don't change my situation. I still don't know where this ship will take me. I'm using my days in the stateroom for contemplation."

Billie tried to understand what Valentina was saying.

"But it's obvious where we're going. We are on our way to New York," she said naively. "Whether we want to go there or not. I would rather travel back to Rome. I like it a great deal more than Philadelphia.

"Yes," Billie continued carefully, "I can imagine what you mean, but I don't know your story. I don't have any idea why you're here and where you want—or don't want—to go."

She fell silent and lowered her eyes, revealing her large dark eyelashes. Henri waited for her to unconsciously try to straighten her nose, but in vain. Her face, which was often such a bright sky, clouded over.

She drew squiggles with the handle of her silver demitasse spoon on the white damask tablecloth, which then became a figure eight, a never-ending loop. Henri reached across the table and tried to stop her hands, but the table was too wide; he would have had to lean far over to reach her and didn't want to be rude. He couldn't help but notice how different Billie's childish and white hands were from Lisette's.

Lisette had curious, strong hands. They were almost as brown as his and always on the verge of touching something. Both Henri and Lisette understood the world with their eyes and hands, and her hands had been an extension of her passionate disposition. Only when Lisette laid her palms in his did her hands seem tiny. Billie's hands, however, were helpless. She had stopped the loops and now she was drawing straight invisible lines.

"So then, shall we go for a walk?" Henri asked to interrupt her.

Billie looked up and put her spoon down. She nodded gratefully and stood up quickly.

Valentina got up too and looked wistfully at Thomas. He had been waiting for just such a sign. He stood suddenly, excused himself to his table neighbors—despite knowing full well that he was being rude—and made his way to Valentina's side.

"Sorry to be disturbing you, but I see that you are leaving… and I haven't had an opportunity—" he began.

Valentina interrupted him, "Monsieur Sauvignac has suggested a walk on deck and we'd be delighted if you would join us." In reality, she had no idea what Henri and Billie thought about it.

"That is very kind," Thomas said. "But may I invite you for a glass of wine in the lounge first? Perhaps Mrs. Henderson and Monsieur Sauvignac would like to join us after their walk?"

Billie nodded enthusiastically, taking Henri by the arm. "What a good idea. I'd like to show you something on deck, Monsieur Sauvignac. Let's be on our way."

Valentina looked at Thomas with a teasing smile. "Where is your sister, Mr. Witherspoon? Are you even allowed to enter the lounge with me?" But Thomas didn't react to her comment, so she let it drop.

On their way to the lounge, they ran into Captain Palmer.

"This time I am kidnapping her from you," said Thomas with a charming smile. "Last time you were faster than me and I haven't forgiven you for that."

The captain smiled back, looked at Valentina, and answered stiffly, "I wish you a wonderful evening. The decision naturally lies with Madame Meyer." He won't pester me further, thought Valentina, relieved, but it's clear he also won't go out of his way to help me when we arrive in New York.

In the lounge, the Russians were drinking and singing. The nightclub pianist had left his post and was happily drinking a beer.

"I travel to Russia now and then," said Thomas. "It's a fascinating country, full of unrest and possibilities, contradictions, despotism, bureaucracy, and injustice. It has infinitely vast landscapes and tremendous natural resources, which is first and foremost why I go there." He smiled. "But you can tell the country is seething, the czar is in danger. Didn't you say last night that your father is Russian and your husband deals with Russian diamonds? The recently discovered deposits in Siberia promise enormous profits…"

Valentina was surprised by how much Thomas knew about Russia. Suddenly she was ashamed that she had never thought much about it. Her father's world had fascinated her and repelled her simultaneously. "Yes," she answered reluctantly, "my father is Russian, a nobleman, who does business in Paris and beyond."

"And in Antwerp, how did you end up marrying a Russian?"

Valentina felt miserable. He not only had a sister who watched over him, he also knew that she was married. Why was she sitting here with him anyway? Why did he look at her like that? Why was he bothering with her? It had been hopeless from the start. How would she ever be able to tell him why she had boarded the ship?

"Have I offended you? Would you prefer not to answer…?" Thomas handed her the glass. "I don't want to pry. I was just interested…because, well, I…am interested in everything about you."

Valentina took a deep breath, took a sip of wine, and said, "My husband is quite a bit older than I am. And he is Russian, like my father. I believe that played a large role. He asked for my hand very quickly, almost rashly. We met at a ball, my first big ball, where the wealthy assess potential brides and begin haggling over all the future prospects…"

Valentina's cheeks reddened, and she spoke hastily. "I come from a good family, you know, there was always enough money. I am financially independent. Even after the wedding, I had a pension at my disposal that was not put into our community assets. My grandmother, with whom I grew up, luckily took care of that…"

She took a hasty sip of wine. "Even so, the proper path for women in my social class was predetermined: you had to marry, run a large house, and have children."

She spoke faster and faster. "In my case, it got around Antwerp that our family had caused a bit of a scandal—excuse me for not going into it in more detail. I felt that I had to get married as soon as possible, partly because I didn't have a choice anyway and partly because I didn't want to give local gossips any more to chatter about. Getting married seemed like the best solution." Her voice sounded less confident as she continued, "I would have had to give up singing anyway since I couldn't embrace it as a profession. Being a singer, perhaps even going to appearances alone, would have just created more of a scandal. Singing is only permitted in parlors as a way to entertain guests. There, women can demonstrate their good bourgeois upbringing, all their piano and voice lessons, but singing on the stage was out of the question…"

Thomas took her hand and pulled her up from the chair. "Come, it's a beautiful, warm evening. Why don't we take a walk on deck?"

Yes, that seemed like a good idea. She had already told him much too much. What would he think of her?

It was dark outside on the promenade deck. Only a few stars shone, and the moon was concealed by clouds. Thomas put his arm around Valentina. She didn't resist.

She knew she shouldn't have allowed it, that she should have reminded him that she was a married woman, but she held her tongue and instead savored how wonderful it felt to have his arm around her.

From the very start, it had been different with Viktor.

Viktor. She had met him at a private ball given by the van Apels family. She had just turned eighteen and wore a gossamer pale blue ball gown with navy blue ribbons on the bodice. If she remembered correctly, she had had a pale pink rose in her hair that night.

He had invited her to dance, and he was a good dancer. Later that evening, Madame van Apels, the hostess, had asked all the guests to sit down and listen to Mademoiselle Valentina, who would perform a few songs. The regal Madame van Apels, dressed in a dark purple velvet gown with a purple feather in her hair, loved to be the center of attention, and the audience feared that she herself might want to perform a few songs. Ginette, Madame van Apels's daughter, for whom the ball was staged and who was a friend of Valentina's, would accompany her friend on the grand piano. Valentina sang a Händel aria.

Lascia la spina,
Cogli la rosa;
Tu vai cercando
Il tuo dolor.
Canuta brina
Per mano ascosa,
Giungerà quando
Non crede il cor.

Her clear, bright mezzo-soprano was fuller and richer than one would have expected from the slender young girl in the inno-cent ball gown. When she sang, it was as though another being emerged, one who only expressed herself through music. Viktor fell in love with Valentina on the spot and decided he wanted to marry her.

From his chair, Viktor observed Valentina, whose hair shone honey colored in the light of the flickering candles that stood on the grand piano. He imagined kissing this lovely girl, who produced these beautiful sounds that made his heart swell with happiness.

It turned out that Gruschkin was a full seventeen years older than Valentina. Although a large age difference, it was hardly unprecedented, and his financial circumstances were solid. He could reliably demonstrate to the grandmother of the bride, Madame Meyer, that he could offer her granddaughter a life not only befitting her social status, but even more resplendent than that.

He had an office close to the main train station that was still under construction. It promised to be a superb, even splendid, example of new architecture. Largely in the hands of the local Jews, diamonds were big business in Antwerp, and Viktor Gruschkin had grasped on his first trip to the city that this was where his future prosperity lay.

He was also among the first to grasp that the diamond discoveries made in Russia in 1826 would be extremely profitable. He left a position at a bank in Kiev and established himself in Moscow. He went on to start a business with the diamonds found in the pits of Sakha. His travels took him from Eastern Siberia to Antwerp, where he sold the diamonds. He had finally moved to Antwerp and knew that marrying a woman from the best social circles could be beneficial to him.

Valentina's grandmother had regretted very much that her husband, one of the most well respected lawyers in Antwerp, was no longer alive, as she would have liked to hear his opinion on the merits of the applicant. She would have preferred that her granddaughter take the time to look around, flirt with other men, and wait for a while before making a decision. She had spoken with Valentina about it, but her granddaughter had only stared obstinately out of the window.

"I have decided, Grandmaman. I will marry him," she had explained.

"But he is the first man who asked you to dance at your first ball. You are beautiful, you are young, and we have money." Madame Meyer wondered at her granddaughter and couldn't understand her behavior. She looked for reasons she might be behaving this way, but came up with nothing.

"You can't be afraid of being left out in the cold and not finding a husband? I know that was the case with your mother and your father."

Mathilde Meyer took a deep breath and continued decisively, "But you needn't worry about that. In the meantime, grass has grown over the scandal, except in your mother's heart. The story, as nasty and mortifying as it was, won't stop anyone from proposing to you, if that's what you're afraid of." Madame Meyer was determined to prevent Valentina from making a rash or premature decision.

"There really isn't any reason to decide so quickly. The ball season is just beginning. Many men will invite you. You can think about whom you like best, and if you don't decide this season, it isn't a calamity."

Valentina continued to gaze into the garden.

"Are you even listening to me, Valentina? Valja? Do you hear what I'm saying? You can get married next year or the year after next. Anytime. I'm not pushing you."

"What do you have against Gruschkin?" Valentina turned with sudden intensity toward her grandmother.

"I don't have anything against Gruschkin," she replied. "I only fear that you don't love him. And I know that a marriage lasts a lifetime. It would be worth your while to consider that before you commit. Even though you can never know whether it's the right decision…" She paused because she hadn't really meant to say that.

"See," Valentina interrupted. "You never know, in any case, whether it's right and whether you will be happy."

"No," Madame Meyer answered and left the room.

Valentina and Thomas stood quietly at the railing. Valentina suddenly noticed that she hadn't said anything for a while. She had freed herself from his embrace, but she already missed his arms, more than she had ever missed Viktor's.

"Mr. Witherspoon," she said, "I am sorry. I don't know what to say. I'm sorry for everything. You see how much I enjoy being with you." She looked up at him but couldn't read his face in the dark. It wasn't until he bent his face down to hers that she could see he wasn't smiling. Then she closed her eyes, and he closed her mouth with a kiss.

Wednesday, July 27

The air was damp and salty, and a gusty wind blew across the deck. The sky was filling with dark cumulus rain clouds, promising a powerful summer storm.

It was early morning and Henri was one of the first people on deck. Henri breathed the salty air deep into his lungs. He hoped that the wind would clear his head of his scattered dreams, in which Victoria Witherspoon had grown taller before his very eyes, losing her slight stoop and turning into an attractive woman in her late thirties. Lily had crossed through his dream as well, but when he awoke, his first thoughts were of Billie. In his mind, he heard her laugh. It was so impetuous, but it also had a desperate quality to it, like the loud, needy cry of a child. Madame Meyer was an enigma, but Billie was too.

Billie was so different from Lisette, who had been like water in a glass, or a small, clear brook that trickled from rock to rock. At least that's how Henri had always seen her.

Or wanted to see her.

He stood and looked out across the sea. Once again, he wished he had firm ground beneath his feet.

"What are you thinking about?" A voice startled him, and Henri turned around. It was Lily. She wore a sailor dress with a large collar and was twisting her dark ponytail around her finger. She looked at Henri with a suppressed smile, taking a mischievous pleasure in the fact that she had been able to surprise him.

"Good morning, Miss Mey!" Henri called out to her. "You're up early. Who brought you up on deck? I'm an old man and don't sleep well anymore. But you?"

Lily stopped twirling her ponytail. "I'm an early riser. I probably don't sleep any later than an old man because my mama makes me go to bed so early. Papa brought me. He knows how much I love the beautiful morning outside. He'll pick me up before breakfast. Until then," she held up a notebook that lay in her lap, "I plan to write down my thoughts."

"May I ask? Do you keep a diary?" It was in vogue these days for girls and women to keep diaries in which they recorded their thoughts and feelings.

"No, it's not a diary," she stated firmly, shaking her head. Her ponytail swung back and forth and then settled down.

"I write down what I observe. The weather, the cloud formations, the movement of the waves, the colors of the sky and sea at different times of the day." She held out the open book to Henri. He took it and glanced inside. Her handwriting was delicate, ornate, and very precise.

"Have you been doing this for a while?" asked Henri, impressed.

"Oh, yes," she replied proudly. "I've been writing since I was twelve. I have a book for plants, one for animals, and this one here for weather; and I recently started one for people."

"For people?" Henri marveled. "What do you write in that one?"

"Oh, everything that I see, anything that gets my attention: how people look, how they move, how they eat, how they laugh."

Henri pulled at his wiry moustache. "Then you were probably observing me at dinner last night. You gave me a sign, but I didn't know what it meant." He wanted to grin but tried to look stern.

"I wanted to encourage you. You were sitting there with two beautiful women. Even though it looked like a prime seat, that had to have been difficult." Lily laughed. "It struck me that you were like a bear sitting between Snow White and Red Rose and couldn't decide which of the two you thought was more beautiful."

"Oh, really?" asked Henri, amazed at her insights. "And which do you believe the bear prefers?"

"Excuse me? I didn't hear you." Lily looked embarrassed after being so forward.

"Don't back down now, dear Miss Mey."

"No. I really don't know. I wrote down in my book that the first time I saw her, Madame Meyer behaved as though she no longer cared to be alive. Mrs. Henderson looked like she wanted very much to be alive, but didn't know how she was going to make that happen. But those are just my impressions. Forget I said anything."

That she wrote about people was her biggest secret. She wanted to keep that to herself. She had confided more in Monsieur Sauvignac than she would have liked.

"You certainly see things more clearly than I do," Henri said. Lily was quiet.

"Do you know what you want to do later in life?" Henri asked to change the subject. The sun broke through between the clouds. Lily squinted and shielded her eyes with her hand.

"Yes. I would like to be a scientist, either a physicist or a biologist." She paused briefly. "Or a writer."

Henri returned her notebook to her.

"That sounds interesting," he said. "And gutsy. You have a lot of big plans."

"Oh, yes," she nodded, "I do. Mama, of course, won't hear anything of it. She believes that women should marry and that married women don't have time to study."

"Do you think so too?"

Lily looked at him thoughtfully. Her expression was sad.

"Mama doesn't want to understand that I won't get married. She's still in denial about the fact that I sit in a wheelchair. I can't have children."

"Maybe you can't have children, but can't you still get married? There are many couples who can't have children…" Henri interjected.

Lily was indignant. "You know as well as I do that a woman in a wheelchair is different. I am not only thwarted from having children. I am impeded every single day and always will be in everything I do. Do you know what that means? Just try to imagine it." She was remarkably severe for her age.

"You can still fall in love and be loved by a man." Henri was convinced of his own proposition. At least he tried to be, but she sensed his uncertainty immediately.

"You don't even believe it yourself." She shook her head scornfully. "But it doesn't matter whether you're right or not: I don't want to get married. I want to study or write. In America, in London, even in Berlin, Zurich, and Vienna, women are allowed to study. Our family is from Vienna, and we still have relatives there. I could go study in Vienna." She paused and looked out to the water. "Oh, the sparkle on the waves!" She pointed out to sea.

"Maybe Mama is right," Lily said, gathering her thoughts. "If a woman is married, she doesn't have any time for herself and scholarship. I would rather have time for my writing. Frankly, it would bore me to run a home, even if I could. And the boring gossip that Mama exchanges with her friends is enough to put you to sleep." Lily's face reflected the boredom that she obviously felt in her mother's company.

"You may find it's different to spend time running a household when it's with someone you love," countered Henri. A moment later he could have boxed his own ears for saying such a thing. What in the world gave him the right to play teacher, he of all people?

"May I?" He rolled Lily right up to the railing and stood next to her. They both looked out at the shimmering sea. The billowing clouds soon slipped in front of the sun, diminishing the brilliance all around.

They didn't speak until Lily's father came to take her to breakfast. Two deckhands picked up her wheelchair and carried her down the stairs.

Lily waved briefly to Henri. In his thoughts, he caressed her cheek. He imagined for a moment what it would be like to take her in his arms, how she'd drape her thin young arms around his neck as he picked her up out of the wheelchair to carry her where she most wanted to go, to a lecture room at the University of Vienna. There he'd set her down gently on a chair in the auditorium and stand beside her on the stairs. A professor in a black suit would come to the lectern, greet his students—including his only female student—and begin his physics lecture on the forces of gravity. Lily would squint slightly as she listened and would soon forget Henri.

Henri ran into Billie on the stairs to the dining room. She was alone.

"Good morning, Mrs. Henderson," he said formally. "May I accompany you to breakfast? How is Mr. Brown?"

Billie gathered up the skirt of her saffron-yellow dress but caught her black-buttoned boots on the hem on the next step anyway. Henri grabbed her arm to support her. She gave him a stern glance but didn't protest.

"He still doesn't have any appetite," she answered neutrally. A moment later she became a little chattier. "A stomach thing that he gets occasionally. Dr. Kirschbaum recommended rest, chamomile tea, and zwieback. He should get some fresh air too."

She looked off into the distance as she continued down the steps. "I'm going for a walk with him on the deck after breakfast. If it's warm enough, he can lie on a deck chair."

She nodded, satisfied with her plan, appearing to have forgotten that Henri was still leading her by the arm. To his surprise, she sat down next to him in the dining room without making any pointed comments. Billie never ceased to puzzle him.

"I'm hungry," she said and went on to order an omelet with ham, porridge, pancakes with maple syrup, and tea. "Coffee doesn't agree with me," she explained almost apologetically, unfolding the ornately pleated napkin and laying it neatly in her lap.

"Mrs. Henderson…Billie," Henri said because this seemed like a good moment. "I would like to speak with you later in a bit more detail. We've had some misunderstandings."

She raised her eyebrows but didn't comment further, to Henri's surprise.

"William will only drink broth at lunch," she said, not making any attempt to hide how well she knew his habits. "Then he will probably go lie down. We could meet on the top deck, by the lifeboats. Most of the guests will still be in the dining room then and it isn't as crowded as the promenade deck." Billie bit her full lips and tugged the napkin in her lap back into place. Had she just set up a conspiratorial meeting with Henri? She lowered her eyes, confused, and tried to look more reserved when she looked up again. Her attempt at hiding her feelings was a failure.

"That would be perfect," replied Henri. If he had been smoother, he would have thanked her for the granted tête-à-tête by kissing her hand, but it didn't occur to him until it was too late. "In case it rains, let's meet in the drawing room," he added.

The steward brought breakfast.

She took one look at her omelet and turned pale. "Could I please just have toast and marmalade?" she murmured. She looked like she might throw up.

"Of course, Madame," the steward answered. "Should I remove the omelet?"

"Yes, please," answered Billie weakly. She had started to stand, but sat down again.

"Are you alright?" Henri asked. She looked miserable.

"Oh, I'm OK," she responded. Whatever it was, it was obviously distressing. "It's just a little bout of nausea," she continued. She looked at the colorful dome that arched over the dining room. "It just happens in the morning. It goes away after that."

When Henri was quiet, she added, "I'm not sick. Don't look at me like that. Here comes your porridge and my toast…" Henri was happy that she sounded like her old self again.

The blue-eyed steward smiled at her. He got on Henri's nerves with his persistent friendliness. "Thank you," he said abruptly.

149

Billie hadn't noticed anything. With a pained expression, she studied her toast.

"Billie," said Henri, "you don't have to eat the toast if you don't want to. Maybe you have the same stomach upset as Mr. Brown?"

She looked at him, startled.

"No," she said. "No. But I need some fresh air. Do me a favor. Finish your breakfast and be at the lifeboats at twelve thirty." She stood up hastily and ran from the room.

Henri turned up punctually at the lifeboats. Billie hadn't been very specific about where to meet among the twenty boats moored along both sides of the upper deck. Henri walked along them slowly so as not to miss her.

He found her right away.

Billie looked better. She still wore the same saffron-yellow dress.

"Let's sit in a life boat," said Henri.

"Here?" asked Billie and pointed with the tip of her closed parasol to the boat that was right next to them.

She is just like Lisette, thought Henri.

"No, maybe not right here by the door." He pointed back toward the rear of the ship. "Back there, the last boat. The end of the world—at least on this ship. What do you think?" he asked.

She led the way. Small curls frizzled at the nape of her neck. Although she wasn't wearing her dove hat, this hat also sat on her head like a bird, tilted slightly forward, looking as though it might lose its balance with every gust of wind and then would have to fly away to avoid falling.

The boat was covered with a canvas tarp, but Henri bravely climbed up the small steps, loosened it, pulled it back, and helped Billie into the boat. There she sat, enthroned, in her saffron-yellow dress with its small matching hat, high above the stern of the *Kroonland* in a rowboat, in the middle of the sea. She tilted her head back and squinted at the sky. The wake foamed below them, leaving a trail of white behind them.

"I am happy," Billie said seriously, "that you said you wanted to speak with me." Her head was still tilted back, and it looked as though she were choosing her words from the distant sky.

"I am tired of fooling myself and others so I'm going to tell you the truth." She stroked the wood of the bench lightly with the palm of her hand and spoke to the clouds after a brief pause. "My name is Miss Billie Henderson, I'm twenty-eight years old and I work in the fashion department of a department store in Philadelphia. My father was a saddler; he manufactured suitcases and purses and had a small workshop. He died when I was fourteen. There were three of us, all girls; I am the oldest. After the death of my father, my mother ironed linens in the laundry room of a large hotel. I applied to be a salesclerk since the four of us couldn't make ends meet with my mother's work. The others were still too young to work, and we abandoned my father's workshop."

Billie looked at Henri thoughtfully. "My parents had been very happy together. We had a very good childhood."

After a pause, she continued, "I found work in Wanamaker's department store. The first week, the head of the department called me into his office. 'You know, my dear,' he said, 'that your salary isn't enough to live on. Not for you alone and, of course, not for a family. You need to find a good gentleman who will support you if you can't find a man who will marry you.' Of course I didn't have a man who would marry me. I was just fifteen. I only knew boys from our neighborhood who were the same age as I was, fifteen, sixteen. They wouldn't have dreamed of getting married."

Billie took a deep breath, as though it troubled her to continue speaking. Henri took her hand to signal her to go on.

She sighed and her voice suddenly took on an oddly passive tone. "The department head helped me to find a gentleman; he recommended one of his acquaintances."

She sighed. "The other girls said, 'You have to get in good with the department head or you'll be thrown out.' The man that Mr. Welsh put me in contact with was bald and had pudgy fingers, but he was kinder than Mr. Welsh."

Henri was quiet. My God, he thought, she had been such a young girl at the time.

"The gentleman paid for a small apartment for me and took me out to eat once a week, sometimes twice. So there was always something left over from my salary for Mother, Josie, and Ann."

Billie clutched her parasol tightly with both fists, as though she wanted to break it.

"We were together for a while, Mr. Reed and I. I no longer recall exactly how long. Then he left me because his wife found out about the affair. 'Billie, my angel, I'll come back to you as soon as my wife has calmed down,' he said. But obviously she didn't calm down. In any case, I never saw Mr. Reed again. There were a few others after that. You get used to it. Except for one, they were all nice to me."

Henri didn't say a word. His instinct on that first afternoon when she had mentioned her stateroom number had been correct. She needed an arm, a shoulder, someone who saw her for who she really was. He hadn't wanted to hear her story a couple of days ago. Suddenly though, it was different. He knew that he was meant to be on this ship to hold her hand and to listen to her story.

Lisette was dead.

But Billie was alive.

"Then I met Mr. Brown," Billie said, interrupting his thoughts. "William. That was three years ago. I waited on him in the shop; he was looking for a fox-fur stole for his wife at the time. I sold him one, a silver fox. The fur was so soft. I put it around my neck to model it and show him how it looked on a woman, but also because I wanted to feel the fur on my cheeks. He looked at me and how I stood there. I laid the fur in front of my mouth, the silver hair tickling my nose; I detected his look. It wasn't lecherous or even wistful. It was lonely. He asked me if I would have dinner with him. I nodded. Why not? He picked me up at closing time and gave me the stole. Shortly after that, I left Mr. Wyland, the gentleman I was with at that time. I tried not to fall in love with Mr. Brown, but he was so kind. We've had many beautiful hours together."

She hesitated. "I think I did fall in love with him. He treated me very well."

She looked up at the clouds. The sky had clouded over, and the last traces of blue had just disappeared. The wind had picked up too.

"I don't know exactly how many children he has. Four, I believe. I actually don't even know why he comes to me. He speaks so proudly of his family and so lovingly of his wife. He's been paying for my room for three years. As long as I wasn't in love with him, it didn't matter to me, but now I can't help asking myself why he comes to me when he has everything at home and is such a loving husband and father. I don't understand men. But no one ever said that I had to."

The smoke gushing out of the smokestacks billowed in the wind, and the waves swelled, peaked with whitecaps. It looked as though it would start to rain at any moment. The ship rolled noticeably.

Billie began to shiver. Henri removed his jacket and laid it over her shoulders. "Keep talking," he said, because he was afraid Billie would never start again if she interrupted her story now.

"Anyhow, William had to go to Paris and Rome for work," Billie continued, albeit hesitantly. "His wife doesn't like to travel. So he came up with the idea of taking me along. He spoke with the head of the department at Wanamaker's, working it out so that I could start back again when we returned. If not in the fashion department, then at least somewhere in sales."

She reflected for a moment.

"The fashion department is my favorite area. I love the beautiful material, the dresses, and furs. But it doesn't matter. Because I got to see Paris and Rome. Who gets to take such a trip!"

Billie shivered more intensely.

"We should go inside. The wind is too intense," Henri said, sitting down beside her. He put his left arm around her and took her hand with his right. It fit so well in his that he was almost frightened.

"Shortly before our departure from Rome, I felt strange. I was sick and had to throw up as soon as I woke up. William sent me to a doctor, which was terribly uncomfortable. I had never in my life been to a doctor. And then to an Italian doctor! The *dottore* questioned me, examined me briefly, and said, 'You are pregnant, Signora. Congratulations to your husband.' "

Billie didn't look at Henri. She pulled her hand out, shoved it under her thigh, pulled it out again, then pressed both hands together and laced them tightly, as though desperately trying to compose herself. Henri saw that she was fighting back tears.

"But..." he said.

She guessed what he wanted to ask and shook her head. "No, I haven't said anything to William. I told him that the doctor said

I had a stomach ailment. But William suspects something. He has experienced enough pregnancies at home."

Resigned, she lowered her head. "You're not supposed to fall in love. A woman like me isn't supposed to fall in love under any circumstances. Do you understand?"

"But Billie," Henri said, "you have to talk to him."

She shook her head firmly. "I won't do that," she said.

"You must," Henri said. "You have to tell him!"

Henri was ready to burst. He felt an irrepressible anger rising in him. "What if he loves you?" he asked. "What if he would be delighted?"

"What do you know?" Billie said angrily.

The wind had turned, and the smoke from the smokestacks was blowing flecks of black soot onto Billie's summer hat and her saffron dress. The wind caused her dress to billow out, and tore at her hat. Black flakes of soot fell on Henri's shoulders, hands, and knees. "Come," said Henri, "quickly." And he pulled her out of the boat onto the deck.

"Excuse me, Madame, Monsieur..." The first officer stood in front of them. "We're closing the promenade decks. A storm is brewing. It will be too dangerous here outside."

At that moment, the skies opened and it began to rain violently.

A strong gust of wind drove the water diagonally across the sky, the drops beating noisily on the planks. The officer discovered the open lifeboat and cast Henri and Billie a suspicious glance. He tried to pull the tarp over the boat and swore as the wind ripped his cap from his head.

Henri seized Billie by the hand and pulled her toward the door. She braced herself against the wind, trying alternately to hold onto her hat and to lift up the heavy, wet hem of her dress. She ran in an unusual zigzag, staggering as though drunk, as the ship heaved and sank in the rolling sea. A sheet of white foam sprayed across the deck.

Once inside, soaked to the bone, they faced one another.

Billie looked in embarrassment at her hat, which she held in her hand. The bow had been crushed by the rain, the hat saturated with water. Billie's brown curls shone wetly, and stray drops of rain dripped down her forehead. Her nose shone bare in her alarmed, unpowdered face.

The rain had darkened her dress, and the skirt and sleeves clung to her body. Her teeth chattered.

"You'll catch cold," Henri said, standing in a small puddle that had formed around him. "Go take your clothes off. William will be worried about where you are. Pregnant women shouldn't get sick."

He pushed a wet strand of hair carefully off her forehead with his index finger. She looked up at him, her mouth soft and scared; she was a young, lost girl, who at fifteen had done what she had to do, as though she was a grown-up.

Billie turned to go. Henri looked at her back, the collar of her dress crushed by the rain, her neck extending gracefully from it like the stalk of a flower.

He wanted her to fight back. For herself. For her child. For her life.

"Billie," he called after her. She stopped and turned. He took her in his arms.

"You must tell William the truth!"

"Oh, no I don't," answered Billie. "It's none of your business."

The storm raged for hours, whipping the waves ever higher. The rollers crashed against the walls of the ship like an enraged animal attacking a steel giant. The ship careened violently in the rolling sea.

The few passengers who weren't sick gathered in the common rooms. The lounges emptied quickly. The dining room was closed. There was no sense in setting the tables, and the passengers had no appetite.

It was worse for the travelers in steerage. With no fresh air, dim lights, overcrowding, towering stacks of luggage blocking every step, and incessant noise from the engine rooms, the sleeping rooms were unspeakably bad even under the best of circumstances. The storm made them even worse. The doors to the decks had been closed, the few toilets were difficult to reach, and the luggage careened, abandoned, through the corridors. The sour smell of vomit hung in the air.

Thursday, July 28

The storm intensified during the night, and by Thursday morning, it still hadn't abated. The lights in the corridors and the vestibules flickered; the violent movement of the ship had loosened the lightbulbs, and the generator had come to a standstill.

Victoria, shattered by the fight with her brother, was in a panic, not only because of the storm, but also because she felt that she was about to lose Thomas. She couldn't say what was worse: the storm, which evoked a fear of dying in her, or the prospect of carrying on without Thomas, who gave meaning to her life.

Thomas regretted behaving so harshly to his sister, all in the name of a woman who wasn't really free and who could probably never be his. He knew how much Victoria suffered, but she had locked her stateroom from the inside and refused to let him in. At the same time, his heart was drawn to Valentina. He knew that it wasn't a fleeting infatuation. He belonged to her, no matter what her previous life was like. It wasn't even her beauty that dazzled him; it was the certainty of having found the person who was for him.

Valentina, too, was overwhelmed by seasickness. Hard as she tried to envision Thomas's kiss, the nausea eclipsed everything, punishing her for her moment of happiness. It was a clear sign that she must remember Viktor and her marriage. Not only that, there was also Richard, at whom she'd thrown herself in her message. He still hadn't replied to her.

Billie didn't think at all. She simply hid in her stateroom and gave herself over to her misery. Henri would have liked to go to her, but he wavered between his newly discovered solicitude and his vanity. His stomach had revolted against the weather, and he was reluctant to reveal his helpless condition to a woman whom he increasingly wanted to like.

William Brown, who hadn't been feeling well before the storm, put off thinking about how things would proceed with Billie after the trip with a certain relief. He had definitely noticed her odd behavior, but he couldn't grapple with his potential feelings until he felt better.

The captain forgot about the stowaway. There were more important matters to worry about now.

Jan Bartels, battle tested, thought of Valentina with a mixture of tender concern and satisfaction. His Valentina's life depended on his capabilities as a sailor. He was still there for his ship and for her, though the way she had used him really wasn't a credit to her.

At midday on Thursday the storm subsided. Few passengers ventured from their staterooms, and the *Kroonland* resembled a phantom ship.

In the lounge, the Russians held their ground bravely; that is, four of them did. Andrej, the singer, was in his stateroom, so seasick that he could only lie on his bunk and look mutely at the ceiling. The others, however, didn't want to be alone in their misery and sat with tea and vodka in the lounge. Fjodor had clamped the vodka bottle between his knees as a precaution.

Over the course of the afternoon, passengers began to emerge from their staterooms, pale and haggard not only from seasickness, but also from the fear of losing their lives.

In one corner of the lounge, Madame Vanstraaten held her young daughter on her lap as though she could protect the little one and herself from getting sick. Madame Borg had joined her, and the two women spoke, in an effort to combat the fear that the storm had unleashed in all of them.

"Willem is in terrible condition," said Madame Borg. "He looks healthy and rosy, but he can't stomach anything. The smallest irregularity rattles him. I have to keep everything away from him. And now this storm. He is so miserable that he asked me to leave him alone. When he doesn't feel well, he prefers to be alone." Madame Borg looked unhappy. She folded her hands.

"A couple should stand together in sickness and emergencies. But over the years my husband has pulled back more and more. When it became clear that we would never have children, he became entirely uncommunicative." Madame Borg patted her small blond ringlets to make sure her hairdo was still in place.

"Not that he has ever blamed me for not having children, but his silence is itself an accusation, a rejection of sorts. I have to drag everything out of him."

Young Olivia sneezed violently. Madame Vanstraaten pulled an embroidered handkerchief out of her purse and wiped her nose. She used the opportunity to adjust the bow on Olivia's head again. "Olivia, dear, you're bored, aren't you? Why don't you see if you can find a game to play over there?" She pointed to a corner across the room.

Olivia nodded obediently and went to the dark walnut cupboard that held various games. Her white knee-highs slipped and she carefully pulled the stockings up again.

Madame Vanstraaten watched her daughter. When she was out of earshot, she said with a bitter smile, "Yes. All men seem to get more tight lipped with time. At some point, you stop talking. Even when you have children. Don't let yourself believe it has anything to do with not having children. It's about getting into too many habits. Too many transgressions. Too many misunderstandings. We haven't spoken to each other in a long time. Sometimes I'll say something if I think my husband is being too strict with the children—he is frightfully strict," she sighed, "but he never listens. I am like air to him." She looked at her daughter tenderly. "He doesn't think Olivia is his daughter."

Madame Borg cleared her throat, surprised. Sympathetically she leaned closer to Madame Vanstraaten. "My God, you poor thing!" she said, shaking her head. "What an insinuation!"

"It isn't an insinuation," Madame Vanstraaten said soberly, as though the storm had made her realize she didn't have anything more to lose. It did her good to speak the truth, to anyone.

"My husband won't divorce me, but he hasn't spoken to me since this transgression. Such a lapse is unacceptable in his world. I don't exist anymore for him as his wife. I only exist to raise the children, his children. That is my only right and the only task that he still allows me."

Madame Vanstraaten smiled wistfully and continued, "It would have been easier if he had sent me back to my family and filed for divorce. My parents are generous, kind-hearted people."

Madame Borg, who would have so much liked to be a mother, stared, aghast, at Madame Vanstraaten, who had just shattered her assumptions about family life. Madame Borg was simultaneously flattered and shocked that Madame Vanstraaten had confided in her.

"But," Madame Borg said, "isn't it a concession that your husband didn't let you fall socially? You can continue to lead a normal middle-class life. The children haven't been taken from you. You have not been called out and shamed..."

Madame Vanstraaten made sure that Olivia was out of earshot. The little one had found a domino game and was sitting at a table, patiently laying out the dominos in a long snake. Madame Vanstraaten smiled her melancholy smile and responded, "Oh no, my husband's treatment isn't meant to be merciful. It is my punishment, a punishment that he inflicts anew every day, that is never atoned, and will be in force for the rest of my life. My husband is very thorough. He directs, controls, and specifies what we need to do every minute of every day, and how we are to feel, as sinners and failures, as weak flesh, as reluctant, lazy creatures."

Her voice broke off. She sat up in her chair, opened her purse, pulled out a new, folded handkerchief, and pressed it into her hands. She didn't put it to her eyes.

Madame Borg didn't reply. She wasn't sure she should tell her husband this story; he probably wouldn't believe it anyway. Madame Vanstraaten glanced at her daughter. The little girl looked up and smiled weakly. She was obviously still feeling nauseous.

"Come, Olivia," Madame Vanstraaten called softly and got off her chair. "Let's go see how the others are doing. Maybe they need some tea or zwieback."

The little girl put the dominos back in their case, stowed the game back in the cupboard, and grabbed her mother's hand. "It's good that at least the two of us aren't seasick anymore," Madame Vanstraaten said to Olivia and nodded once more to Madame Borg as they left the room.

Henri, among the first to feel better, went to look for Billie. He made the rounds through the sitting rooms. The smoking lounge reeked of stagnant cigar smoke, but it was still better than the smell that lingered in the corridors. A few gentlemen sat on the brown leather benches that lined the walls of the room, but only one of them was smoking. One of the electric bulbs on the white-painted coffered ceiling had gone out, leaving one corner of the room dark. A large damp spot darkened the carpet, and Henri pictured auburn cognac, white Riesling, and purple burgundy flying through the air on teetering silver trays.

The dining room was deserted. The swivel chairs turned their wooden backs dismissively to the long tables; the top of the piano was closed. Now it was clear why the chairs were fastened to the floor.

Henri didn't run into Billie during his explorations.

Toward evening, the decks were opened. The wooden planks were saturated, and water still dripped from the railings. A cool, strong wind had ripped blue holes in the overcast sky. The sea was still churning, but the dark green waves, though still capped with white foam that sprayed into the air, didn't roll with the same frenzied force as before. The wind swept the wisps of clouds together, then scattered them again, a relentless shepherd tending his herd of clouds.

Finally the sun appeared deep on the horizon, a large, yellow, glowing ball that grew gradually redder. The sun painted the surrounding clouds in flaming crimson and orange.

Henri stood, wrapped in his old black coat, before the vast, glowing sky. If Billie didn't respond to his knocks again, he would knock on Mr. Brown's door. How had she spent the last few hours? The more he thought of Billie, the less he found himself thinking of Lisette. Now, however, she was on his mind.

He thought of how she'd always put her hand wordlessly in his whenever they went for a walk in Paris. Lisette coped with life better than he did, but she was still always afraid of losing herself in the big world.

"I am afraid of people. You know that," she explained when he enclosed her hand in his. He never ceased to be surprised by this trusting gesture. "The world is too big, too difficult for me. I know that you don't believe me, but that's how I feel." Occasionally she had pulled her hand back, thrown her arms partway up in the air, and called out, "I just want you to hold me!"

If only he had done that! What had kept him from doing that? Why had he refused her? Today he would have taken her in his arms and simply said, "Yes, of course!"

"Monsieur Sauvignac!" a voice behind him startled him out of his memories. Valentina had been observing him for a while. Wrapped in a brown blanket, she leaned against the wall beside the door. She was very pale. The wind had loosened a few strands of her hair and kept ripping them out of her hands as she tried to pin them up.

"Madame Meyer!" Henri said delightedly and leaned next to her against the wall. "I was just wondering how you were doing, presumably not too differently from the rest of us."

She tried to smile. "I wasn't seasick right away. But then...It is difficult, not knowing how long it will last. Yes, I was...miserable. After all those hours inside, I just had to get some fresh air, as you can see."

In her pale face, her nose looked sharper than usual.

"I was just going to look for Miss Henderson," Henri explained. "But maybe we can meet later in the dining room? That is, if you can imagine eating again..."

Valentina hesitated. "Oh, God, I don't know," she said. "I don't think so."

When Henri returned to his stateroom, he found a message from Billie shoved under his door. She had filled an entire page with a few sentences in her clumsy, sweeping handwriting.

Henri, I will speak with him. I don't know when, but I will do it. I was so nauseous that I threw up a thousand times! I'm not coming to dinner. Until later.

Henri looked at the slanting and crooked page in his hand as though it contained poetry. When had he become such a romantic? Some flecks of ink decorated the paper, and the text contained more than a few spelling errors. But every objection that he raised against his feelings for Billie was futile. He stashed the letter in the inside pocket of his jacket so that he could pull it out and look at it again. It was Miss Henderson's jasmine-scented emissary, and he planned to take good care of it.

Come to me after you have spoken to William. Stateroom 11. Promise me! Look for me in the dining room or in the lounge if I am not in my stateroom. Henri

He rang for a deckhand to be his *postillon d'amour.*

Lisette kept quiet. It was almost as though she had disembarked. No memory of her surfaced in his mind.

The few passengers who had ventured out of their staterooms looked like they were lost. They walked cautiously and held on tightly to the massive walnut handrail, as though the storm was still tossing the ship about. The purser stood at the door to the dining room and greeted the passengers who appeared for dinner. Although all of the lights were lit, the room seemed bleak. The light didn't play on the crystal glasses or on the silverware as before. The stewards hadn't set all the tables and had removed the floral decorations to avoid any new spills.

Although he knew several of the guests, Henri sat alone at a table. The good-looking steward brought him a menu. Henri was overcome by a slight touch of nausea as he read the list of courses.

Grapefruit Cocktail
Quenelles of Foie-Gras President
Cold Consommé Madrilène/Okra Soup
Plymouth Fillet of Dried Salted Mullet
Cold Asparagus, French Dressing
Saddle of Lamb with Fresh Spring Vegetables
Boiled Potatoes Sautéed in Butter
Skewers of Roast Vermont Capon
California Salad
Washington Pudding/Delaware Apricot
French Pastry
Dessert
Coffee

Soup, asparagus, and some capon seemed like sensible choices, and Henri opted for water. As he waved to the steward to put in his order, he saw Valentina standing in the doorway. She looked searchingly around the room, but neither Thomas nor Victoria was there. Valentina didn't know whether to feel unhappy or relieved since her doubts had gained the upper hand.

Henri jumped up and asked her to join him.

"I see that you are taking a chance," he said and handed her the menu.

She smiled weakly and ordered a clear broth.

"I don't know how daring I am," she answered, "but I'm trying to eat something."

She looked discreetly around the dining room, unsettled by the thought that she could have possibly overlooked Thomas in her nervousness. But he really wasn't there. Stupidly, she felt hurt.

"Dear Madame Meyer," Henri said. "You have dared to do something outrageous. You have defied all conventions. I don't know if I could do that."

She looked at him, amazed.

"But I didn't give it as much thought as you seem to think!" she exclaimed. "I left because I couldn't live anymore as I had been living." She didn't understand how anyone could find that daring.

"I'm sorry that I took the liberty of saying that, but do you know a single woman who has done something like that? It could be that under certain conditions, men are bred to make radical decisions. But you are a woman. Yours is a world of convention and constraint, as it is for all women. To liberate yourself from that—"

She interrupted Henri with a quick, impatient hand movement. "I have never felt like I was a part of that conventional world. I have never belonged to it. You get used to being different."

She smiled at him. "As an artist, isn't it the same for you?"

Henri nodded. "Yes. Of course." He broke off. "If that connects us—that we both feel like outsiders—may I call you Valentina?" He hinted at a bow, and put his hand to his chest, "Henri. You mentioned your name to Miss Henderson…Valentina… Also, we are connected by the storm we came through, if further arguments are necessary to persuade you…"

"Yes. It could be that this ship is creating some unusual and irresistible alliances…" As she spoke, she thought of Thomas Witherspoon, who still hadn't appeared. It seemed that she hadn't seen him for an eternity.

"We'll toast to that when we can drink wine again, OK? But permit me one more question: why do you think of yourself as an outsider?"

Valentina hesitated. How far did she want to trust Henri Sauvignac with her story?

"I can understand your question," she replied. "It's true I have had a very privileged life. I was brought up by my grandmother, who was always very good to me. And I was fortunate to be born into an affluent family."

She stopped, and something seemed to cloud her thoughts then.

"What happened to make you go to the harbor and board this ship? The ship should have sailed hours earlier! How could you have known that it would be delayed?"

"What happened? Why did I go to the harbor? My God, you are asking intimate questions. That is a long story. Do you really want to hear the entire thing?"

She didn't expect an answer and continued, "Every story has a prologue. I was raised by my grandmother. In Antwerp. I rarely saw my mother. Her health was delicate and she spent most of her time traveling to various health spas in Europe. I have never seen my father. He left my mother before I was born."

Henri looked at her incredulously. What was she saying? He felt a searing heat rise in him and loosened his collar with his fingers.

"What's the matter?" asked Valentina, suddenly upset. "You look flushed. Don't you feel well? Here, drink a glass of water… Monsieur…Henri?"

"No, no…I'm OK now," he murmured, further loosening his collar. "Please continue."

He put his hand on hers apologetically. "Please! Your father left your mother before you came into the world…"

Valentina wondered why his voice suddenly sounded so husky.

"My mother met my father in Paris, in the drawing room of the Montagnol family. The Montagnols were good friends of my grandfather from his student days in Paris, where he studied law at the Sorbonne. My mother lived with them for several months to become a woman of the world. She was just eighteen at the time; my father was twenty-three. My mother played the piano superbly. Everyone always asked her to play something. On this particular evening, it was September 1876 in the Montagnols' drawing room, she accompanied my father on the grand piano. My father was not only dashing and charming, but he also had a voice that melted women's hearts."

Valentina disappeared into her thoughts. She had imagined this scene so many times she almost felt she had been there. "She fell head over heels in love with him."

"You obviously inherited a great deal from your father," Henri said. "Your voice…and your beauty."

"My mother is also beautiful," Valentina added hastily, compelled to come to her defense. "I only know what my father looks like from one picture that a Parisian salon painter painted of my parents on their wedding day. It is hanging in my grandmother's house, despite the disgrace my father brought to our family. In the picture, my mother is playing the piano. She looks very proper and is looking at my father full of adoration…" Valentina paused again, as though she were standing before the painting as she described it.

"My father, thin, tall, dark haired, in black tails, is leaning against the grand piano." She had memorized all of the details; she could picture how her father spoke, sang, leaned over the piano to her mother, smiled at her and asked her to dance—even how he kissed her for the first time.

Then she said suddenly, angrily, "He never even tried to see me."

Every emotional pain is immortal and has the capacity to be resurrected whenever it is mentioned. Valentina's story took place many years ago, but the feelings were still raw. Her eyes filled with tears.

"He never explained himself? Never wrote? Never saw your mother again?"

"No," answered Valentina. "He never wrote. He simply disappeared in the dead of night."

"Ah," said Henri. His voice was raw as he added, "I know someone who never tried to see his daughter. I…"

She hadn't heard him and continued.

"My parents got married in Antwerp, six months after they met. My grandfather had been against the liaison. Even though he had studied economics in Moscow, my father didn't have a profession. He had been on an extensive European trip with his wealthier cousins and was then supposed to take over his father's estates."

"I remember," Henri cut in. "Your father is Russian. You mentioned that when I wanted to introduce you to the Russians here on board..."

"I was given the Russian name Valentina. I don't know why, because it must irritate my mother. It is my grandmother's name on my father's side, which no one in my family knows. Every time my name is mentioned, she thinks of my father and what he did to her. I am a thorn in her side, the living, omnipresent sign of her disgrace." She blushed, with a certain irony, as though humiliated by the fact of her own existence.

"My mother couldn't get over the shame. Everyone in Antwerp gossiped about it—that the handsome Andrej had abandoned her without a trace when she was seven months pregnant. They hadn't even been married a year. Thank goodness my grandfather didn't live to see it, since they had married against his wishes. My grandmother had given her half-hearted consent, and then they had moved into her house. After my father left, my mother became sick. My grandmother said she became apathetic and didn't sleep anymore. Ever since my birth, she has suffered from one female ailment after another."

She looked at Henri, worried that she might be boring him, but he only nodded to indicate that she should continue.

"My mother traveled from hot springs resort to hot springs resort, from one health cure to another. She still does to this day." Valentina shook her head. "She followed the miracle doctors; at first she adored them, but then she got rid of them when their cures failed. She only came home now and then." She shrugged her shoulders. "My resemblance to my father wasn't just a lucky coincidence. 'Valentina,' my mother would say, 'be polite and listen to your grandmother. You know I can't take care of you. Be thankful that Grandmaman is so good to you.' Then she'd sigh"— Valentina imitated the sigh—"she'd stroke my hair absently and say, 'Don't turn out like your father!' Then she'd turn back to my grandmother and describe yet another failed treatment that had led her from Baden-Baden to Bad Ragaz to the Saturnia thermal springs."

Valentina broke off abruptly. Thomas Witherspoon was standing in the door looking pale and even taller than usual. He pushed his hair off his forehead and looked around the room. Valentina couldn't take her eyes off him, as though he might see her more quickly if she focused her gaze in his direction. She didn't notice that she had fallen silent and that Henri was waiting for her to continue with her story.

She had simply forgotten that Henri was there.

Thomas finally noticed her, and Valentina rose out of her seat, looking as though she wanted to rush toward him.

Valentina suddenly remembered Henri as Thomas approached the table and greeted them. Thomas was polite enough to include Henri in the conversation, but Henri saw that the evening had taken a new turn.

Henri stood up. All of a sudden he felt tired and cold. He wanted to be alone. Valentina still didn't have the slightest idea why her story was so important to him, but he did.

"Please, sit with us," Valentina finally said, blushing at Thomas. She looked up into his green-gray eyes and thought, No, just as she had the first time she saw him. And just as before, she thought: I want it, but I can't and I won't.

Henri used the opportunity to offer Thomas his seat and say his farewells. "I hope, Mr. Witherspoon, that you and your sister weathered the storm without too much trouble. Excuse me if I retire now. I am sure you will be the best possible replacement for Madame Meyer."

His final words bordered on rude, but he had noticed how Valentina's affections clearly lay with Thomas. "Valentina…" He bowed slightly and disappeared.

"Monsieur Sauvignac addresses you by your first name…," Thomas noticed.

"My God, how are you?" Valentina leaned toward him. Thomas looked very poorly. "You warned me a couple of days ago and advised me to enjoy my *entrecôte*. You were right," she continued. "All day I've felt as though I'll never be able to eat again… You look pale."

"Yes, I am not seaworthy yet." He made a boyish grimace. "It's good that my occupation keeps me on firm ground. Victoria and I both suffered."

The steward asked whether Thomas cared for anything. Thomas requested only black tea and turned back to Valentina.

"I would have liked to check on you, but I thought it might be too brash. I asked Dr. Kirschbaum if he had spoken to you, but he only said that you were in your stateroom. It was horrible for me that I couldn't come to you. Today I was determined to find you."

He gave her a disarming smile, and a shiver spread through Valentina's body. She worried about her lack of self-control, but she knew she must suppress her feelings.

"Yes," she said helplessly. "Yes." He must have noticed how confused she was, that she was in love with him. She had already caused enough trouble. She had to compose herself. If Richard had gotten her message, he could be waiting for her on the quay in New York…And how would she explain that to Thomas?

"You look wonderful," Thomas broke into her thoughts. "The storm couldn't have done you much harm…"

"That isn't true!" she protested. "But where is your sister?"

He shook his head and turned serious.

"Neither one of us does well at sea, but Victoria even panics on land when there is severe weather. Our mother died in a fire, and lightning can start fires. Poor Victoria. She is still in her state-room." He didn't mention his argument with her.

"I am sorry," Victoria said, putting her hand on his, but pulling it back quickly when she touched his warm skin. With Richard, it had been different, she thought. Viktor didn't even cross her mind. Thomas lifted the hand she had touched.

"You pulled your hand away so quickly. Is there something wrong? Or would you try it once more?" He put his hand on the table again and moved it closer to her.

Dear God, thought Valentina, how am I supposed to save myself from him? Desperate, she said brusquely, "Mr. Wither-spoon. I am married. You know that. There is a great deal more that you don't know. All of it makes it impossible for us…to be together. We must part ways."

"But Valentina," Thomas didn't understand the reason for her sudden rejection. "I know that you are married. And you know that I know it. All the same, whatever happened before is in your past. But now we have met. We have only the future to consider…"

"No," she responded, almost unkindly, "you have a future and I have a future. We have no common future." She paused and looked him straight in the eye. "We will never have a future together."

Thomas was quiet, looking as though he hoped she would retract her statement. When she remained quiet, he withdrew his hand and said stiffly, "Forgive me for offending you. I imagined that you felt as I did. But it seems I have let my feelings get the better of me. I didn't realize you felt so differently."

He got up and added stiffly, "I am sorry that I have erred. How could I have been so stupid? Forgive me. I am going to go look after Victoria now."

You couldn't have known, Valentina wanted to exclaim to him. I haven't told you everything. It is true that I feel just as you do...!

But she didn't say a word; she rose from her chair, confused and silent, as though waiting for him to right the situation.

And in fact, she did hear a voice. "Can I be of some help?" But it was only a steward who had come up behind her. Valentina shook her head.

Thomas had already bowed and was gone.

Richard. She had to write him. She had to find a way out of her situation. Richard was one of the kindest people she had ever known. No one had looked attractive to her after the death of Charles—except Richard. Young and easy-going, he had a bright future ahead of him. And she had met him—and written to him—before she knew that there was a man such as Thomas in this world.

The sky had been vast in Engadin. She had finally been able to breathe, despite the darkness that gripped her heart. Richard had lightened her sad, tired, downtrodden soul. He had all the confidence that she had lost. He believed that life was good and that it was right to live fully. Or perhaps it was the vastness of the landscape, the mountain air, and the mild fall sun that had brightened her mood, just as Dr. Koch had predicted. Valentina couldn't be certain.

The young American had kept his promise and had come over from Pontresina to pay his respects a few days after Valentina and Madame Brochet had moved into their rooms in the Kurhaus hotel.

The Kurhaus had proved to be a good choice. In recent years, it had emerged as a luxurious spa on par with Baden-Baden, while also offering a magnificent landscape, splendid air, and abundant sunshine. St. Moritz had become an international destination, and Dr. Koch hoped that, in addition to the baths and mountain air, the social life would distract Valentina and help cure her.

Dr. Koch had booked them a drawing room and two bedrooms, which could be combined into a suite. The imposing, classically styled house had accommodations for three hundred guests and their servants. Valentina explored the hotel with Madame Brochet before she reported to Dr. Brügger, the spa doctor, for her prescription for the baths. The house was vast, containing, among other things, a dining room that seated four hundred, a ballroom, two beauty parlors, and a library filled with international newspapers. Madame Brochet sent a telegram to Antwerp saying that they had arrived safely.

On the afternoon of their first day, Dr. Brügger examined Valentina and put together a spa plan for her. He encouraged her to take walks because the fresh air would do her as much good as drinking the water and taking the bathing cures.

The mountain air made Valentina tired, for which she was grateful. She finally was able to fall into a deep slumber, during which she enjoyed the rare luxury of forgetting about everything. She was also thankful for the steady daily routine, which made it difficult to think about much. In the morning, she went to the baths. The spring water was warmed with the aid of a steam engine, and then a bath was drawn. Valentina shivered in the tub because the water was cooler than her body. But the acidic-smelling carbonated bubbles that formed on her skin tingled pleasantly, invigorating her skin, and soon created a languorous warmth. When the bath attendant helped her out of the tub and wrapped her in a towel, her skin was bright red, and Valentina looked at it in amazement. The attendant explained that it wasn't cause for alarm, that the water always caused a reaction.

Richard Livingston hiked a full hour from Pontresina, which he did willingly in hopes of meeting the beautiful Madame Gruschkin. He didn't dare visit every day since he was aware of the fact that she was in mourning. Yet he couldn't get thoughts of the beautiful Madame Gruschkin out of his mind. It drove him almost to despair that he couldn't put her out of his mind, regardless of where he was. In his mind's eye, he saw her sitting in the stagecoach in her black traveling clothes, with her frail, narrow waist, hands in her lap, her pale face concealed beneath the black veil of her hat. She was so beautiful that a slight shudder ran up his spine whenever he thought of her. When she had pushed back the veil and looked at him, a tug in his body had spread from his loins to his heart. He had stared at her eyes, which reminded him of an Egyptian statue that he had once seen in a museum.

He had to see Madame Gruschkin again, even though his instincts told him otherwise. In New York, he had been court-ing a girl who had every right to believe that he would ask her parents for her hand in marriage upon his return. He had been in love with Cynthia for two years. Now that he had just been made partner in a reputable architectural firm in New York, there was no longer any obstacle. He could finally establish his own livelihood and a family.

As promised, he had sent Cynthia a telegram in Pontresina saying that he had arrived safely. Although it was true, he had the unhappy sensation that he was deceiving her because he didn't mention meeting Madame Gruschkin. He knew that it would have been unusual to mention a fellow passenger in a short telegram, but he also knew that the brief encounter could change his life—that, in fact, the fortuitous meeting had probably already changed it.

He met Madame Gruschkin and her companion, Madame Brochet, in the foyer of the spa hotel. Though it was early afternoon, the grand electrical lights that hung from the ceiling were already lit. Richard swept his gaze across the large room and the balustrade, which rose on slender white columns in front of the curved staircase, but he didn't see the women until he looked in the mirror above the mantel. Madame Gruschkin was sitting quietly while Madame Brochet read something to her from the newspaper.

When he approached and greeted them, he noticed that Madame Brochet appeared happier to see him than did Madame Gruschkin. It was as though she did not even recognize him. But Richard Livingston wasn't easily deterred. His tenacious ancestors were a stubborn lot, and his friendly, even-keeled disposition meant that he wasn't easily hurt.

"How wonderful!" Madame Brochet let slip out when she saw him. He bowed politely, smiled, and said, turning to Madame Gruschkin, "Madame, may I refresh your memory? We traveled here together in the stagecoach from Chur. I know that the early sudden snow made more of an impression than my company, but

I am very happy to see you again. Perhaps I can describe some of the other highlights of the region, if you should need a guide. I already told you that my family on my mother's side is from here. I can tell you all about the mineral springs, the trout, the excellent Veltliner wine, and the bear hunting…"

He was reckless, but he wasn't being tactless. Most important, Valentina didn't stop him. She offered him a seat, and he thought he might have even glimpsed a brief smile as she pointed to the empty wicker chair beside her.

Madame Brochet was relieved. She thought the conversation might flow more smoothly now, and she thought how enjoyable it was to sit at a table with such a handsome, entertaining young man.

In the days that followed, Mr. Livingston accompanied the two ladies on a stroll through the resort facilities and to the spa concert. When he didn't come to visit for a couple of days, it wasn't only Madame Brochet who missed him, but also Valentina. She wouldn't have known how to describe what she felt exactly, except that it was more pleasant when he was there. Valentina even persuaded herself that the only reason she missed him was that he knew the region so well.

The next time, when he suggested a walk along the lake to the dairy farm for afternoon tea, they both agreed to go. From that day on, they took walks all over the area. Valentina felt that the baths were restoring her strength. Whether she liked it or not, she suddenly had an appetite. For the first time in over a year, she slept at night as she had before Charles's accident. Although her newfound energy didn't fit with her mourning and her feelings, she didn't fight it.

Although she remained reserved, Richard noticed that she was changing. She listened when he spoke, which she hadn't done in the beginning. She even began to ask questions, gradually becoming more curious about the region Richard knew so well.

Now and then she smiled. Richard found himself falling in love with the shy, reserved Madame Gruschkin and her rare smile. It was a bit like someone falling in love with a flower that rarely blooms, one that you can look at but not pick.

One day he suggested, "If you like, we could take the horse-drawn omnibus to Maloja. From there the streets descend steeply into a mountain valley and into Italy. In three hours, we could be in Chiavenna..."

Madame Gruschkin appeared to be everything he wasn't. She was mysterious and musical, graceful and melancholy, like the elusive fog banks that rose up over the dewy meadows every morning, hinting that summer was coming to a close. He began to feel that he was only complete when he was with her. They complemented each other and enriched each other's lives. After a few weeks, he knew that he would give up Cynthia for her; Cynthia, who was so much like him—bright, transparent, and vivid—embedded in her family and content with the direction of her life. She wanted children and a country house and a social life full of balls and galas, charity bazaars and afternoon teas.

No matter what he told himself, he couldn't tear himself away from the thought that only Madame Gruschkin could teach him the true meanings of pain and passion, ecstasy and tranquility, sorrow and joy.

It was already the beginning of October. Soon winter would burst in. Richard's mother used to say that in Engadin there are nine months of winter and three months of cold. But that wasn't true. The last few weeks had been splendid. The needles of the larch trees had turned golden and blazed against the blue sky. They covered the walking paths with a thick carpet of gold. Snow, which already dusted the tips of the mountain massif, would soon reach the valley.

The last hotel guests of the season were leaving, and the social life wouldn't blossom again until Christmas, when the winter guests came. Madame Brochet had already booked tickets for the stagecoach back to Chur and the train trip to Antwerp on October 5.

Before parting ways, they took one last excursion with Richard. They climbed on the double-decker omnibus, which was harnessed with five horses, to the Maloja Palace. It was already too cold on the upper observation deck, so they sat in the enclosed lower level. The view along the lake was the perfect ending to their stay.

At some 6,500 feet above sea level, the Maloja Palace was the most stunning hotel that Valentina had ever seen. Madame Brochet wanted to explore it all—the ski lift, the different parlors, the hotel's own bakery, the in-house print shop, and the painting studio. Valentina encouraged her to look around at her own pace. In the meantime, Richard and Valentina walked to the boat bridge of the hotel. Richard knew that he wouldn't have another moment alone with Madame Gruschkin and that if he was ever going to speak his mind, it had to be now. The sun was already low, bathing the lake in golden light. A couple of boats rocked on the shimmering water, and a cool breeze rose from the surface of the lake. Valentina shivered and pulled her short black cloak more tightly around herself. Her chin disappeared into the fur, and Richard blew off a couple of larch needles that had dropped onto her shoulder. Valentina smiled.

"I will miss you," she said wistfully, "as well as this valley, where I can finally breathe and better bear my sorrow. At home, everything will remind me once again of Charles's death…" Her eyes slid up to the snow-covered peaks. Then she said, "I'm not looking forward to going back. In fact, I'm dreading it. I thank you, Mr. Livingston; I thank you for being such a pleasant distraction, for your presence…" She fell silent and looked down at the railing of the bridge on which his tanned, powerful hands rested. Cautiously she put her hands next to his. Richard gently stroked the fur trim of her gloves.

"It is I who would like to thank you, Madame Gruschkin," he said softly, though there was no one nearby to hear them. "You have surely noticed how much it means to me to spend time with you. You are leaving tomorrow, and if I don't say anything now, we will never see each other again. If that were to happen, I can assure you that my life would become poor and meaningless." He placed his hand on top of hers, but he didn't grasp it.

"I can only speak like this because this is our farewell, because I won't ever be able to say it to you if I don't say it to you now. I know that you are in mourning. I know that you have lost your child. I know that you have a great deal on your mind, but I would like to offer you…"

Appalled, she pulled her hand out from under his. Undeterred, he continued, "Please look at me, just for a minute. I want you to know that I am in New York for you, if you ever want that." He took her hand, held it tightly, and kissed the slender fingers in the glove with great fervor. He gazed questioningly into her face as he did so.

"I love you," said Richard. "Come with me to New York. Begin a new life with me. In a new country. A life you won't dread. That you will despise less, in which nothing will remind you of the past."

Valentina looked at him with huge eyes. "I don't understand," she said.

"But it's quite simple. I love you. I would like to live with you. I would like to take care of you. I can take care of you. Don't you believe me?"

The sun sank lower. The shadows over the countryside lengthened. Valentina turned her face away, but Richard turned it gently back toward him.

"I ambushed you with my declaration of love in a completely unauthorized manner..." His voice sounded bitter.

She shook her head slightly.

"No," she said, "not unauthorized. And I don't cherish you any less for it. In fact, I cherish you more, though I shouldn't say such things." She blushed. "But you know that I can do nothing, that there isn't any possibility of my responding to your declaration. You indulge in a dream, a dear but crazy idea...You must forget these thoughts. Will you promise me that?"

"No," he said, shaking his head.

Suddenly they heard a familiar voice.

"There you are!" called Madame Brochet from a distance, approaching quickly. She seemed relieved. "The omnibus is leaving any minute! I have gotten the driver to wait for us ...Come... quickly..."

She turned back toward the hotel, where the vehicle was waiting.

The next morning the roads were covered with snow. The stagecoach left early, and Mr. Livingston had already said his goodbyes the previous evening. To Madame Brochet's regret, Valentina hadn't invited him to dine with them one last time. He kissed their hands. Before he left, he handed Valentina a small envelope that he had been carrying in his coat pocket all afternoon. Inside was his address in New York, which Valentina read over and over. Then she threw away the note and the envelope.

When the stagecoach left St. Moritz that morning, Madame Gruschkin's face had once again assumed the vacant expression that Madame Brochet knew so well.

Henri slept fitfully during the night. He was inconsolable, alone with his shame.

Valentina couldn't know of the parallels between her story and Henri's life. But Henri did. It was as though she had placed Lisette's tanned hand in his and said, "Look. Here she is. Once more, one last time. I brought her here so that you could speak to her once more, before she leaves you forever. Before you have to live your life alone."

Valentina would take Lisette with her, up into the starlit sky, down into the depths below. As Henri lay on his bed in the dark, he stared into the abyss in which he found himself.

He hadn't found any message from Billie in his stateroom and that seemed suddenly significant too. Didn't she belong to the life that would begin as soon as Lisette was gone? Didn't he have to say something to Lisette in farewell?

Henri felt for his clothes in the dark and dressed without turning on the light. He slipped into his shoes, sat on the bench, laced them in the dark, opened the stateroom door and shut it softly. The nighttime illumination cast a pale light over the corridor. He climbed the stairs, as though alighting from Hades, his own realm of shadows in which he was trapped. He opened the door to the top deck. It had to be about four thirty in the morning because the first pale strands of light were beginning to appear on the horizon. The air smelled of life; dawn was near.

Shivering, he pulled his coat more tightly around himself and leaned over the railing. The waves below were as black as the sky, a mirror of the night. He wanted to ask Lisette for forgiveness. And he knew that he had to do so outside, where he could see the infinity in which he now found her around him.

A June day three months before Lisette left him came to mind. It had been hot and muggy, and a powerful thunderstorm had blown in that afternoon. Toward evening, the storm had subsided. A breeze moved through the trees, the leaves rustling and moving in unison, like the waves on the sea. The wind had dried the damp ground, and the next day promised to be hot again. He and Lisette had gone to the country, somewhere near Pontoise, for the weekend, where they celebrated with friends because Henri had gotten some new business that would keep him financially secure for the next few months.

The glow of the sunset elicited an exclamation of admiration from Lisette: the clouds glowed a delicate plum pink; the horizon was a line of cherry-red that bled into the sky as though a painter had drawn it on wet watercolor paper. They took a walk and said little. In the pools and ponds, frogs began to croak and in the descending darkness, fireflies swirled in the air. They hovered over the meadows and among the trees, silently wavering and magical lights, a soft pulsing of flaring stars twinkling in the grass.

Later that night, he and Lisette had made love without saying a word. It had been a special night, the most beautiful that he had ever shared with her.

All of a sudden, Henri felt happy. His inner turmoil deserted him. He remembered how happy he had been that night, and he understood that Lisette would always be a part of him, no matter how much he tried to deny it to her and even himself.

No one was supposed to penetrate his core, no one was supposed to see—not even he himself—his longing and fear of rejection. But he could see now that that had been stupid. He had destroyed so much with that kind of thinking.

When Lisette left him, he hadn't been as surprised as he had made himself out to be. He had behaved as though he didn't know why Lisette had asked him to marry her one last time. She was pregnant, that had been it, but she hadn't mentioned it. He had been thankful for that and had acted as though he didn't know. He had continued to delude himself until now. She had looked at him with a mixture of sorrow and pride when she left. But her sorrow had enveloped him as he realized how he had betrayed her—and his own love for her.

Morning came. The pale streaks on the horizon spread across the sky.

"Lisette," Henri said softly. "Can you hear me? I love you. I love you more than I ever thought possible, more than I ever could have admitted. I betrayed you. Although you were the one to go, I abandoned you when you needed me. I denied our child and myself."

The red sky of dawn had blossomed on the horizon. It colored one cloud pink and then a second one. Venus, the morning star, could still be seen. Henri took a deep breath. The damp, salty air burned his eyes. "I am ashamed," he said. "My God, I am happy that no one can see me. There are some things that you have to do alone."

The sun rose, flaming into the sky, coloring sky and sea a molten gold. Henri closed his eyes to the dazzling radiance. Warmth flowed through him, as did, oddly, a sadness that could not be differentiated from happiness.

Lisette forgave him. He saw her standing before him. There had always been a tenderness about her, despite her strength. She, who had always laughed so easily, nodded seriously at him. Then she turned and left. She was already far away when she turned around once more and waved to him. But now, it seemed—he couldn't discern her face clearly from this distance—she smiled.

Friday, July 29

The ship slowly came to life. Soon the first passengers would appear on the promenade deck. Henri was still outside, knowing he wouldn't be able to go back to sleep. For the first time since the *Kroonland* had left Antwerp, he enjoyed being on the ship; he found himself thinking of America and the world's fair in St. Louis with curiosity and interest.

Actually, it was a huge honor to be invited on this trip, a recognition of his work and a fantastic opportunity to get to know a new continent.

The sun climbed higher, the sky was a welcoming blue. Henri smiled. He had what was called a Sunday feeling. Sunday had never meant much to him, since it had never been any different from the weekdays for him. But now, here it was.

As a child, his Sundays had been tightly regulated. Berthe, the cook, always put on a freshly starched apron and wore a black dress with a white collar, which she saved for Sundays. She adorned it with an oval enamel brooch with pink and red roses. Henri's father had given Berthe the brooch for her ten-year anniversary with the Sauvignac family, much to the dismay of his wife.

She wore it exclusively on Sundays, a symbol of triumph in the tacit battle she had fought over the years with Henri's mother.

Henri's mother didn't like Berthe's heavy, greasy cooking; she maintained that Berthe's food pressed on her soul. She watched her figure, admiring the beautiful Empress Sisi of Austria with her slender waist. Since she had Austrian relatives, she permitted herself to be loyal to a foreign royal house. Henri's father defended Berthe's cooking, claiming that his men worked hard and needed to eat well. He would then look at his wife with a conciliatory sigh and say, "Hopefully you won't decide one day to only eat meat drippings like Empress Sisi." His eyes would then glide satisfactorily back to Berthe's breasts, surging with excitement at the conflict.

It was a movement that fascinated young Henri. He had often tried to get Berthe to run so that he could watch her bosom rising and falling. His father obviously had the same fascination. Henri had observed how he chased the cook through the house, laughing as he did so, whenever Henri's mother visited a sick aunt in Brussels. Berthe was, despite her size, swift and sprightly, and Henri's father, more burly than agile, became breathless more quickly than she did in this pursuit. Hidden behind the door of his nursery on the top floor, Henri could see clearly, however, that Berthe yielded freely and let herself be caught. She chuckled when his father grabbed her bouncing hips, and when he whispered something in her ear, a blush spread from her cheeks to her wheat-colored hair.

Henri's father didn't let her go. He kept his mouth to her ear and did something there that elicited a snicker and then a faint moan from her. Berthe's room was in the attic above Henri's room, and the older Sauvignac directed her there now. He stood behind her, pressing his body into her back, and his hands held her breasts like two melons as he pushed her up the stairs. She was still as red as a lobster, a color Henri had never seen on his mother's face, which was inclined toward pallor, her cheeks a pale yellow like aged parchment.

Henri softly closed the door to his room so as not to be seen. The maid was in town, he knew, as did Berthe, who had sent her to do the shopping. Henri's father should have been in his office in the middle of the afternoon.

Henri stood right behind the door. The wood creaked on the steps as they made their way up to Berthe's attic room. When the door upstairs closed, Henri crept cautiously up the stairs. He knew exactly where he needed to step to avoid the spots that creaked. He and his friend Paul had practiced it many times when they played at hiding a treasure in the attic. While he and Paul only dreamed of a treasure, his father had a real one and set about enjoying himself.

Henri stood in front of the chamber door and blushed when he peeked through the keyhole. He knew Berthe's room well. In front of the dormer, there was a rectangular table at which she often did her needlework. In front of it was a chair, to the left a bed. To the right, next to the door, was a cupboard in which she stored all of her possessions. If he found the right position, Henri could see the top of the bed through the keyhole. His father had pulled off his coat and thrown it over the chair. He kept his gray vest and shirt on.

Berthe lay on her back; the older Sauvignac shoved her skirt up and knelt between her legs. Henri saw only the vest and the black, thick hair on his father's head.

Mesmerized, Henri watched a patch of sweat spread slowly on his father's vest, turning the silvery gray of silk to a dull gray.

Unfortunately he couldn't see much of Berthe's body since his father was in the way. The fantasies, which featured her body from his father's point of view, occupied him for years as he fell asleep and often enough during the long boring hours at school.

Berthe wasn't fat, only shapely and very sensual, and that gave Henri's fantasy unlimited sustenance. He watched her as she cooked, dipping her round finger briefly in the sauce, licking it and dipping it in again, her tongue traveling pleasurably over her finger a second time to taste the sauce before adding some salt or pepper. She pounded the pepper in a brass mortar, the pestle grinding in a circular motion against the bottom of the container as it squashed the black peppercorns with a soft cracking and crunching. When she added salt, she grabbed a pinch of it with her thumb and index and middle fingers out of a white porcelain jar labeled SALT and tossed it into the pot. She playfully sprinkled it over the roast or the vegetables. He watched how she thoughtfully donned her hat and carefully pinned it with a hatpin whenever she left the house. She stuck her tongue out slightly between her lips when she did it. From then on, he watched women's tongues and lips obsessively—a passion that remained with him even as an adult.

Berthe's hatpin had a pearl on the end, presumably a fake one—unless his father had occasionally been very generous in his gifts to her—and Henri imagined how he would run the hatpin lightly over her naked stomach, making her skin shiver slightly. He imagined her getting goose bumps and then the skin smoothing out again. And he fantasized a thousand times how he would undress her and bit by bit expose her magnificence.

He didn't yet know what, exactly, happened at the decisive moment. The older boys at school whispered and snickered about it, but Henri was only twelve years old at that time. He simply loved the idea of Berthe's naked beauty robbing him of his senses, enabling him to do whatever it was that men supposedly did with women.

Berthe filled his cosmos, became the measure of all things. He watched her sweating in the kitchen when she was heating the heavy stove, opening the iron hatch with thick potholders and putting in wood, the first embers flaring up and scattering sparks. When she stood up, beads of sweat stood on her forehead, but he had watched her stoke the fires of hell in which he, full of sinful thoughts as he was, certainly would have to stew someday.

Henri's mother never sweated. In contrast to Berthe, she powdered herself and avoided the sun.

On Sundays, the family usually went for a walk, after which Berthe, the brooch on her bosom, would serve the Sunday roast and stewed apples. Henri's mother didn't love Sundays; on the contrary, for Sunday meals were even heavier and longer than usual.

Henri loved his mother but didn't know whether she loved him back. In his mother's presence, a veil sank over the world, making it impossible for him to see the world clearly. A languid aura hung over everything when she was in the room. Although he often threw himself affectionately into her arms, wanting to be held, he understood that this was a burden for her, a bold demand that she couldn't reciprocate.

Her presence cast a vague, uncertain aura over everything; his own emotions felt surreal. His presence seemed to be a burden that she couldn't bear and could only be mollified when he was absent. Henri strove for recognition of his existence— and yet he worshipped his mother precisely because she was so untouchable.

In his childish imaginings, she was a queen whose every wish had been fulfilled but who would remain unhappy until the right man succeeded in saying the magic word that would break the spell. Whenever Henri came to her, flushed and excited or upset about something that happened at school, she patted his head absently and said, "Later, Henri, later..." He knew that he was not the one who could save her.

Henri realized that his father received as little affection from her as he did. However, he did not know that Paul Sauvignac had been his mother's second choice; his mother had hoped to use her beauty to marry above her class, but it had not worked out.

The fine weather had lured other passengers on deck. Fresh air seemed to be more important than breakfast.

Henri was still caught up in his memories when someone behind him cleared his throat and said stiffly, "Good morning, Monsieur Sauvignac."

He turned around and looked into the cool eyes of William Brown.

"Am I disturbing you?" Mr. Brown asked politely.

"Of course not," Henri replied, though he felt a little awkward.

His opposite was impeccably dressed, as always. Mr. Brown wore a lightweight navy blue linen suit with a white dickey, blue shoes, and a flat straw hat with a blue hatband. His face appeared calm and controlled, though Henri noticed a red flush on his neck that rose to his cheeks.

"I heard that you weren't feeling well," said Henri. "How are you? We missed you in the dining room. And then the storm let all of us have it..."

"You could say that…"

The deckhand was bringing deck chairs back on deck and lining them up in rows facing the sea.

"Would you like to sit down?" asked Henri, pointing to the deck chairs.

"I don't think it is necessary that we sit next to each other as though at a summer resort," Mr. Brown answered. "But of course we could sit for a little while if you'd like." He pointed to a white wooden bench.

Henri didn't know what Billie had told Mr. Brown, which made him uneasy.

The American took off his hat and laid it on his knee. A gentle breeze blew through his hair and a strand fell onto his forehead. All of a sudden he looked much younger; he pushed back his hair self-consciously.

"To be honest, I would rather not be sitting here with you. Miss Henderson brought you into her confidence in a way that doesn't make me very comfortable. Sometimes she is so spontaneous," Mr. Brown said, sounding reproachful. "You will understand when I ask you for your complete confidentiality."

Henri nodded. "Of course. I will not do anything with what I know."

"Thank you," Mr. Brown replied curtly. "Let's not beat around the bush. It is obvious that Miss Henderson has already made you aware of everything." He cleared his throat. "Miss Henderson has been," he cleared his throat again and turned the straw hat in his hands, "my lover for some time. I brought her on this trip. I wanted to give her the opportunity to see something of the world, to experience something she normally would never be able to. I hoped that she would keep wonderful memories of it for a long time. But, as she obviously told you, she is now pregnant. Naturally, I would pay for an abortion. Even if she wanted to raise it without my help, she has to understand that I don't want an illegitimate child. Not because I couldn't give Miss Henderson financial help—that's not the issue—but because the situation would make me susceptible to blackmail. I have four children and a wife whom I love. My life is in order, as the saying goes. Any evidence of a relationship with Miss Henderson—a child—jeopardizes my current, highly satisfactory life. I also want to protect my family from any humiliation."

He paused as though he was expecting an objection from Henri. Then he added, "And I want to run my practice without scandal."

Henri kept quiet. Mr. Brown clearly took his silence as approval because, with a quiet, composed movement, he put his hat back on.

Finally Henri said, "May I ask you something, Mr. Brown?"

"Please."

"Do you love Billie?"

Tiny beads of sweat appeared on Mr. Brown's upper lip. He contained himself, but his tone was sharper. "I don't know what gives you the right to ask such a question. But since Miss Henderson has already made you a witness to our intimate relationship…"

He paused and fixed his gaze on the horizon.

"Yes. I love Miss Henderson, even though that probably surprises you. I love her the way a man can love a woman other than his family that means everything to him. In every life there are unfulfilled longings, even when you have everything that you could possibly want. Miss Henderson was a gift to myself. She is tender, curious…"

He searched for the right word.

"…alive."

They both kept quiet and stared out to sea. "Do you mean you love Billie because she is so alive?" asked Henri.

Mr. Brown nodded and put his index finger thoughtfully on his lip as though to indicate that he wanted to bring the conversation to a close. Despite himself, he continued, "But Billie has to realize that she has to blend into my lifestyle. Things are what they are. If she accepts that, then we could stay together as long as my situation permits. She doesn't have any choice other than to live as she does now, whether it's with me or someone else. It's a lifestyle that debases women and—let's be honest—who would want to marry such a girl…?"

Henri tried to remain calm. He didn't have any reason to feel superior, and yet it sounded threatening when he said, "Pardon me, Mr. Brown. I know I don't have any right to comment on the matter, but—"

William Brown interrupted him with a curt hand movement. "I am not interested in your opinion, Monsieur Sauvignac."

He was obviously determined to end the conversation— and to have the last word. "You and I," he continued, "we aren't friends. A fluke brought us together. You have, may I say, shown more interest in Miss Henderson on this trip than I have. Or do you deny it? OK. This is a conversation between men. I am counting on your discretion. That is all I can ask of you. To conclude, Miss Henderson has known since day one what she could expect from me. I've never kept her in the dark about that."

He stood up. "But I can assure you that I will help Miss Henderson straddle the next few weeks financially. The department store has promised her a position. It won't be any trouble for her to continue working there if she doesn't have a child."

He grabbed his hat and adjusted his collar. "And so that you are clear, Miss Henderson is in agreement with my suggestions. I think she has recovered her sense of reality and we are unified over all further steps."

Henri had risen too.

"If you don't have anything more to add…?"

"No," said Henri. "I don't have anything more to add…No wait, one thing. Billie likes you a lot. She has fallen in love with you. Right from the start, when you went to buy that fox stole for your wife."

William smiled painfully. He was already leaving.

"And she is expecting your child," Henri added.

"I already have four," answered Mr. Brown, "and I already have a wife. I would be grateful to you if you would leave Billie and me alone now. She is still my lover and has given me to understand that she would like to stay that way."

William Brown and Henri Sauvignac parted without even the hint of a bow or a handshake.

Valentina decided to pay a visit to Dr. Kirschbaum. He had said that she could come by anytime, and Valentina was unhappy. It had been so long since she had felt anything and suddenly her feelings were in a constant state of flux. When she thought of Thomas and his embrace she was joyful, then, the next minute, she was overcome with doubt. What would he think of her if she confessed that she, as a married woman, planned to meet another man? How could she explain to Thomas that, despite everything, she had fallen in love with him?

What should she say to Richard? How could she disappoint him after she had written, "Will you be there for me?"

One thing had become clear to her over the last few days: she would never go back to Viktor. As impulsive and rash as it had been to run away, it had been the right thing to do. Viktor was who he was, and she didn't reproach him for it—but she didn't want to live with him anymore either. It had been wrong to marry him. Viktor loved her in his own way, but she didn't love him. She had only admired his strength and determination; he had been a replacement for the father she had never had. It had been a mistake, though, right from the start.

She knocked on Dr. Kirschbaum's door.

"Madame Meyer!"

He seemed pleased to see her and welcomed her into his consulting room. "You have decided to take Madame Klöppler up on her offer. That dress doesn't hold a candle to your evening gown, but it suits you. What brings you to me? I see you have gotten through the storm in fine shape."

"You probably didn't have any remedy for seasickness," smiled Valentina, "or am I mistaken? No, I don't have any physical complaints. However, I remembered your offer of support in other respects…"

"Then we don't have to sit around in my office," said Dr. Kirschbaum spontaneously. "Let's go for a walk on deck."

Valentina's thoughts flowed more easily as she walked, but she still wasn't able to find the place to start.

"Everything that you say is part of patient confidentiality," the doctor said, "even if it doesn't concern a physical ailment."

"When you examined me, you wanted to know whether I knew someone in America who could help me after our arrival," Valentina began. "I thought about it and I do know someone, a man whom I got to know during my visit to a spa and with whom I am on very good terms…" She faltered. "I sent this man a message through the ship's radio…"

"Have you received an answer?" asked Kirschbaum.

"No, not yet, which is upsetting. But there is still something else. This man confessed to me a few months ago that he had tender feelings for me. I was married at the time, and I had lost my child not long before."

Again she paused.

"And now you are on your way to him and you no longer know whether that's what you really want?"

"Yes," nodded Valentina, visibly relieved.

Dr. Kirschbaum deliberated. Then he nodded. "Tricky. Is there something else that has just now triggered this change of heart?"

Valentina blushed.

"Ah." Dr. Kirschbaum didn't say anything more, but quickened his pace as though he suddenly understood. "Would you like to hear my opinion?" he asked.

Valentina nodded.

"I believe that you should start to consider what you would like to do with your life, completely independent of what other people want of you and what you believe you owe them."

He looked at her kindly.

"That may sound odd, and I assume you have had a different upbringing, but I am of the opinion that every person, whether man or woman, discovers his own talents and aptitudes and that we as human beings have an obligation to face up to the dreams that we keep hidden deep within ourselves. Only what we do out of love is successful in the long run. But first we have to figure out what it is that we love."

Dr. Kirschbaum handed Valentina a handkerchief. "The storms within us are often more tempestuous than the storms at sea," he said soberly, "but...Ah, Mr. Witherspoon...Good afternoon!"

Dr. Kirschbaum noticed that Valentina's blush deepened.

Thomas bowed formally to Valentina and then turned to the doctor. "Excuse me for interrupting your conversation, but it's important. I would like to ask you to come see my sister. I am very worried because she..."

"Dr. Kirschbaum...quick, quick, come!" A young sailor interrupted Thomas as he came running down the deck. Breathless, he stood before the doctor and gasped, "A boy fell down the steps in steerage, and it looks bad. He's not breathing."

"I'm coming," said Dr. Kirschbaum with a glance at Valentina, who had turned deathly pale. "Mr. Witherspoon, would you be so kind as to accompany Madame Meyer to her stateroom. She needs to lie down. I'll need the doctor's room for the victim. Please order coffee for Madame Meyer." Turning to Valentina, he continued, "Drink at least two cups; you'll feel better." Then he turned back to Thomas. "I'll come to your sister right afterward. Don't worry..."

He hurried after the sailor and left Valentina and Thomas alone.

"Thomas," said Valentina, "Mr. Witherspoon..." They stood in front of Valentina's stateroom door.

"I'll order coffee for you as Dr. Kirschbaum has asked," Thomas said stiffly.

He is being so formal, Valentina thought desperately. How can I get him to relax?

"Would you like to sit down with me for a minute?" She unlocked her door. His eyes were almost as cold as his sister's.

"I really should go check on Victoria..."

Valentina screwed up her courage. "Your sister isn't going anywhere, Mr. Witherspoon. She'll be with you for the rest of her life. Won't you come in for just a moment? I'm asking you."

She didn't wait for him to answer. She simply entered her room, lay on her bed, and closed her eyes.

Thomas rang the steward, ordered the coffee, and sat down on a chair beside her bed.

What did she want?

Valentina remained silent, feeling the dizziness that had come over her slowly dissipate.

"You're probably asking yourself what I suddenly want from you," Valentina finally said.

His expression was still reserved, but his eyes had lost their coldness and she saw that the warm sea green in them had returned.

"I am married. That is a fact, but I am not going to return to my husband. If I weren't married, I would have behaved differently. As it was, I was afraid even to touch your hand."

He looked at his hands. Although they were large, his hands were slender and delicate, like those of a musician; they could almost have been the hands of a woman.

"Why?" he asked. "They don't look violent, do they?" He finally twisted his mouth into a smile.

"They don't have to look violent to be dangerous," she said, adding, "You have beautiful hands...Do you play an instrument?"

He laughed. "I fumble around on the piano. I didn't get very far. I am more successful as a geologist. But I love music, yes. My mother was a gifted violinist, and she would be turning over in her grave if she knew how little I've done with her musical legacy."

"Oh," said Valentina, "then our mothers would have gotten along; my mother was an excellent pianist before she got sick."

"What about you? Do you have a similar confession to make?"

"I used to sing."

"And you don't anymore?"

"No, not since my son died. But that is another story."

"What kind of a story?" asked Thomas. "What does that mean? I know so little about you. All I know is that when I saw you for the first time on Sunday evening, I knew that you were the one I have been waiting for my whole life. I was not surprised that you were led to my table—it couldn't have happened any other way. Everything suddenly fell into place. I didn't ask why you wanted to be left alone. I didn't press you. But my feelings never changed."

She sat up, leaned her back against the wall, and looked straight at Thomas. "I will tell you the story of the white dress. That will tell you a great deal about me.

"July 23, the day that the *Kroonland* cast off from Antwerp and I boarded the ship, was the anniversary of my son's death. My son, Charles, died on July 23, 1902. He was two years old. My husband and I were spending our summer holiday by the sea, in Normandy, in the town of Cabourg. We had rented a house. My birthday is July 22, and I was turning twenty-three. In the spring Viktor, my husband, and I had spent a few days in Paris, and Viktor ordered an evening gown for me from a famous Parisian fashion designer. He picked out the fabric and the pattern himself; the dress was supposed to be delivered shortly before my birthday and was to be a birthday present for me. It was this dress, of course." She stroked the heavy white satin of the dress, which lay on the bed.

"The dress was delivered on time and I took it, all wrapped up, on vacation. I wanted to wear it for the first time on my birthday. A huge ball was taking place on my birthday at the Grand Hotel Cabourg. That afternoon a small concert was going to take place, and I had been asked to sing. Though it meant that I wouldn't have much time with Charles that day, I liked singing and agreed, knowing that I would get to spend all of the following day with him."

She touched her hair with her hand. "The ball that night was a raucous affair. 'Exactly what I hoped for you on your birthday,' my husband said. I don't know why, but I felt unusually anxious. It may have been because the dress was laced so tightly at the waist; in any case, I felt as though I couldn't breathe properly."

"There's still some coffee here," said Thomas. "Here, have another cup. Dr. Kirschbaum said that you should drink coffee."

"Thank you," said Valentina and took the cup. She continued, "I'm feeling better already. In any case, it got late. Viktor had had a lot to drink. I wanted to go home, but he had met some Russians he knew in the hotel and didn't want me to spoil his fun. When we finally left, it was three in the morning. Charles and the nanny were sound asleep. Viktor was in high spirits. 'Let's drink another bottle of champagne to you, my little dove,' he said. I was half asleep, but he…" Valentina paused.

"…wanted to make love to you," finished Thomas.

Valentina nodded.

"Then we fell asleep. I took care of Charles myself in the mornings; the nanny knew that I always got up early to do that.

But that morning, I slept in. Viktor always got up late when we were on holiday, especially when he had had so much to drink. I woke up close to ten o'clock. Sometimes Charles toddled barefoot in his nightshirt into our room, but he hadn't done so this particular morning. I slipped on a dressing gown and went across to the nursery. The door was open, but the door to the nanny's room was closed. Obviously she was still asleep. Charles was not in his room. We had forgotten to lock the house door that night; I had drunk more than usual too and hadn't paid any attention. Now I saw that it was wide open. I ran into the garden."

Valentina's voice had gotten huskier and she faltered. Thomas didn't interrupt her.

"I found him in the pond. The garden had a pond. It wasn't deep, but Charles was just two. He lay with his head under water."

She fell silent.

"There's not much more to say," she finally added. "I was never all that close to him to begin with, but we grew further apart after that. When I accused him of killing our child, he struck me in the face." Her index finger traveled across the tiny scar on her upper lip. "This was from his signet ring. It wasn't fair of me to blame him. I felt guilty and lashed out. Neither of us had locked the house door, and in the end, I was the one who hadn't woken up. But I blamed him because we'd had so much to drink and stayed out so late, which is why I slept in the next morning. It no longer matters who's to blame."

Thomas took her hand. This time she was glad he did.

"Viktor had always cheated on me, but after Charles's death, he didn't even try to conceal it. We each mourned in very different ways. Sometimes he brought the girls home at night. I stopped singing. I completely lost interest in life. Our family doctor sent me to a health resort in St. Moritz last fall. There…" she broke off and fell silent.

"There?" asked Thomas.

"Well, that is a whole other story," said Valentina.

Thomas knew that he still had a great deal to learn about Valentina, but this much was clear: if she didn't tell him everything, there would always be some obstacle between them.

"Valentina," he drew her to him and kissed her. "Please, tell me that story too. Tell me everything, so that nothing can ever come between us again. I want to prove to you that nothing can separate us."

Valentina thought about what Dr. Kirschbaum had said.

"Soon," she said and closed her eyes so that nothing would distract her from the bliss of the next kiss.

Meanwhile, in another stateroom, Henri Sauvignac held Billie in his arms. Her face was puffy from crying. She had wrapped herself in her robe and clutched Henri as though they were shipwrecked and adrift at sea.

"I don't want to get up," she whispered into his chest, "I never want get dressed again. I never want to see another person."

Henri had to smile. He gently pushed her away so that he could look into her eyes, stroked her tangled hair, and said, "What? Never again? Even if I dress you myself, as though you were a little girl, button up your shoes, take you by the hand, and invite you to a beautiful lunch in second class?"

She looked at him, surprised, leaned her head against his chest again and murmured, "Why in second class?"

"Because no one knows us there and everyone will think that you always look as you do now. No one will have any idea that you've been crying."

She laughed despite herself and rubbed her forehead on his jacket.

"You smell like the sea air," she said softly.

"And when you have eaten, we can go sit somewhere on deck in a deep deck chair and look out at the sea. Then you too will smell like the sea air."

"Turn around. I'll get dressed," she said with a hint of a smile.

"Don't be ridiculous, Billie. It's not like that. I'll wash your face with a washcloth and get you dressed piece by piece, with every accessory that peculiar women's fashion demands. You must stay quiet. Be a good girl. And above all, as I dress you, imagine me undressing you later because I have an immense desire to look at your freckles."

Henri set to work slowly and painstakingly dressing Billie. Her face took on a faraway look that was both blissful and a little sleepy. Her brown curls were coiled in an unruly mass. Henri wondered when the last time was that Billie had wanted to be dressed by someone. It was probably a long, long time ago. He sat her on the bench, pulled on her black boots, and buttoned them.

"You'll have to pin up your hair yourself. I don't know how to do that," he said when she was finally dressed.

She nodded. Then she pointed to a small bottle on the vanity.

Henri picked it up, opened the crystal container with the dove-shaped stopper, and held the vial to his nose. It was a sweet, delicate mix of rose and jasmine. He moistened his index finger with the perfume, kissed the small hollow of Billie's throat, and dabbed a bit of essence on it.

"My work is complete," he said. "How beautiful you are."

She walked over to the vanity and began to comb her hair. Henri watched her, and she smiled at his reflection in the mirror.

"I didn't think you would come looking for me," she said. "Why should you?" Suddenly tears well up beneath her lashes. "Did William tell you everything he said to me?" She looked at Henri. The sob that followed was so fierce and sudden that he winced.

"I am afraid he told me everything and more," he answered.

"He said: You can't have everything in life." Tears streamed down Billie's face. "And I thought: He's right. I should stay with him. Who knows what the next one would be like."

"Mr. Brown said that you can't have everything in life," Henri said sarcastically. "Talk is cheap, but look at him—he has everything that he wants."

He didn't know if she understood what he said because she didn't respond to him. She simply continued, "Who knows whether I will ever have a relationship—after the abortion, that is, if I don't die from the abortion itself."

Henri took her in his arms.

"You will find someone," he said. "You have already found someone."

She didn't react. He found it odd that she had no idea what he wanted to say to her. He had a lot to learn about women, an embarrassing realization, since he had always prided himself on his expertise.

"OK, come on," he said, "Let's get some lunch. Then you can tell me about your conversation with William and why I didn't find you in your stateroom until now."

As he led Billie to the second-class dining room, Henri thought about how foreign the world of men was to him. He obviously belonged to it himself, but he hated the hypocrisy of men, whose behavior was considered ethical when it was really just a pathetic way to protect their own interests. He found himself thinking of his father and Berthe and the day she left the Sauvignacs' house.

He had been thirteen at the time, and Berthe was still the model for his fantasies.

"Boy," she had said the night before, putting her rosy, soap-smelling hands heavily on his shoulders, "tomorrow I will be leaving. You will get a new cook who cooks with less fat."

"But I don't want you to go!" he had cried, a kind of despair washing over him that he didn't fully understand. "Papa doesn't want you to go either!"

"The madam has arranged it, and she is responsible for the house staff. I have already packed my things."

"Where are you going?"

"To my mother in the country. I have no other choice. I only have lodging if I am employed."

"Send me your address when you have a new job."

She hugged him then. Her body felt soft, and he wished he could have stayed in her arms forever. She smelled of soap and tarragon, an herb that she loved. When she released Henri, she had tears in her eyes.

The next day the maid served them. Henri's parents sat quietly at the table. His father didn't touch his plate. Henri's mother's knife scratched the china.

From that day forward, Henri's father was only home sporadically in the evening. He arrived punctually at six for dinner, as before, but he didn't stay and read his newspaper with a cognac and a cigar in his wing chair. Often he went out and didn't come back until late at night. Never a talkative man to begin with, he was now almost silent.

Henri's mother attributed this to his Armenian heritage too.

Henri smiled when he thought of his father. He hadn't been a revolutionary, but he had tried to live without hypocrisy. He hadn't broken out of the framework of the middle-class mold, but for the first time, Henri now understood why his father consented to his stonemason apprenticeship—to give his son the freedom that he himself never had.

Suddenly Henri saw clearly that his father had truly loved Berthe.

Henri and Billie entered the second-class dining room and sat down. They were both hungry. Billie ordered scrambled eggs with bacon and devoured them. Two minutes later, she turned pale, then she flushed, stood up, and looked to Henri for help.

"Henri, the bathroom. Did you see where the bathrooms are?" she whispered imploringly. Henri asked the steward, and Billie ran off.

"Isn't your wife feeling well?" asked the steward sympathetically.

"Yes, yes," said Henri, "my wife is just pregnant."

"I knocked on your stateroom door a thousand times," said Henri. "Why didn't you answer? Why didn't you come to me after you spoke with William?"

They were now seated on the promenade deck in second class. Billie was feeling better.

"Why? Because I was in William's stateroom, that's why." The wind played with her brown curls, which had come loose from her bun. She no longer looked like she'd been crying. The fresh air did her good.

"But I knocked on his door too when I couldn't find you!" Henri said, raising the corner of his mouth and scratching his moustache. "He said he didn't know where you were."

"I know," she answered, "he was pleased to send you away. 'Dear Billie' he said to me afterward, holding my wrist tightly, 'I must advise you not to seek the company of this man. He'll give you ideas that in the end will make you unhappy. The truth is that you don't have many options.' How right he was, Henri! 'I will help you,' he said. 'I will speak to your manager at the store. He will excuse you for a few days. I'll continue to pay for your room and we can continue to see each other, but only if you don't speak of this to your colleagues and your family.' I answered, 'You leave me no choice.'" Billie's expression changed from one of resignation to disgust. She grabbed Henri's hand.

"But I realized at that moment that I found him disgusting. He had drawn me to him, saying 'I knew that you were a smart girl and would come to your senses…Billie, you know that I love and desire you and that you are my good fortune, don't you? You understand that I have no choice. I can't simply change my life. I have responsibilities. To my family, to the company, to myself.'"

"Just not to you," Henri cut in impatiently.

Billie looked at him, suddenly irritated. "What do you mean by that?" she asked.

Henri didn't explain himself. "And," he asked, "how did you answer him?"

"I didn't," said Billie, staring into the distance. With an awkward shrug, she continued, "I just didn't say anything. He held me tightly and kissed me." She paused and frowned. "He disgusts me…"

Henri stood up, pulled Billie out of her deck chair, put his arm around her, kissed her on her upper lip, and said, "Let's go for a walk. Soon we'll be off this miserable ship and then we can go to St. Louis."

"We're going to St. Louis? What do you mean?" cried Billie. "Are you now telling me what to do too?"

She disentangled herself from his arms and began to pace back and forth. She calmed down and said, "Henri, everyone is telling me what to do; only I never have any say." She shrugged. "I don't have any money, I don't have any education, I have a job, but I am dependent on Mr. Welsh and dependent on Mr. Brown. I am dependent on the back-street abortionist and can only hope that she doesn't kill me. I have to say, I don't like any of it one bit."

"Let me finish," said Henri, grabbing her arm again.

"Don't say anything to me!" Billie said, stamping her foot and pulling her arm away. "Not you too!" She looked at him angrily.

"That's exactly what I have been avoiding my whole life," Henri said with a deep sigh.

"What do you want to avoid?" asked Billie.

"If you don't let me finish talking, I can't explain it to you." She nodded. "OK, I'm listening."

Henri cleared his throat, his eyes glittering darkly. "First of all," he said, his mouth twitching, "first of all I want to tell you what it would be like if you came with me to St. Louis. The world's fair is there. Some of my work is going to be on display…"

"I know that the world's fair is there," said Billie.

Oh God, how can this possibly go well, thought Henri. We'll turn out just like the Borg couple.

"Why are you looking like that?" asked Billie. "Did I say something wrong?"

"No," said Henri. "Secondly, I hoped that you might leave Mr. Brown and return with me to Antwerp."

"But what would I do there?" Billie exclaimed, pressing her index finger to her nose. Then she said with a radiant smile, "Only if you marry me, Henri."

Henri groaned. "You are worse than Lisette…"

"And who is Lisette?"

They had circled the ship several times and now they stood at the railing. Henri leaned over and looked into the depths.

"I'm going to jump if you don't stay quiet!" He would never have any peace again! She would have to find a job in Antwerp so that he could work in peace.

"Lisette is a woman that I loved very much, without knowing it." He drew Billie to him before she could protest.

"Now be quiet and listen to me. Lisette modeled for me. She did it to earn money for her own art. She drew better than I did, and she studied painting. We were together for several years; she was the most fantastic lover you can imagine." Billie opened her mouth to say something, but Henri shut it. "I didn't know you then! She wanted to get married, but I didn't. I had sworn I would never get married because I didn't want to be like my parents, like every other married couple I saw around me. So she left me. I didn't know that she was pregnant. I could have figured it out, but I didn't want to know. I looked for her after she left, but I didn't find her. She had erased all traces of herself."

Billie's face was full of compassion. "That is just terrible!" She pressed Henri's arm. "Go on."

"Months later, I got a letter from a woman with whom Lisette had lived after she moved out of her old attic room. 'Dear Monsieur Sauvignac,' the landlady had written, 'I would like to inform you that Lisette Morisot, who rented a room from me, died from puerperal fever." Henri could recite the letter from memory. " 'She mentioned you several times in her final hours and called for you, but I didn't know your address until later, when I found it in Mademoiselle Morisot's documents. The daughter that Lisette Morisot bore was taken to the orphanage in Orleans, where the family of the deceased is from.' "

Billie stiffened in his arms. Henri paused, expecting an outcry, but she just looked at him incredulously.

"You see," he said, "I am a scoundrel. No better than your Mr. Brown."

"And the child?" asked Billie.

"I never went to Orleans."

"How long ago was that?"

"Over a year ago."

Billie looked at him. "Let's go inside," she said then. "I'm cold."

"In a moment, Billie." He held her back. "Lisette told me once, 'Your heart is as unreachable as the dark side of the moon.' But we can change things. You don't have to stay with William, and my heart is not the moon. You can start a new life, and I can too. I would like to live with you, Billie. I would like to travel with you to St. Louis and then return to Antwerp. We will marry and travel to Rome..." He smiled at her. "I want to make love to you in Rome; I can already picture it..."

The horror of his story was still etched on her face. She clearly had doubts about him, but then she put both of her hands on his chest and nodded, slowly and thoughtfully.

"Open up! Miss Witherspoon, please!" Dr. Kirschbaum knocked again on her stateroom door. "It's Dr. Kirschbaum. Your brother asked me to stop by."

Thomas stood quietly next to him.

"Miss Witherspoon! Your brother told me about your argument and that you don't want to see him. Please, at least open the door for me."

Silence.

"I'm going to get the key to her stateroom," Dr. Kirschbaum said to Thomas. "Stay here."

Thomas didn't protest. He should have insisted earlier that someone break down the door. The chambermaid and the steward said that Victoria had ordered tea and a small meal in her stateroom, but that had been the night before.

Dr. Kirschbaum returned with two assistants.

"Only in case of an emergency," he said to Thomas and opened the stateroom door.

"I want to examine her alone. Wait here," he said and disappeared into the stateroom.

"Come quickly," he called out moments later, "Briggs, Keller, come here. We must bring her up to my office." Then men picked Victoria up and carried her off. Thomas looked after them, aghast.

"You're welcome to come with us, Mr. Witherspoon," Kirschbaum said quietly, "I have to pump out her stomach. Your sister is unconscious, but there is still hope. Come along." He hurried after the men.

Thomas hastened after them.

"Do you know if she regularly took any other drugs besides the morphine?" Kirschbaum asked.

"Yes, she swore by Veronal. She said it was the most effective pill for insomnia..."

"I've said forever that Veronal should only be available by prescription!" Kirschbaum exclaimed heatedly. "There isn't any sleeping pill that is better for..." He paused.

"Presumably she took an overdose," he added soberly. "Wait here." He pointed to a chair in the outer office and disappeared into the treatment room.

Valentina had never seen Thomas like this before.

"Tell me what's wrong. What happened? You are completely beside yourself!" She pulled him into her arms.

"Yes. Something happened. Victoria tried to take her life. I told you that we fought. Fought bitterly…Then the storm came. She is afraid to death of storms, but she wouldn't let me come to her. When she wouldn't let me in today either, didn't even react to my knocking, I was suddenly afraid. I shouldn't have spoken to her like that. I should have taken more time to explain things to her…"

Valentina took a step back, appalled.

"It's because of me," she cried, upset. "She did it because she was afraid of losing you to me. She won't share you, and you too had trouble distancing yourself from her. She is all that is left of your family. How could I put myself between you two?"

Thomas drew her to him. "You are both right and wrong. It will take time for Victoria to learn how to live without me. She needs to understand that she won't lose me. But at the moment… But wait, you haven't even asked how she's doing."

"But of course she must still be alive. Otherwise you would have spoken differently."

"Would I? Until now I haven't said how things are going for her. Yes, she is going to survive. Dr. Kirschbaum will keep her under observation, but now I must go to her. I wanted to tell you that I'm not coming to dinner."

Valentina nodded helplessly. "Oh, Thomas! I am so sorry. I hope she will be better soon."

He hugged her briefly. "I must go to her now, Valentina. I'll see you tomorrow."

Saturday, July 30

How could she have hoped that she and Thomas could be together?

Love is one thing; the real world something else entirely. Even writing to Richard had been nothing more than a pipe dream. He hadn't answered. Too much time had passed since their farewell in St. Moritz, and she hadn't given him any reason to hope. Richard was perhaps with another woman. Maybe he had gotten her message and destroyed it to avoid arousing suspicion.

She would have to accept Richard's silence and break with Thomas, just as she had had to accept Charles's death. She had fled to the *Kroonland* to free herself, but there wasn't any freedom, not even in America. There wasn't any freedom from oneself either, unless one took one's own life. Freedom only exists under certain conditions, dictated by the world you live in.

Valentina reached for the golden-brown dress that Madame Klöppler had loaned her, put it on, pinned up her hair, straightened her shoulders, and went to see Dr. Kirschbaum.

"I couldn't save the boy," the doctor said, grasping Valentina's arm cautiously. "It isn't anyone's fault. When the decks were finally opened again after the storm, everyone pushed their way out. In steerage the density of people is atrocious; the air was beastly. A couple of children competed to see who could get outside the quickest; one of the boys plunged down the steps...He broke his neck."

Valentina pulled her arm free to bring her agitation under control. "How old was he? I would like to visit the boy's family, Doctor. Do you think that would be possible?"

"Yes, of course. The boy was eleven. His name was Mischa Adamowicz."

Valentina was turning to leave when Dr. Kirschbaum stopped her. "By the way, Miss Witherspoon, whom I think you have gotten to know, is doing much better. She will soon return to her stateroom. Perhaps you would like to stop by and pay her a visit. It's curious, days go by when absolutely nothing happens, and then suddenly all hell breaks loose. Ah..." Something else came to mind. "Have you gotten an answer to your radio message? We arrive in New York tomorrow."

Valentina shook her head.

"Then I would definitely follow up with the radio operator. Some things in life you have to accept—no one knows that better than you do—but you don't have to be fatalistic about it. The art lies most often," he smiled, "in being able to distinguish between what you have to accept and what you don't." On that note, he accompanied her to the door.

The passengers in steerage hardly expected a visit from first class, and the emigrants stared at Valentina mistrustfully.

"I am looking for Mischa Adamowicz's family," Valentina asked beseechingly, but most of them didn't understand her or declined to answer. At last she aroused the pity of an older woman, who led Valentina to the boy's family.

The endeavor was pointless. The dead boy's family was from Poland and didn't understand one word the stranger said. Nevertheless, Valentina grasped the hand of the mother, embraced her tightly and said, "Madame Adamowicz, I know you don't understand me, but I would like to tell you that I understand your pain. I lost a child like you..."

Tears of compassion filled her eyes, but it was hopeless. One of the bystanders, who knew a few words of French, intervened. He understood what Valentina wanted to say and he interpreted for her. The Polish woman nodded slowly in understanding. Her face lit up, and she returned Valentina's handshake.

Valentina couldn't do anything more. Each person is alone with his pain, even when others share the same fate.

The radio operator greeted Valentina politely. She asked whether he had sent out two messages from her that should have been brought to him several days ago. He looked in his records and pulled out the message to her grandmother. He couldn't find a second message from her. When Valentina inquired further, he said that he remembered quite clearly that this was the only message he had received. He had never been given a second message.

Jan, thought Valentina, Jan had read the letter. He was jealous. How could I have been so naïve? He had saved me, but he also wanted to punish me for asking another man for help...

Jan was in love with her. How could she not have seen that?

Because I didn't want to, she thought guiltily.

Without knowing it, Jan had done her the greatest favor by not passing on the message. Richard didn't have any idea that she was on her way to New York! She would have liked nothing better right then than to give Jan a kiss!

As soon as she was off the ship, as soon as it wasn't dangerous for her to contact him, she would explain everything to him.

Despite herself, she was looking all over for Thomas. Everyone she knew on the ship seemed to have disappeared. Not only could she not find Thomas, but there was no sign of Henri, Miss Henderson, or even the impeccable Mr. Brown.

Only the Russians of whom Henri had spoken could be seen, playing shuffleboard raucously and laughing on the promenade deck.

She had just decided to walk over to the navigating bridge when she noticed the young girl in the wheelchair that Henri had mentioned to her. The girl was writing in a notebook; her dark curls fell loosely over her face when she lowered her head, and she pushed them repeatedly behind her ear as she wrote. She wore a pale blue summer dress, white stockings, and white button boots, which made her look like a child. As Valentina approached her, she saw the girl's dark, scrutinizing eyes. Lily said, "Good afternoon, Madame Meyer."

"Good afternoon. You know my name!" Valentina was surprised.

"Everyone knows your name," answered the girl. "The whole ship has been talking about you. My name is Lily. Lily Mey. You can call me Lily. I am just sixteen." She smiled pleasantly at Valentina.

Valentina returned her smile and replied, "Monsieur Sauvignac has told me about you. He is very impressed with you."

"But why?" asked Lily, amazed. The compliment seemed to embarrass her.

"He said you are a very intelligent girl, that you write down everything that you notice all around you." Valentina leaned against the railing. "I see you are taking notes at this very moment. May I ask what you are most interested in?"

Lily nodded. "Of course. I am interested in all natural phenomena. And in people."

"Monsieur Sauvignac told me that you would like to study. Physics, I believe?"

Lily looked at Valentina, surprised. "He has told you quite a lot about me. Oh well. It's true. I would like to study physics or be a writer."

"And what excites you about that? Excuse me for being so forward, but I am genuinely interested. I think it's fantastic that you have such a clear idea about your future. You have an advantage over a lot of people."

"I would like to learn about the stars, about the universe. And you can only do that if you have studied physics. The universe is infinite, limitless. And the imagination is too. If you write stories, there are also infinite possibilities, a universe of possibilities…"

She looked out into the sea and continued, "My world is very narrow." She lifted her hands from her wheelchair and let them fall again. "I can't live alone and there are many things I will never be able to experience. My world is small, but still, the universe is there." She looked penetratingly at Valentina. "And I would like to be part of it. I would like to participate in the huge, infinite universe."

Valentina nodded. "That sounds wonderful," she said. "I have never thought about it before, but I can understand that very well. You're right. That is what we should all be striving for." She smiled again.

"This is the first time that I have seen you during the day," said Lily. "Your dress is beautiful, but when I think of you, I picture you in your white evening gown."

"Oh yes?" said Valentina. "So you think about me?"

Lily felt like she'd been caught, and she blushed. She always spoke too quickly, revealed too much about herself. But it was too late.

"I thought I would like to write a story about a woman like you sometime. A woman who showed up on a ship in a white evening gown. A woman no one knew…"

Valentina laughed. "And what kind of a story would that be?" she asked.

Lily looked out to sea and thought. "It would be the story of a woman who has a special talent. She is sad because she can't live like other people. She is also afraid to be who she is and is running away from herself. But then she realizes that you can't run away from yourself, just as a person can't run away from his shadow." She chewed on her pencil. "Have you ever watched how shadows follow people? In the afternoons, you can see it beautifully here on deck."

Valentina said, "I'll have to pay attention to that. Thank you for telling me the story."

Lily shrugged her shoulders. "It could also be a different story." She looked out into the sea. "The sea tells everyone a different story."

"So," said Dr. Kirschbaum, "you have survived the worst. You should rest in your room for a while. This evening at the farewell dinner, you may not want to eat too much, but you are safe to go."

He smiled encouragingly at Victoria Witherspoon. He didn't rise from his chair to show her out of his office. He thought of his conversation with Thomas Witherspoon and instead looked for a way to get his patient to talk.

"You now know that medicine can be poisonous. Some Veronal can help you sleep, but too much of it can be fatal." He chose his words carefully since he wasn't sure whether she had taken the overdose intentionally. "The same is true for the morphine. You already know that the effect of any drug declines over time. Whatever it is that afflicts a person can grow stronger if you don't succeed in eradicating the ailment with the treatment."

He stroked his beard, not looking at Victoria as he continued, "I know many migraine patients who become addicted to morphine. They think it is the only way to relieve their other problems as well. Could it be that you have also taken it for relief from panic and anxiety? And Veronal, as well?"

His voice was so soft and his tone so neutral that Victoria relaxed. Although she resented Thomas for mentioning it to Dr. Kirschbaum, she appeared relieved that he had broached the topic.

Dr. Kirschbaum gave Victoria a glass of water. For the first time, he looked at her not as a patient, but as a woman in her prime. At first glance, she was not especially attractive because she dressed in a very ordinary, understated manner, almost carelessly, as though she didn't want to attract attention—especially a man's. As he looked at her more closely, he noticed her beautiful hands and delicate skin, and her face would be attractive if her eyes didn't look at the world so defensively. Yet behind the cool, mistrusting eyes, Dr. Kirschbaum perceived a deep fear of loss, of loneliness, and of life itself. Observing how Dr. Kirschbaum looked at her so kindly, Victoria realized how colorless and dull she looked in her gray, black, and beige clothing.

"Yes," she said, "I was afraid of the storm. It's like that with every storm, even onshore. I have been afraid of thunderstorms since I was a girl. Thunder and lightning tear not only the sky to shreds; they can also tear a family to shreds…"

"Do you mean to say then that thunder and lightning have destroyed something in your life?" The doctor leaned forward attentively. He could read by her expression that he had hit the mark with his observation.

"Yes," said Victoria, and her usually closed face took on a helpless expression. "Lightning struck our family. My mother died in a fire when I was twelve and Thomas barely two. It was during a thunderstorm. Lightning struck our house and set it on fire…" The old fear washed over her anew. "My father wasn't home. I pulled Thomas out with me to the street. He didn't understand what was happening and whined and screamed. My mother was on the top floor. I screamed for my mother as the fire blew out the windows. The firemen arrived too late. For my mother, they came too late."

She fell silent and even Dr. Kirschbaum was quiet. He stood up, picked up the carafe, poured some more water for Victoria, and sat down again beside her.

"I am afraid," Victoria said softly. "I always have the same fear. At night when it is dark, if it is thundering, if I hear of accidents, if…"

"Your brother goes away and you can't protect him," added the doctor.

Victoria nodded.

"You can't protect him, Miss Witherspoon," said Dr. Kirschbaum. "Even though you saved his life once, you can't protect him from everything."

She looked at him horrified, her gray eyes filling with tears. The doctor's words were cruel.

She shook her head and gripped her forehead as though she wanted to drive his words out of her head. She touched her temples, but no headache was brewing. The terrible sentence wouldn't let itself be wiped out. It resounded in her again and again: Even though you saved his life once, you can't protect him from everything.

Dr. Kirschbaum knew how terrible the truth was. He also knew that he had to go even further if he wanted to help her. He continued, "You are not allowed to run his life, no matter what kind of danger he finds himself in. It is his life. Though you are connected to each other, you, Miss Witherspoon, have a separate life, independent of your brother. You must lead your own life, with its own dangers that you must face and learn to tolerate."

He sensed that he shouldn't say anything more.

"You should get some rest before this evening," he said. "I believe you will fall asleep quite quickly. I will check up on you later, tomorrow at the latest. Maybe then you will want to continue our conversation."

He looked into her face, which, surprisingly, no longer looked quite so distressed. On the contrary, she looked relaxed, and a small smile, without a trace of bitterness, brightened her face.

Dr. Kirschbaum smiled as well.

"I'm looking forward to seeing you again," he said.

The Last Formal Dinner,
Saturday, July 30

Billie looked more bewitching every day, and William Brown sincerely regretted losing her. He slipped into his white vest, tied his bow tie, and looked at himself in the mirror. As he slapped some eau de cologne on his freshly shaved throat, he asked himself what his future could possibly look like.

He had assumed that everything he came across in his life would conform to his plans. That was true for his wife, who was busy with the children and asked few questions. It was also true for Billie, who was in a tenuous position and had few alternatives. That she had obviously fallen in love with him was both flattering and appealing. When she had explained to him that she was leaving him, he became painfully aware of what he was going to lose.

He tapped himself reassuringly on the cheeks, but it didn't help. Sadness, almost a kind of desolation, spread through him. He felt as though he was slowly being swallowed by quicksand. He was successful, of course, and he would remain so. He looked after his family, and that wouldn't change either. Upon his arrival in New York, he planned to send his wife a telegram to say that he would soon be arriving safely in Philadelphia. Yet the prospect of being back in Philadelphia suddenly seemed lackluster to him.

Mr. Brown slipped into his patent leather shoes and suddenly realized that the days he had spent in Rome with Billie would have to hold him for the many long years ahead. He wasn't entirely unhappy, but he knew that something was lost to him forever.

He left his stateroom and closed the door behind him.

He would have to learn to get by without the spontaneous ease and innocent tenderness that he had experienced with Billie. He hadn't realized until that moment that that was what had made life bearable.

Perhaps at some point he would look for another lover. You could always buy youthfulness and some degree of tenderness.

Perhaps.

Billie had put on her evening gown and said to Henri, "Could you please make sure that the next time I go out, I don't look so flushed? What will people think?" She kissed Henri cautiously on the mouth.

"They will think that you have behaved very naughtily and didn't have anything to do before dinner other than make passionate love to a man. And they will ask themselves which of your two companions was the lucky man."

Billie looked at him, shocked. "Do you really think so, Henri?"

"No," he laughed, "people are too preoccupied with themselves. I just can't wait for you to say in a dignified voice, 'I believe I will go to my stateroom now. I am tired.' "

"Why?" asked Billie, as she unconsciously tried to straighten her nose.

"Because then we will both get to go do what we like to do best."

"You are a monster, Henri!"

"We have a great deal in common," said Henri and kissed Billie on the mouth before she could say another word.

"Come in," said Victoria. She wore a lovely mauve-colored dress that Thomas had never seen on her before. It suited her and gave her a much softer look.

Her brother put his arms around her. "It's wonderful that you're coming with me. I'll bring you back as soon as you get tired. But it will do you good to eat a little something. And tomorrow we'll see what happens. One step at a time."

"Lotte," said Valentina, holding the door handle as the chambermaid laced her corset, "have you ever been in love?"

"No, Madame," said Lotte, clearly shocked by the question.

"There isn't anyone on this ship among the many sailors, deckhands, and stewards that you like?"

"Sure, Madame…one of the chefs…"

"Then just pay attention that you don't make an awful mess of it the way other women so often do."

"What do you mean, Madame?" asked Lotte.

"Never mind," said Valentina, "You will do it properly."

"As you say, Madame," Lotte said and disappeared.

The ship's orchestra was ready. When the first-class guests paraded down the grand staircase to the dining room to dine together one last time, festive music welcomed them at the door.

The excellent menu, good wine, music, and the passengers' impending arrival in New York created an aura of exhilaration.

Even for the poorly fed emigrants jammed together in steerage, the end was in sight. They celebrated and danced in happy anticipation. Though uncertainty, fear, poverty, and death loomed ahead, tonight they felt infinite hope.

On the face of it, the seating arrangements that had formed in first class over the course of the journey hadn't changed much. Mr. Brown and Billie had agreed to appear together for the gala dinner before parting ways the next day. Mr. Brown liked to observe proprieties. Henri planned to arrive with Valentina, who had agreed with Thomas that he should look after his sister.

Madame Borg had looked for seats for herself and her husband far from the Vanstraaten family: the revelation to which she had become privy during the storm still distressed her.

The Vanstraatens sat in their usual places at the table, as they likely would until the first child left home. Anselm Vanstraaten, the younger son, picked his nose, for which, judging by the frigid glare of Monsieur Vanstraaten, his mother would have to atone later.

Lily had wanted to sit closer to Monsieur Sauvignac and Madame Meyer, which Lily's father would gladly have complied with, but which his wife Hermine would never agree to. She was as elegant as always in a sapphire-blue dress and silver fox stole. Her daughter, who placed little value on appearances, indifferently wore the same sailor costume and childish dress as before. She spoke excitedly to Henri across the table about sculpting.

During the course of the week, the Russians had almost drunk themselves into a delirium. Henri had been too preoccupied with his own affairs to join them, and he was quite happy about that, the way things had turned out. But he asked himself whether one day he might regret not having celebrated with the boozy bachelor party. He didn't yet have a clear sense of how prominent a role Billie would play in his future.

Madame Klöppler appeared to be satisfied that Valentina had worn one of her creations and had publicized it widely to the passengers on the *Kroonland*.

Many of the first-class passengers retired to the smoking lounge and the public lounge after dinner. Some played cards while others chatted. And even the most puritanical Americans took advantage of the access to the ship's excellent wine list.

William Brown excused himself from dinner and made his way to the smoking lounge to think about his future with a cigar.

"I must thank you, Valentina," said Henri on the way to the salon. But his companion wasn't listening. She had focused her gaze on Thomas, who was accompanying his sister back to her stateroom. Dr. Kirschbaum had promised to look in on her after dinner.

"Go on ahead," Thomas had said to Valentina, Henri, and Billie. "I'll be there soon."

"What did you say?" asked Valentina. "I'm sorry, I was lost in thought…"

Henri looked at her with more patience than he normally had. She hadn't heard anything he'd just said.

"I thanked you," he said dryly, and his thick black moustache twitched.

"For what?" Valentina looked at him blankly. She gathered the train of her white evening gown and placed her foot gracefully on the step in front of her.

"For being you," smiled Henri, "the stellar queen and goddess. Far away from us mortals here on Earth." He paused. "No, pardon me. I didn't intend it in a mean way. You can't know why

I am thankful, and I won't elaborate now. It would be too long a story."

Valentina looked at him with an apologetic smile. "We don't know each other very well."

"That doesn't matter. Sometimes people help others without having any idea they are doing it. Come on; let's find a nice table in the lounge."

Billie had already found one.

"There!" she cried. "Look, there's a good one," and she pulled Henri toward it.

The Russians decided it was time for some music. They welcomed Henri with a wink when they saw Billie on his arm. "Now you'll finally get to know the Russians I mentioned," Henri said to Valentina. "Didn't you say your father and your husband are Russian?"

Valentina nodded and looked at the men without much interest. Where was Thomas? She longed for him.

One of the Russians was seated at the piano, and the other four raised their glasses. Fjodor had provided some bottles of vodka. Then Andrej struck up a Russian folksong and the others joined in. Abruptly Valentina became alert. The man who leaned on the piano had a wonderful voice; it was soft, deep, and smooth. She lowered her glass and stared at the singer. He sensed her gaze upon him, raised his hand in greeting, and waved amiably.

Valentina suddenly realized that there were different kinds of happiness and different ways of finding it. Music was one of them. She knew the next song that the Russian sang. His friends didn't know it, so Andrej sat at the piano and accompanied himself. Valentina moved her lips wordlessly. It was as though he were singing it for her alone:

I have been blind since I saw him.
Wherever I look, I see him alone…

She had performed this very Schumann song once upon a time. Despite herself, she joined in softly. When the Russian noticed, he smiled and nodded to her invitingly; she smiled back and followed him, softly, cautiously, without forcing her voice, which she hadn't used for so long. She began to breathe more deeply, the tightly laced dress restraining her. The dress was obsolete. It wasn't the right dress for this new Valentina, who sang.

Thomas entered the lounge at that moment. He was happy to see Valentina there; ten minutes without her seemed like an eternity. He sat down quietly so as not to disturb her.

"How beautifully you sing," he said when the song was over. "I will do whatever it takes so that you can sing in New York. You can make a career of it, I know it, and I will have a famous wife whom I may accompany to her concerts."

"Yes," she said. "Maybe so."

Sunday, July 31

"We will soon be in New York," the captain said to Valentina with a certain satisfaction. "I informed you at the start of our journey that we must transfer you to the inspector since you are a stowaway. The immigration authorities have already been informed by radio. This means that you will be taken with the immigrants in steerage directly from the ship onto a ferry to Ellis Island, where you will be interrogated."

Valentina listened to him dispassionately. It was clear that he didn't plan to help her after she had refused his "offer."

Captain Palmer appeared to have forgotten the incident and continued objectively, "Some inspectors are on their way by boat. They'll dispatch the first- and second-class passengers, who will then be able to go ashore without any further formalities as soon as we arrive in the harbor."

He lifted his gaze and scrutinized Valentina with a cool glance. "Unfortunately I have to ask you, Madame Meyer, to remain in your stateroom until you are transferred to the Ellis Island authorities and to hand over to me everything that was loaned to you during your crossing."

He looked at her without emotion and pointed to Madame Klöppler's dress, which she was wearing. "Including that, so you'll have to put on your own dress."

"Captain, I appreciate your efforts on my behalf and you have given me a great deal of freedom on the journey, but couldn't I ask Madame Klöppler to give me the dress? Naturally I will pay for it as soon as I reach my attorney and can have money transferred to me."

The captain smiled with folded hands. "I would love to permit that, but I have to deliver you as you were presented to me after your discovery."

"But I presented myself!" cried Valentina. "I also have one more urgent request: I would like to speak with Mr. Witherspoon, a first-class passenger; it will only take a few minutes. I can't imagine that that wouldn't be allowed..."

Valentina was visibly upset. How was she supposed to communicate with Thomas? He planned to be by her side and vouch for her to the authorities.

"I'm sorry," Palmer shook his head, "the rules are effective immediately. We are already in New York territory, and I can't make an exception. Ah, and one more thing..." He was just about to leave her stateroom when he turned around once more and pulled Valentina's earrings out of his pocket. "I'd like to return your earrings to you. I am confident that you will settle up with the Red Star Line for all of your expenses when you have access to your account."

He slipped the diamonds into her hand and left.

In front of Valentina's stateroom, an officer stood guard.

The Statue of Liberty emerged from the early morning haze on July 31, standing proudly on the glassy-smooth water. The travelers in steerage greeted her with loud cheering.

The men waved their hats, and the women began to gather their family's possessions. Everyone pressed on deck. The long-awaited skyline of Manhattan grew larger as they approached. Wasn't it a miracle? Some of the houses seemed to touch the sky!

They had arrived; they were in New York at last.

Dr. Kirschbaum wasn't in his consulting room, which flustered Victoria. Where was he? She had hesitated for a long time before mustering the courage to go look for him, and now he wasn't there. It was difficult for her to admit how disappointed she was. Well, she would just have to send him a letter to thank him once again, but it wasn't the same as seeing him in person.

"You look well, Miss Witherspoon," Dr. Kirschbaum called to Victoria from down the corridor, although he had hardly recognized her in her summery, white linen dress. "Were you looking for me? I'm sorry I wasn't here. Can I do something for you? Would you like to go inside?"

Victoria shook her head. "No, no, that isn't necessary. I'm not ill. I just wanted to say good-bye to you. And to thank you…"

"For pumping out your stomach? No, no need to thank me for that. It was my pleasure to get to know you." He meant it too.

"You didn't handle me with kid gloves, and I'm not referring to the stomach pumping," she said. Her remark sounded harsher than she had intended.

Dr. Kirschbaum smiled. "I know." He didn't apologize and that pleased Victoria. She asked herself how old he might be. His beard and his hair were white, but the laugh lines around his eyes made him look young.

"Perhaps that's why I wanted to find you today. You offered to continue our conversation. That isn't easy since you will be at sea, but should you find yourself in New York and don't have anything else planned…" She pulled a piece of paper out of her purse and handed it to him. "This is our address. I would be delighted if you'd come for tea. I'd like to ask you what you know about morphine rehabilitation programs. And," she took a deep breath, "I would also like to talk to you about my brother…" She felt awkward discussing something so personal, but knew that she must say what she had come to say.

"It is difficult for you that your brother has fallen in love."

"Yes," she answered.

He pocketed the note with her address and said with an odd twinkle in his eyes, "I would love to come visit you. I'm sure we can find things to talk about other than your brother."

At this marvelous suggestion, she ran her hands awkwardly down the linen skirt of her dress and said demurely, "I have to go now."

But she liked Dr. Kirschbaum more and more with each minute.

Thomas was furious. The immigration officials had made it abundantly clear that he could not speak with Valentina or officially vouch for her. It didn't make any sense for him to try to do anything for her on Ellis Island. They were currently processing more than a thousand immigrants a day there; special requests simply could not be accommodated. Besides, Valentina had gotten on board illegally and she had to be interrogated by the inspectors.

Thomas felt more powerless than he had in a long time and began to lose his temper.

Slowly the *Kroonland* was piloted into New York Harbor. Curious bystanders, friends, and relatives waited on the quay. The smokestacks emitted irregular billows of smoke. The ship's horn sounded across the harbor. The passengers stood crowded together on the decks. No one wanted to miss the arrival into the harbor. The children leaned out over the railing and waved to people on shore. The passengers in steerage had gathered their baskets, crates, and bundles around themselves: The women wore headscarves, the men hats. They had put on their coats despite the heat, just so they didn't have to carry them. Some fifteen hundred people waited eagerly to set their feet on firm ground again.

The crowd on the quay welcomed the ship. Names were called out and children were held high. Hackney cabs stood waiting. Even a few automobiles could be seen.

The first-class passengers were the first to disembark, followed by the second-class passengers. However, the emigrants who had been waiting patiently in the corridors were told that they would not be allowed to step onto the Promised Land yet. They had to be taken to Ellis Island first and their fate would be decided there.

Dr. Kirschbaum stood on the railing and watched the passengers disembark. He didn't have any trouble picking out the small figure of Victoria Witherspoon. She had looked back at him repeatedly and now raised her hand in a wave. He waved back. He found her to be a remarkable woman.

Dr. Kirschbaum experienced a melancholy moment as he wondered what place he would call his home. The sea wasn't a proper home. It was a desert on water where he would always be alone. Maybe it was time to change that, he thought, before he turned from the railing and disappeared inside the ship.

Billie had shoved her hand into Henri's. She became silent, over-whelmed by the prospect of the completely new life that would begin once she was back on American soil. She had peppered Henri with endless questions. She eventually noticed that he didn't yet have answers to many of them. The future had to unfold first.

Henri was quiet too, dwelling on his own thoughts. He sud-denly had not only a wife, but also a child fathered by another man. The small being still hidden in Billie's stomach definitely con-cerned him—Mr. Brown could resurface again at any time. It was deeply distressing to him that Mr. Brown was leaving such a huge imprint on his, Henri's, life. He loathed the self-righteous man and wanted nothing more than a clean break from him. What if the child took after his father and wanted to look for him one day. This thought brought another to mind that was equally unpleasant. He was well aware that he too had a child who might one day try to find him. Billie was not the only one bringing a messy past into the relationship. They were each other's equal in every way. And yet, it was precisely this awkward legacy that gave him hope. Billie's child and his child gave him a future, restored life to his existence. He would be asked to give them what his father had given him: love, understanding, and trust. He smiled when he thought of his father. Yes, he realized he wanted to give it a try.

Henri looked at Billie. Her cheeks had flushed with excite-ment, her eyes shone. She was bursting with anticipation. She too was ready for a new beginning, a fresh start filled with real love.

Henri squeezed her hand. Without looking at him, she squeezed his hand back, tenderly and firmly.

Outside on the quay, the journalists bolted like a mob toward the first passengers who came down the gangway. Stowaways weren't unusual, but a woman in a white evening gown, who snuck onto an ocean liner without a ticket, money, or luggage, was sensational news. The news already had been leaked before the arrival of the ship. Journalists wanted to question as many passengers and crewmen as they could to spice up their stories for gossip-seeking New Yorkers.

The woman herself, who had become known as the "woman in white," was nowhere to be seen.

Valentina waited in her stateroom for the ferry that would take her to Ellis Island. Richard Livingston wasn't standing on the quay, as he hadn't received any message from her.

She hadn't seen Thomas since the night before. Once she thought she heard her name being called, but the voice had been drowned out by a jumble of other voices.

Here she was at last, in New York. The man on whom she had pinned her hopes didn't know about her arrival; the man whom she loved had been ripped from her. She was completely on her own, and for the first time since she'd run away, she was afraid. Now she had to pay the price for her impulsive behavior: She had to take her life into her own hands.

When she had stepped onto the *Kroonland,* she hadn't had any vision of a future life. Now she not only had to envision her own future, but figure out how to turn it into a reality.

Since boarding the ship, Valentina had become a new person. July 23 seemed like a day from a past life.

This past July 23 at dawn, Viktor Gruschkin had left a brothel on the harbor where he was a regular guest. The well-worn wooden stairs groaned softly under his heavy steps. In the foyer, he had taken his hat, coat, and cane and left the establishment, which looked much less seductive in the early morning light than in the dim evening hours.

It had been a pleasant evening. Nana, the woman he had been given, had only been in the brothel for a few weeks. She was a plump mulatto, probably from the Belgian Congo. He had visited her several times now, becoming increasingly intrigued after each interlude.

The devil only knew how she had come to be here. Someone had probably promised her a better life. When he saw her for the first time, she had been sitting on a plush red chair in the corner of the parlor. Her white corset was lightly laced; her petticoat covered her knees, and she rested her hands primly in her lap, as though she had never had to spread her legs. At the table next to her, resting on a filthy white lace tablecloth, stood a gas lamp. The light was turned down and suffused her dark skin with a soft bronze sheen.

The other women sat together, chatting, laughing, yawning, and staring into space. They had greeted Viktor Gruschkin like the regular he was and tried to pull him over to their tables. Viktor, however, didn't let himself get sidetracked. He headed straight for the new girl and examined her. Then he ran his hand appraisingly down the length of the corset. He then shoved his hand into the top of it and pulled one of her warm breasts out with a practiced movement. It hung like a dark fruit over the top of the corset.

The others fell silent and watched. The girl turned her head and looked away. She seemed to be looking into the distance, lost in her own thoughts. Perhaps she was imagining palm leaves rustling gently in the wind, or a beach on which her bare feet left a trail of impressions; maybe she saw pelicans diving in the water or pink flamingos standing beside a shallow watering hole, one leg pulled up high. Gruschkin wedged his other hand between her knees and pushed her skirt up. She continued to look away. It was warm; the air in the parlor was stifling. The windows were open wide, but there was not a hint of a breeze. Gruschkin moved his hands higher between her thighs, which were damp and sticky. Before his fingers probed any further, he decided that yes, this was the girl for him. He felt dizzy. His blood pressure was too high. The others gawked openly at him as they fanned themselves. Madame gave the newcomer a brief nod to indicate that she should follow Monsieur Gruschkin up to the second floor.

Viktor found the new girl more tantalizing than all of the other women he had been with there, and he liked her. She was gentle and good-natured and had a beautiful bottom. Her lush breasts had beefy black nipples, which he found arousing. When he made her sweat, beads of perspiration gathered between her breasts, and he imagined he was licking the salt of the earth as his tongue traveled upwards from her belly button to the valley between her breasts. Her stomach was like a soft pillow from his childhood. He fell asleep between her thighs that night and didn't think it necessary to get up and return home for decency's sake. He had paid for the entire night, and besides, he was a good customer. He and his wife had had separate bedrooms for quite some time.

In the morning, after leaving the brothel, he planned to make a detour back home before stopping by the coffeehouse for breakfast and then heading to his office. The sound of his steps on the cobblestones echoed in the narrow alley and blended with the clatter of hoofs and the rattle of the first hackney cabs and trucks.

Viktor Gruschkin cheated on his wife without meaning any harm. He loved Valentina. He swelled with pride and love for her when she sang. "My little dove. My little bird." As Viktor Gruschkin entered the house, he reflected with satisfaction on their new home, which was equipped with every modern comfort: electrical lights, central heating, and a British-style bathroom. Jan Bartels arrived at the house around the same time to pay a visit to his mother, though his real motive was to try to catch a glimpse of Valentina.

After a few hours in his office, punctually at twelve thirty, Viktor Gruschkin returned home. One could set his watch by him when it came to lunch. Griet Bartels, the cook, recognized his steps as he walked up the stairs. At twelve thirty on the dot, Griet pulled the fish out of the oven and stuck a knife into the potatoes to check that they were done.

Monsieur Gruschkin pushed open the apartment door forcefully. He smiled happily when he smelled the fish from the hallway. He took off his hat, put down his cane, washed his hands, and called to his wife.

Instead the maid came running.

"Good afternoon, Monsieur Gruschkin," she said. "Dinner is served. Madame would like to apologize, but she isn't feeling well. She doesn't plan to have lunch." The girl tried to discreetly lead him into the dining room as she spoke, but he remained in the hallway and hit his hand angrily against the potted palm. "What is it now? I don't like to eat lunch alone. Everyone knows that. Go to Madame," he was getting worked up in a rage and his voice grew louder, "and tell her I have had enough of her antics." He was getting flushed and he felt a twinge in his left eye, a sign that a headache was coming on.

"As my wife knows, we have been invited to the de Wael family's home this evening. It is a very important invitation for me." With his hand, he massaged his forehead. "We will leave the house at seven, and I want to see Madame in the white evening gown that I had made for her in Paris."

Babette bit her lip and nodded. She knew that Madame would refuse to wear that dress, but, as though reading her thoughts, Viktor Gruschkin added menacingly, "I insist on it. Tell her that. And I won't tolerate any—do you hear, any!—opposition."

Gruschkin dropped into one of the high-backed chairs in the dining room, poured himself a glass of water from the crystal carafe, and yelled into the kitchen, "The soup! Where is the soup?"

His good mood had dissipated. After the soup, he ate Griet's fish without paying her a single compliment, which he usually did when his favorite dish was served. Soon after, he returned to the office.

His office was stifling in the scorching afternoon heat.

He opened the windows in hopes of a breeze, but the air was still. So he closed the window and pulled the drapes closed to keep out the blazing sunlight. The heavy burgundy curtains bathed his office in a dull, dark pink light.

Gruschkin sat back down at his heavy walnut desk and tried to attend to his important correspondence. He had trouble concentrating. There was trouble with his business. Anton Wiesenthal, an important customer, had tried to slash the price he had paid for the last batch of diamonds. Though Gruschkin himself couldn't detect any impurities, Anton had claimed that they were of lower quality...

Viktor tried to deflect his anger by thinking of Nana. Most of the time it helped him to picture her dark breasts bulging out of her corset. But today he had become so agitated that he had to go further. His thoughts drifted to the night before. He loved the sound of her naked bottom slapping against his thigh when she sat on him. Viktor sighed and beads of perspiration formed on his forehead. When his doorbell rang, he was abruptly brought back to reality. He dabbed his forehead quickly with his handkerchief, drank a glass of water in one gulp, and sat for a moment to collect himself. Then he got up clumsily and opened the door to Frans. He remembered now that he had ordered the driver to come to his office.

Frans brought with him the new shoes that Gruschkin had had made, but that was only a pretense.

"Well, Frans, what do you have to report?"

Frans, tall but anxious, looked smaller than his master. He stood before Viktor, the shoebox still in his hand. He set the box on the smokers table and removed his hat. He was proud to have something to report for once. Since Madame Gruschkin rarely went out, he usually couldn't satisfy his master's desperate desire to learn anything about his wife.

"You know," said Gruschkin to his driver, "that everything Madame does interests me. So tell me..."

The driver stood up straight and, lowering his voice conspiratorially, said, "Today there was a visitor at the house. A gentleman visitor."

Viktor Gruschkin felt a surge of heat rush to his cheeks. He was already irritated enough today. Now this! He sat down and asked Frans, "Do you know who the visitor was?"

"Yes, Monsieur. It was Jan Bartels, Griet's son. He was with his mother in the kitchen." Gruschkin leaned forward impatiently in his chair. "And what else?" he asked curtly. "Did my wife receive the young man?"

"No, Monsieur. She didn't receive anyone."

Frans's answer didn't reassure Viktor. Quite the opposite. He pictured his wife receiving a man in the parlor. Any man. He imagined her shaking hands with him, sitting beside him on the sofa, putting her hand on his arm, whispering intimately. He gasped. A fire rose up in him and pressed against his eyeballs. His brain blotted it out.

She never smiled at him anymore. He sensed that she was disgusted by the idea of having to sleep with him. She used her grief like a protective shield. He felt guilty even stepping into her bedroom. When he slipped under her covers, she moved aside and stiffened. Her cool, dispassionate flesh insulted him. He then slept with her out of rage at her rejection, but also from helplessness because he didn't know how to pull her out of her torpor. She never said a word, but he sensed her resistance to him increasing. He felt ashamed that he couldn't reach her heart. Afterward he usually got up, dressed, and went to the brothel, too angry to return to his own bed.

Frans still stood there, expectantly. Gruschkin returned to his senses.

"Anything else, Frans? Is there anything else at all?"

"No," he replied, bowing slightly.

"Then go! And take the shoes with you."

"Shall I take you home, Monsieur Gruschkin?" asked the driver.

"No," responded Gruschkin tersely.

Frans said good-bye, but Gruschkin didn't react. He had already buried himself in his papers again.

⁂

Back at the house, Babette, the maid, burst into tears. She ran into the kitchen to ask for Griet's help.

"Griet," she cried, "Griet, you must help me with Madame." Griet set down the kettle of hot water that she had just taken from the stove and turned to Babette.

"Madame won't put on the Parisian dress. You know that. I knew that she would refuse, but Monsieur ordered me to tell her that tonight he wants to see her in it and that he won't tolerate any opposition. But Madame won't let me dress her. What can I do? Monsieur will let me go in his anger…"

"Where is Madame?" asked Griet tersely.

"Madame is in her room. She has just gotten out of her bath."

Griet only nodded and murmured, "I had a funny feeling this morning."

Out of habit, she cast a quick glance around the kitchen to make sure that nothing would burn in her absence then left the inconsolable Babette to go help Valentina.

Griet entered the bathroom. The enamel tub with the raised back stood on claw feet. Madame loved hot baths, and steam still rose from the tub. The brass faucets gleamed like gold; Viktor Gruschkin demanded that Babette polish them every day. Next to the tub stood a wicker chair and a palm nestled in a glazed chinoiserie planter. The window was covered with white English tulle drapes, but Babette had shielded the bathroom against the bright July light by pulling the dark green velvet curtains closed. In the shadowy greenish twilight, Babette had laid out the Turkish towels and, on a second chair, Madame's corset, slip, garters, and white silk stockings. The bathwater was milky. Babette had scattered a powder into the water that clouded it to spare the bather the sight of her own body. Monsieur Gruschkin made fun of the powder, but women from London to Rome used it.

The white evening gown was laid out in the dressing room.

And there was Valentina. Griet looked upon her with concern. The blazing heat bothered people. It hung over the city for days, in the alleys, the rooms, and lay heavily and oppressively on people's minds. The atmosphere was almost gray from the humidity, although the sun shone in the cloudless sky. It was weather that made the quiet ones more silent and the hot-tempered ones more hot tempered.

"Valentina, Valja," said Griet softly and imploringly to Madame Gruschkin as though she were a child.

"Listen to me, Valentina. Babette told me that Monsieur Gruschkin is insisting that you wear the white dress today. You don't have to explain to me why you don't want to. I know it. But I have a bad feeling. This morning I found unusual innards in a fish…"

Valentina smiled briefly but didn't interrupt the cook.

Griet continued stubbornly, "That can't mean anything good. I believe that. Even though you laugh about it, and Jan too." She paused briefly and looked at Valentina, her beautiful Valentina. "Jan was actually here this morning. He is traveling on the *Kroonland* now. Jan laughed too, but I know what I'm talking about. You should both believe me."

"And you didn't let me know that Jan was here?" responded Valentina indignantly. "I would have liked to see him. You know that!"

Griet wouldn't let herself be distracted from what she wanted to say, and stopped her with a wave of her hand. "Babette said you didn't want to see anyone and Jan had to get back to the ship. They were delayed, but they will sail with the evening tide."

She took a deep breath and continued, "But what I really want to say to you is this: You should wear the dress this evening if Monsieur wants you to. He will not change his mind. He made that quite clear to Babette. He was furious this afternoon and he will only be more so if he comes home to find you being stubborn. You are as beautiful as a goddess in this dress, and he loves you in it, despite everything that has happened. He wants you to be the most beautiful and vibrant of all the guests tonight because this evening is important to him. I can understand that."

Valentina looked withdrawn. She turned her face away so that she wouldn't have to look at Griet and pulled the large towel over her breasts as though she felt a chill. "You can go," she said curtly.

Viktor returned home at six o'clock to freshen up and get dressed for the party. Griet heard his footsteps on the stairs and quietly closed the door to the kitchen. Babette slipped in quickly. Only the valet greeted his master and asked him what he would like. Viktor demanded that he lay out his tails, top hat, white vest, a fresh white shirt, and a white bow tie, and disappeared into his room.

He hadn't been able to rid his mind of his gloomy thoughts all afternoon. Even though he didn't know Jan Bartels, he knew that Valentina and Jan Bartels had played together as children and had liked each other. It didn't even matter that Frans had told him that Valentina hadn't received him. He had never liked the fact that Griet had nursed Valentina when she had to send Jan to the country. It was too much for him that his wife had brought the old cook into the household with her.

No one should be closer to Valentina than himself. If it had been possible, he would have preferred that no one ever had been close to Valentina before he met her. All afternoon, Viktor had been haunted by the idea that Valentina could be in love with Jan Bartels. Valentina had never mentioned his name, but perhaps that was intentional.

Viktor Gruschkin cut a fine figure in his tails. He was a bit stocky and not very tall, but he had thick blond hair. He looked like a man who was successful and knew it. He had come a long way, he thought with a certain vanity. Whoever would have thought that he would someday be accepted into the richest circles in Antwerp? His father, a bookkeeper, had worked in the same office his whole life, earning and speaking little. He had been miserly and mean-spirited. Laughter and joy died away when he entered a room. His mother had stopped singing.

Viktor had little in common with Boris Gruschkin. Viktor was shrewd, with a quick wit and good business sense. Unlike his father, he yearned for a better life: he liked to drink and indulge himself and didn't have any trouble spending money when he had any. Viktor had always been inclined toward violent outbursts, and if he had been drinking, toward violence. Music, however, soothed him; he loved opera and singing. He described himself sometimes as a Russian dancing bear that could be tamed with sweet sounds.

Valentina had tamed him.

Viktor looked at his pocket watch. It was ten minutes until seven. He hadn't seen Valentina yet. He would knock on her door shortly and pick her up if she didn't come out herself. He was longing to see her and his patience was wearing thin. He was especially eager to see her as she had once been, when she still sang and he had held her in his arms like an expensive present.

Viktor Gruschkin stood up the moment he heard the pendulum clock strike seven in the parlor. He proceeded to his wife's room and as the last chime's echo faded in the parlor, he knocked on her door.

Valentina opened it. She wore an elegant black dress with a high lace collar.

"We can go," she said.

Viktor looked at her. He felt another twinge again behind his right eye, a short, piercing pain.

Then his rage erupted, more aggressively than earlier. He took a step into the room, pushed Valentina back and slammed the door behind him. For a fraction of a second, he was aware that he was losing control, but the red tide of fury only swelled within him.

He seized Valentina's neck with both hands and shook her.

"You want to defy me?" he gasped. "Have you forgotten that you are my wife? That you are only a woman? That you must do as I say?"

He released her neck and took a step back as though he wanted to give her the opportunity to answer him. But Valentina remained silent.

"Why don't you say anything?" he screamed. "Don't I deserve an answer? You don't want me in bed, you don't want me at the table, you wear these horrible black clothes like an accusation against me. Every day you tell me anew that I am responsible for your unhappiness."

"Today is the anniversary of Charles's death," Valentina said quietly.

"Yes, today is the anniversary of Charles's death. Do you think I didn't know that? But it is the *second* anniversary of his death. It has been two years and I want you to stop mourning. I want to live normally again." He was still screaming.

"I can't live normally," replied Valentina with hostility.

He looked at her, surprised that she had spoken, but then he understood what she said and seized her again.

"You simply don't live with *me* anymore, that is all. Do you think that I don't know that other men come here? That you are distant with me because you are only thinking of your lovers and how you will escape from me now that we have laws that permit women to get a divorce?"

"You are crazy," Valentina said. "Your jealousy controls you more than your grief. That's right: You can't forgive me because I think more about our child than about you. You are jealous of your own child, of a dead child..."

He suddenly had a splitting headache; her pale, beautiful face contorted into a grimace before his eyes; he lunged and struck at this stranger's face.

"You will put on the white dress," he said calmly, as though the blow that he had dealt her had restored his composure. He stepped behind her, undoing the first few buttons of the dress she was wearing. Then he ripped off the rest of the buttons in a single movement. He turned Valentina around again like a toy to look at her.

He saw tears in her eyes, and that satisfied him. If she said one more word, he would strike her again and silence her.

"I will call for Babette to help you get dressed," he said impatiently and reached for the bell. "Babette!"

"Yes, Monsieur," Babette cowered with fear, curtsied, and avoided looking at Madame.

"Help Madame put on the white dress. She needs another corset. And lace it tightly; the dress has a narrow waist, as Madame knows. I want my wife to wear the diamond earrings that I gave her for our wedding. I will wait here by the door. Hurry. I don't like to be late."

Viktor went into the bathroom and looked in the mirror. His face looked tense from his headache, and his expression was grim. He, Viktor Gruschkin, had hit his wife. It was the second time he had done it, and he waited for the remorse to swell up in him. The fact was he didn't feel he had done anything wrong. Both times he had had cause, and he was, he assured himself, a more generous husband than many others.

He went into the parlor, poured himself a glass of vodka, drank it in one gulp, and went to wait by Valentina's bedroom door.

Babette opened the door, peeked out to make sure Viktor Gruschkin was not standing there, and let her mistress step out with a mixture of dread and devotion.

Yes, she was a queen in this dress, hovering between reality and a dream state, reminiscent of otherworldly beings, fairies and goblins, dragons and dragon slayers. Babette had never seen such an apparition as Valentina, but she was afraid because she knew that this particular dream was the result of a brutal scene.

Viktor gazed at his wife. She was just as he wanted her to be. He was already giving her his arm when an agonizing thought ran through his mind. He grabbed Valentina's purse, which she wore on her wrist over long white gloves. He took the purse and opened it as he usually did when they went out. He rifled through it, but didn't find anything that would arouse his suspicion: a comb, a powder compact, some rouge. No perfume. No money except a few coins—the limit of what he allowed her. No suspicious letters or papers. He closed the bag and returned it to her with an uncertain smile.

They left the house together. Viktor gave Frans the address, and they were on their way.

Much as Viktor Gruschkin had done, the de Waels had chosen the best possible address for their new house. The boulevard ran where the fortress walls protecting the old city of Antwerp had once stood. In this era of widespread development, it had become a central avenue. Viktor Gruschkin planned to meet important local dignitaries at the reception. Although the diamond business was in Jewish hands, it was the old Flemish families who wore the jewels, and it was important to move in their circles. This privilege was denied to the Jewish dealers, but since Gruschkin was Russian and his wife came from an influential family, he enjoyed such invitations.

The parlor was lit festively with a mix of electrical lights and flickering candles. The women look soulful and mysterious in their evening gowns in the warm glow.

The long table in the dining room was set for twenty-four. The lady of the house hadn't missed a single detail: The flower arrangements were an exquisite symphony of pink and white. The porcelain and silver tableware gleamed, and the menu and place cards were reminiscent of a formal dinner gala in a grand hotel.

Viktor accompanied his beautiful wife to her chair. After scrutinizing the other women, the hostess knew that Valentina would, without a doubt, be the queen of the evening. Valentina's hair had been pinned up into a smooth bun that emphasized her beautiful profile and the gentle curve of her slender neck. Other than the diamond earrings, she wore no jewelry.

Viktor was still anxious, not because Valentina was quiet, which didn't bother him, but because he sensed that the evening, splendid as it was, followed a set of unspoken rules. Rules that the old, wealthy families of Antwerp had established and that Viktor himself would never comprehend. He was an outsider, a parvenu.

Valentina knew the rules. She had grown up with them and moved through the battlefield of social ambition with ease and grace. It was only thanks to her that he had access to this world of which he had always wanted to be a part.

Because of that, or perhaps because his triumph over Valentina's defiance still wasn't complete, he turned to Madame de Wael, who was telling the group about the premiere of *La Traviata* that she had seen in Paris and her disappointment in the leading lady's musical talent. Viktor paused elaborately, looked at Valentina, and turned back to Madame de Wael. "Speaking of talent, you know how much I adore my wife's voice…"

He looked back at Valentina, who turned away. Her features were steady.

"If you and the guests would enjoy it," Gruschkin cleared his throat meaningfully, "I'm sure my wife would be happy to give a small performance after dinner…"

Madame de Wael looked surprised when Valentina rose abruptly. She stood before the table; her cheeks flushed, her toppled wine glass spreading a red stain across the starched white damask tablecloth.

"Excuse me," said Valentina. As she grabbed her gloves, she saw Viktor's incredulous expression out of the corner of her eye, as well as the scandalized looks of the other guests who turned to stare at her as though she were in a spotlight on stage.

"Excuse me," she repeated, "I don't feel well. I'll be right back."

She left the room. No one spoke. Society held its breath.

Society had its scandal.

Valentina closed the door of the dining room behind her, walked down the hallway with quiet steps, nodded to the valet, and left the house before the servant could even offer her his help.

By the time Viktor recovered from the shock and stood up to go look for her, she had reached the cabstand.

One of the drivers, an older man in a shabby overcoat, approached her and silently opened the door. The man was no longer surprised at the ladies and gentlemen who he conveyed, but this woman would have been a riddle to him—if, that is, he had still had any desire to solve riddles.

"To the harbor, to the Rhine quay. Quickly!" Valentina said hastily and pulled the carriage door shut herself.

Ellis Island

Valentina had been lucky and didn't have to wait long for the ferry. Only a few hours after the *Kroonland* docked at the pier, the steerage passengers, and Valentina in her gown, were ferried to Ellis Island. Not far from Valentina stood the family of the boy who had died on board. They waved her over, but the crowd was so closely pressed together that Valentina couldn't get to them. She felt lost and alone. Thomas, she thought desperately, Thomas, where are you? How could we have lost each other so quickly when we just found each other?

The exhausted arrivals were received in a magnificent new building with an imposing façade. The passengers weren't only tired, they were afraid. They had little idea what to expect from the medical examination and the interrogation of the inspectors, whose English most of them didn't understand. Mothers held their children tightly by the hand so as not to lose them in the crowd. They had to leave all of their luggage behind in the hall of the large building and were worried that they would never see it again. Valentina was shoved up the steps with the crowd.

Valentina had long ago lost sight of the family of the boy.

On the second floor, they were shuffled into long rows. Two doctors at the head of the line examined them one at a time. The passengers wore stickers bearing the name of the ship on which they had arrived and held papers on which the shipping company had written certain details prior to their departure. Valentina already had been reported to the authorities and held Dr. Kirschbaum's medical certificate in her hand. She watched the stooped older woman in front of her with pity. When she finally stood before the doctor, he drew a chalk mark on her dress that indicated she would require further examinations. The woman looked anxiously at her son. A woman with a child in her arms stepped forward. Valentina watched the doctor pull down the girl's lower eyelid. She began to cry loudly. The doctor shook his head and an interpreter tried to explain to the family that no entry was permitted to anyone with eye infections.

Visibly upset, the father tried to explain that they had all been examined before they left. My God, thought Valentina, what will happen now? The man gesticulated desperately and tugged at the interpreter's sleeve as though he could rectify the situation. But the man only shook his head in resignation. Next! But they couldn't simply tear a family apart, thought Valentina. They couldn't just send the grandmother and the child back! Suddenly it was her turn to be examined.

Valentina was healthy and had no trouble with the doctor. The inspector, however, had a multitude of questions for her, including her marital status, nationality, last place of residence, final destination, and financial situation.

"Have you ever been in the United States? Have you ever been in prison? Have you ever been dependent on welfare?" Valentina shook her head.

"No entry permit," announced the inspector. When he saw Valentina's confused expression, he added, "Go over to those offices where special interviews are conducted with those denied an entry permit. Someone will explain the next steps for you to take. Next!"

Tears filled Valentina's eyes. Through her veil of tears, she saw that the family of the dead boy was allowed to pass through. The parents waved happily to Valentina; the oldest son held a paper American flag in his hand, which he brandished fiercely. For a brief moment, the thoughts of their new homeland had displaced the loss of their son.

Valentina waved back through her tears.

Across the Sea and Beyond . . .

Over the next two days, the *Kroonland*'s cargo was unloaded and new cargo was brought on board. There were some changes in the crew. Jan Bartel wouldn't be on board for the return trip. However, the handsome steward was there and served Valentina graciously when she appeared alone in her white evening gown, the only guest in the dining room for dinner on the day that she was turned away by the immigration authorities.

The captain felt generous since he had had his revenge. He again made a first-class stateroom available to Valentina who, like all of the other rejected emigrants, would be sent back on the same ship on which they had arrived. He was sure that she would keep her word and reimburse the Red Star Line. And who knew, perhaps it would still be worth his while to please the lady.

A few days later, a new group of passengers boarded the ship. No, she wouldn't be able to endure it. She wouldn't leave her stateroom. Valentina didn't want to see anyone. She didn't want to face the gossip or exchange a word with anyone.

Only Dr. Kirschbaum was a comfort. She was so relieved at the thought of him. She would ask him to visit her as soon as he could. She wanted to tell him what she had planned.

When they docked in Antwerp, she would take a cab to her grandmother's house. She would visit Viktor, apologize to him for her rash escape, and file for divorce. Then she would sort out her finances with her attorney, get an overview of her financial situation, and start her voice lessons again. She needed to find out what had become of Jan and offer him help.

Then there was Thomas. Unlike the prince in the fairy tales, he hadn't rescued her from Ellis Island and swept her off to his castle in New York. Maybe her expectations were too high when it came to love. She didn't even have his address; they had both been so certain that they would go ashore together and face the authorities side by side.

But maybe that was as it should be. She had to take care of her old life before she could begin a new one. Perhaps she would try to locate Thomas later. It wasn't out of the question. What had Dr. Kirschbaum said? You have to accept a lot of things, but not everything.

Valentina smiled at the thought of Thomas. One thing was certain. No matter what happened, she would remember him for the rest of her life. She would love no other.

Some memories are beautiful, even when they are painful. And some of them have a great deal of power over one's life. She wanted to discuss that with Dr. Kirschbaum too.

Valentina sighed.

Life is odd, she thought. You just never know what is going to happen when it comes to love.

Victoria Witherspoon accompanied her brother to the harbor. She was not excited about the prospect of letting her brother leave without her. However, Thomas had left behind the plans for the expansion of the summerhouse on Long Island, and she wanted to go over the details of the upcoming construction work with the architects in his absence. She definitely had her own ideas about how the house should be configured. She knew he would acquiesce to her ideas since he traveled so much. He didn't even know where he wanted to settle down—and anything was possible now that he was embarking on this new adventure.

"I hope that you won't be mad at me," she said huskily and cleared her throat, "if I don't stand around here sentimentally and wait until the *Kroonland* sets sail again with you on board. I've had enough of ships for now."

She looked sternly off into the distance. "Even if there is something to be said for the opportunity of heading off to new shores."

Epilogue

My friend reached the new world on the *Kroonland*—after the ship came through a powerful storm—and established himself as a merchant in New York. I became a journalist.

I never saw the lady in white again, but she shaped my life in several ways. I learned from a *New York Times* article that was later reprinted in Antwerp that she was discovered on board the *Kroonland* and that she had been denied an entry permit to America; she would be sent back to Antwerp on the same ship. By the time I had read this news, the ship had already arrived in Antwerp and was already back at sea. I had no luck finding her. My friend wrote to me that he had seen her briefly—after a fatal accident in steerage, she had appeared there and asked to speak to the family who had lost their son; he knew nothing more.

With time, I forgot about the woman in the white evening gown.

I married a woman who, from a distance, reminded me of her; the marriage was not very happy.

Almost thirty years later, when I was moving, I came upon the envelope in which I had kept the ring that she had given me as she boarded the ship.

The name Viktor was engraved in the narrow golden band.

Once again, the odd stranger returned to my life. The world had changed a great deal since then; the society from which she had wanted to escape no longer existed. The war had destroyed it. Russia had been shaken by revolution, Mussolini's fascists had come to power in Italy, and the National Socialists were taking over Germany. Storms more tempestuous than the one she had experienced were brewing. Only the stream of those looking for freedom and a new homeland wouldn't end.

The few pieces of the puzzle that I collected about the woman in white didn't reveal much. However, when I held her ring in my hands again, I felt compelled to give her a story, because every person needs a story.

Our own stories, and those of our cities, regions, and nations, emerge from the stories that generations have in their hands.

So I wrote this novel as it could have been. There is no objective truth, anyway.

I am still looking for her.

There is a stowaway like her in every life.

Although I cannot understand it, she is the one who accompanies me and steers my life.

$\mathscr{P}$ostscript

"Woman Crosses Ocean in an Evening Gown on Liner Without Another Dress" headlined the *New York Times* on August 3, 1904. This article is the factual core of this novel.

Detained on board the Red Star Line steamship Kroonland, *which arrived here on Monday from Antwerp, is a young woman whose only costume—the one in which she boarded the vessel, and the only one she wore during the voyage and since the ship arrived here—is a beautiful evening gown of white silk, almost covered with fine lace, with a low-cut bodice and short sleeves and a long train. The woman has not a cent in money...She possesses a beautiful voice and is an expert pianist.*

How the woman happened to take the trip, the officers of the ship do not know; and her presence aboard in her unusual costume she cannot satisfactorily explain, herself..."

Reprinted in the *Herald Tribune* in August 2004, this old story inspired my fantasies. In this novel, I have tried to give the mysterious "Lady in White" a story.

All names and characters—even the main character—are fictitious.

Zurich, December 2007

Thanks

Acknowledgments are usually the last part of a book. I can say with certainty that there wouldn't ever have been a first page without the support of a great many people. At this juncture, I would like to thank everyone for his or her goodwill and support.

Albert Erlanger provided terra firma beneath my feet as I devoted myself fully to writing.

Johannes Thiele, my friend and colleague, and Joachim Jessen, my literary agent, have always believed that I should go beyond nonfiction and try writing a novel.

I owe my thanks to Peter Fritz for the idea for this book. He discovered the newspaper clipping on which the novel is based and felt it could be material for a novel. He supported me steadfastly through thick and thin, which could not have been easy.

Chandler Crawford nominated me for a scholarship at Ledig House in upstate New York. There, as in the bosom of Abraham, I was well cared for and worked for three solid months. It is there that I learned from the Australian author Dorothy Johnston that the characters—not the author—are always right.

Ivo Gay visited his hometown of Antwerp with me.

At the maritime museum in Antwerp, I acquired data about the schedules of the steamships of that era. Dr. Albrecht Sauer from the German Maritime Museum Bremerhaven confirmed that the *Kroonland* had marine radio communication equipment by the Marconi Company at its disposal. The Ellis Island Museum offered me the fantastic opportunity to review passenger lists from that period. I did find the "Lady in White" that the newspaper reported in 1904.

Countess Bredow never tired of phoning to inquire whether I was writing. Her advice was always helpful.

My former colleague, Lia Franken, made a gift to me of her professional stringency. She worked mercilessly through one of the first versions without discouraging me from starting a new version; her work was priceless to me.

My friend Vera, with whom I spent a rainy vacation in England, was patient as I was compelled to make one last attempt. She mostly saw me sitting in front of a stack of papers, pencil in hand.

My girlfriends Claudia Lichte, Ursula Nuber, Katrin Eckert, and Gunda Borgeest gave me my first important reader opinions.

Heinrich Deserno agreed with the ending of the novel from a psychoanalytical standpoint.

Katrin Wiederkehr was a true godmother to the project.

Dagmar Gleditzsch and Petra Sluka kindly wrote expert English reviews.

Jane Starr championed the novel, which she unfortunately only knew from the English reviews, out of friendship.

"The passages that are always most beloved by an author are always deleted by a publisher," Countess Bredow warned me. She was not proven right in this case: Lutz Wolff was a godsend for me. His enthusiasm for the book and his sensitive comments on the manuscript showed me that not only can characters find their authors, but authors can also find their publishers.

About the Author

Dörthe Binkert was born in Hagen, Germany. She studied literature, art history, and politics and earned a PhD in literature. For thirty years she was an editor and editor-in-chief for several major German publishing houses. After writing nonfiction books for years, she published her first novel, *Weit übers Meer* (published in English as *She Wore Only White*), in 2008, inspired by an intriguing historical news article. She has a son, and she currently lives in Zurich, Switzerland, where she writes fiction and nonfiction and works as a freelance journalist.

About the Translator

Lesley Schuldt, a translator for over thirty years, began her career translating financial documents for a bank and general business documents for translation companies. In addition to translating, she taught German and English as a foreign language to students from elementary school through adults. She has been an active member of the American Translators Association since 1978. Since 2003, she has concentrated on literary translation and has worked closely with German authors to introduce their novels to the United States. She is particularly drawn to historical fiction and was intrigued by *Weit übers Meer (She Wore Only White)*, a novel based on the true story of a mysterious woman who stowed away on a steamship traveling from Antwerp to New York in 1904.

She has two grown children and lives in Steamboat Springs, Colorado, with her husband.